Cactus Mystery Press Titles by Narielle Living

Brewster Square Series Cozy Mysteries:
Madness in Brewster Square
Birding in Brewster Square

Paranormal Mysteries:
Signs of the South
Revenge of the Past
Children of the Tribe

For information contact :
Blue Fortune Enterprises, LLC
Cactus Mystery Press
P.O. Box 554
Yorktown, VA 23690
http://blue-fortune.com

Book and Cover design by Wesley Miller, WAMCreate, wamcreate.co

ISBN: 978-1-948979-02-3

Third Edition: April 2018

Signs
of the
South

Narielle Living

Cactus Mystery Press
An imprint of Blue Fortune Enterprises, LLC

Dedication

To my family...

... all of you, for always believing in me. There was never a moment you doubted I could do this, and there was never a moment I was without your love.

Acknowledgements

Writing is definitely not the solitary occupation so many envision, and there are a number of generous people to thank for all the support I received through this endeavor. I would like to offer my most sincere thanks (thank you!) and acknowledge those who helped make this book possible, including:

The York – Poquoson Sheriff's Department in Yorktown Virginia, specifically Captain J.E. Richardson who is always so very patient in answering my questions about procedures and what-ifs; Deputy First-Class Mike Russell and Deputy Shawn Kekoa-Dearhart who were even more patient with me in the Citizen's Academy Class offered by the sheriff's department; and the many officers and SWAT team personnel who helped educate and inform all of us in that class. They are a special group, and any law enforcement mistakes in this book are entirely mine.

Many thanks to those who read the book in its initial stage and offered wonderful insight and critiques, including Jackie Guidry, Julie Leverenz, Steve Fisher, Carrie Pagels and Kim Taylor.

A big thank you to my former students at Everest College for sharing their stories of life in a small southern town. I hope each and every one of you continues your education and goes on to achieve amazing success.

My support group, specifically those wonderful women who insisted on hearing me read the first chapter to them: Cindy Wilson, Tamara Gardner, Sharon Morgan, Liz Urban, Lyn Cooper and Patty Smith. I feel lucky to have known you all.

A special thank you to my dear friend, Darlene DeRosa, who patiently explained motorcycles to me.

And most of all, thank you to my husband and son who are always supportive of me as I immerse myself in the writing process. I love you both so very much, as high as the moon and as deep as the sea.

Chapter One

SHE APPEARED JUST PAST BALTIMORE. Her mother, standing in the middle lane of Interstate 95. A rush of adrenalin like nothing she'd ever known before jolted Ella out of her drowsiness and the vision dissipated. Ella's mother, dead for over a year, morphed into a dark blue Honda about to change lanes.

Ella shook her head, wide awake despite the hours of nonstop driving that had begun at seven that morning. Her hands trembled, sweaty as she gripped the leather steering wheel. This was officially her first ever hallucination. Time to breathe, get some oxygen… in, out…

"I better pull over before we crash." A short whine and tail thump from the thirty-pound brown mutt in the back seat confirmed it. They both needed to stretch and get some food, maybe clear the car of fumes that cause these types of problems. The highway image evoked memories of her mother and tears burned behind her eyelids. Again. God, she wanted a cigarette.

At the rest stop Ella used the bathroom sink to splash cold water on her face and clean the salt of her tears. She went out to the restaurant, bought a slice of pizza, and finished eating it by the time she reached the parking lot. Shivering from the car's air conditioning, as well as the disquiet of her mind, she turned up the Springsteen music on her MP3 player, put the car in gear, and merged onto the sun-drenched highway. A dilapidated white van driving next to her had red letters stenciled on the side that read *Kingdom of Repentance*. Numerous faces, old and young, looked out the van's window at Ella. She smiled and waved, trying to be friendly, but was answered only with unblinking stares. Nobody waved.

"Maybe seeing my mother in the middle of the highway wouldn't be so bad right about now," Ella muttered. "At least it was a friendly face."

A whine from the backseat re-focused Ella's attention. Her dog was always sensitive to her moods, dancing and jumping when Ella was happy and whining when Ella was worried. It was also possible that Daisy was just tired of the long car ride.

Her cell phone rang. She glanced at the caller ID, knowing who it was from the ringtone. She had to answer, it wasn't polite not to answer. Maybe she could pretend there was no cell phone service on the highway. *That won't work, she always knows these things.*

It was her sister, Lisa. "I thought you were going to call once you got there."

"I'm not there. I'm not even in Virginia yet."

"Is everything okay? You've got your car so crammed full of stuff, I can't believe you could see anything out the back window. And I'm sure your dog is stinking up your car."

"I can see, and nothing smells. Everything's fine. I'll call you when I get to the house."

"I can't believe you tried to bring that filthy creature into my house yesterday." Once Lisa got onto a subject, she was like a dog with a bone. Ella smiled at the thought, pun intended.

"Daisy is not filthy; she had a bath a couple of days ago."

Lisa sniffed. Despite Ella's insistence of the dog's health and cleanliness, Lisa's children were not allowed to play with Daisy. Ever. Ella had tried one last time before she left, but Lisa made her opinion clear, and finally Ella admitted defeat and walked a cowering Daisy back to the car. Even though she was only twenty-seven years old, sometimes it was easier for Ella to give in and do what Lisa told her to do.

"Never mind about the mutt, make sure you call Dad. This morning was hard on him."

Ella didn't mention that it had been hard on her, too. She suspected that Lisa was struggling with her leaving, and Ella's instinct was to make it better somehow for her sister. Constant reassurances had become part of their conversational routine.

"I promise I'll call him when I get there. You're still coming down for Thanksgiving, right?" Ella tried to imagine what the holiday would be like, then dismissed the thought; there was no point in staging the drama in her head before it happened.

"You'll have to let us know about the house first. What if it's not as good as you thought it would be? I don't want to go all that way to stay in a rat trap, you know." Ella smiled. Lisa's attitude was back, which meant she was fine.

"I'll let you know. I've got to go; I shouldn't be driving and talking. I love you."

"Me, too. Don't forget to call Dad. And for God's sake, be careful, Ella."

Ella disconnected and tossed the phone on the seat. She knew that for all their fighting, her sister meant well. Lisa cared, even if she wasn't always able to show it.

The tractor trailer creeping up on her tail snapped Ella back to her driving. Looking in the rearview mirror, a surge of anger jolted through her.

"Stop following so closely!" Jerking the steering wheel to the left, she changed lanes without using the turn signal and sped up to get away. "Dumb ass."

Lately, Ella's anger was ready. Even though she'd never admit it to her family, she knew this emotion was related to her mother's death. The anger and sadness lived just outside her heart as one piece, fueling outbursts and draining her energy.

The opening notes to Bob Dylan's *Eve of Destruction* coincided with Ella's squeal of relief. The welcome sign for Virginia loomed ahead, an indication that they were definitely getting close. She hadn't told anyone that she was worried about the choice she had made. It was difficult to get a real feeling for an area from looking at a computer screen, but it was too late now; she'd made a commitment and was going to see it through.

***

The website showed Paterson, Virginia, population 11,566, as an ideal place to call home. Situated on the waters of the Chesapeake Bay and close to the college where Ella would be teaching, Paterson had a decidedly small town persona. From her research on the area, Ella gleaned that town council members fought hard to keep strip malls and big box stores from invading. Surrounded by larger urban areas, Paterson advertised safety and comfort, both of which appealed to Ella.

After crossing the state line into Virginia, Ella paid more attention to her surroundings. The eastern stretch of the state was unremarkable and flat, with no hills in sight. The vegetation on the side of the road was similar for most of the ride: shrubs and oak trees mixed in with the ever present highway wall that loomed as a sound barrier.

When she reached Interstate 64 a gray clouds appeared overhead, muting everything. Grateful that she hadn't had to drive through any rain, Ella focused until she saw the exit for Paterson. *Thank God, we're almost there.*

The road into Paterson, empty of cars, was dominated on each side by loblolly pine trees standing sentry, as if they were allowing only the chosen ones in. Ella shook her head. It had been a long drive, and she was tired. Why else would she have such weird thoughts?

Stay focused on the road.

The burst of noise sounded like gunfire, but the loss of steering coupled with the flapping sound told her otherwise. Heart pounding, she gripped the wheel, frantic to remember what to do.

Don't slam on the brakes. Her father had told her that once.

Bracing to control the steering, Ella slowly lifted her foot off the accelerator and fought the car to the side of the road. Thank God she wasn't on the highway.

Shaking, she tried to catch her breath while the adrenalin coursed through her body. A warm, shaking body of fur wriggled under her arm. "It's okay, Daisy, we're not hurt. We'll be fine."

She wished she felt more confident of that.

She was in the middle of an unknown area, with no friends or family nearby. She didn't even know any local mechanics. She sat, wondering who to call. Her new boss? No, that would make her look incompetent. Her father, for advice? No, that would just worry him. Maybe she should get out of the car first to assess the damage.

A light flashed in her rearview mirror as a police cruiser pulled up behind her car. That would definitely make getting help easier. Lowering the window, she watched as he approached the back of the car, placing a hand on the trunk. When he reached the driver's side, she looked up into the blue eyes of a smiling face.

"Looks like you have a little trouble here."

Ella nodded. "Yes. I think my tire is flat. Unfortunately, I don't know if I can get to my spare."

The police officer looking down at her didn't seem surprised. "Yeah, that's a lot of stuff."

That was an understatement. "I'll be able to get to it once I unpack the car. But for now, I can't just dump everything on the side of the road."

"Hmm, you may be right. Let's get you to where you need to be. We can't have you and your stuff spending the night out here, can we?" When he smiled at her, Ella's mind froze. He was handsome—and very possibly flirting—which made her effectively unable to communicate for the moment. When she didn't respond, he leaned into the window. "Do you want me to call roadside assistance for you?"

She nodded, expelling a breath. Roadside assistance would help her, then she could get to her new home. And maybe Officer... she squinted a little as she read the name tag... Drake. Officer Drake would be kind enough to follow her, and—

The crackle of static cut through her thoughts. She didn't understand a word that was being said from the radio piece attached to his shirt, but it sounded urgent. A frown creased his face. "I'll call for your assistance. Stay in your vehicle until they arrive. I've got to go to an accident."

Ella waved him away. "Go, don't worry about me. Thanks for calling for help." She raised the window and watched him move with considerable speed to get back into his car. He wore his uniform well.

***

Not too far from where Ella sat in her car, a phone rang. The voice that answered was gruff with sleep. "Yeah?"

"It's done. The place has been rented. See to it that everything is taken care of."

The man sighed. He knew there was no way around this. "Why don't you just sell the damn thing? Then it'll be out of our lives instead of having to deal with this renter crap. And I'm always the one dealing with the renters—when we're able to keep them, at least."

"It'll be sold when I die," the voice on the other end said, "and not a moment before. Make sure this one minds her own business. She's a Yankee."

"I'll check up on her. Maybe she'll last longer than the others."

He disconnected the call, knowing he probably wouldn't get back to sleep. Working at night meant that he slept during the day, but if he woke up early it was usually too difficult to get back to sleep. He might as well make the most of this extra time. "I'd better be sure," he muttered. "I'll go over and check that everything is ready. Maybe this one will be able to live there longer than a month."

Chapter Two

313 BURNT RIDGE WAY WAS a small, older home built in 1925 that was hers for at least the next year, according to the rental agreement. The internet pictures had showed a house with just a little over 1,000 square feet, three bedrooms, two baths, and all appliances, including a washer and dryer. With two stories wrapped in gray vinyl siding, a back deck, and a front porch that begged for a rocking chair, the remodeled exterior gave the home a decidedly beach-like feel. For Ella, the best part was that the backyard went straight into the marsh, which eventually joined the Chesapeake Bay. She imagined that at some point she would own a kayak and have all sorts of fun navigating through this portion of the bay. Evenings would be spent on the back porch, grading papers and watching the sun set over the marsh.

From the outside, it seemed almost perfect.

Before going inside, Ella and Daisy wandered through the yard. The lawn was neatly mowed, with an old oak tree in the front. In the far corner sat a gray barn, a sorry, dilapidated-looking structure with a slight lean and in desperate need of paint. Curious about the barn, Ella started to walk toward it.

"What the—Daisy, what is wrong with you?" The dog was cowering in an effort to stay close to Ella. "Go check out your new yard, run and play; you'll love it." Rather than sniff her new grounds, though, the dog stuck close to Ella, bumping into her with her tail tucked between her legs.

The yard inspection didn't last long. Soon, Ella was desperately digging for her keys; there was no time to check out the backyard marsh. She was already slapping at her arms, legs, neck, and face in disgust.

"Oh, God, let's get inside. These mosquitoes are the size of hummingbirds." Clearly Daisy was in complete agreement as she was waiting at the front door before Ella had even finished her sentence.

Any previous daydreams about grading papers on the back deck were washed away in an instant.

"It looks like we're going to need some serious bug spray, Daisy."

After fumbling a bit with the key in the front lock, Ella opened the door and stepped into the elegantly remodeled home. The air in the house was still and stuffy, but she noted that everything was the same as the pictures she'd seen. The walls were painted a pleasing, neutral taupe, and the refinished hardwood floors were gleaming. She walked through the living room into the kitchen, done in light blue and white, lending a spacious, by-the-water feeling to the room. The countertops were sand colored, and the new appliances were white. Off the back of the kitchen was a bedroom with its own bath, again tastefully done in neutral colors.

Absently patting Daisy's head, she told the dog, "I like everything except the blood suckers outside. I guess we can think of the mosquitoes as extra security; nobody will want to try to break into a house when they have to risk running into ferocious insects... at least I wouldn't." Grinning, she wondered if adding giant bats would fix the problem.

Ella wandered through the bottom floor trying to determine where everything should go. Standing in the back bedroom, she put her hands on her hips. *Will it be better to stay here or in an upstairs bedroom?*

From the kitchen Daisy gave a low, throaty growl.

Ella looked out, nervous. The dog stood in the corner of the kitchen growling softly, hackles raised.

"What is it, girl? Do you smell something?" Nothing was there that would provoke her dog, yet the throaty snarl continued even as Ella put her hand on top of Daisy's head.

"I don't see anything. There's nothing here."

The growling deepened, and Daisy looked ready to attack.

A gentle breeze blew across the room, followed by a loud crash. Both dog and owner jumped.

It took a moment for her heart rate to get back to normal. "It's okay," Ella gasped. "We forgot to shut the front door. It was probably the wind. Nothing else."

What else could it be? Ella took one final look around the kitchen before walking out. Daisy followed close at her side. As soon as they were back in the living room, Daisy sat and looked up at her, tail sweeping the floor.

"What on earth was that about? Nothing is there, and nobody is outside."

A voice boomed at her from the front door.

"Hello! Anybody home?"

She looked across the living room, but all she could make out was a large, shadowy figure in the doorway. In an instant, her stomach dropped to her knees as she realized a stranger was at the house and nobody in the world knew where she was—or even where she was supposed to be. Why didn't her sister call at a time like this, instead of always interrupting other things?

"Ummm, yes?" She was desperately trying to remember where she'd stashed her pepper spray, or if she still had any. With no lamps or cutlery, there was nothing else on hand that she could use as a weapon.

The shadowy figure took a few steps into the living room, turning itself into a strikingly average, slightly balding man. Average as he was, he was still taller than her five-foot-five-inch stature and heavier than her 115 pounds. *It's always the ones that look normal.* Her only chance was to turn and run out the back door.

"Sorry," he said. "I shouldn't have sneaked up on ya like that. I'm Jeff Bartok, son of the owner of this house. I just wanted to check in, make sure everything's okay."

She smiled, hoping her expression masked her anxiety. While Daisy was slinking off to the nearest corner with her tail between her legs, Ella stepped forward on her own shaking legs and shook Jeff's outstretched hand.

"Hi, I'm Ella. Ella Giancetti."

As she stared at him with growing suspicion, her initial fear turned into outrage. Did he think he could just show up, open the front door, and walk right in? Maybe this guy was watching the house, or lying in wait for her to get there. What were the odds he would appear as soon as she arrived?

Jeff took a slow look around, pretending to look at everything. "So, Ella, where's your stuff?"

"The movers will be here tomorrow," she said, immediately regretting her words. It was abundantly clear that not only was she new in town, but she was also alone and vulnerable. Her outrage soon faded, though, and the trepidation returned.

Jeff nodded slowly before looking at her. "Where ya gonna sleep tonight?"

Ella hesitated. She really wanted to tell this guy it was none of his business where she slept. But, if this man was the son of the owner, then he probably was going to be around to check on things. In fact, he was probably the one to call if something happened, like a pipe bursting or killer mosquitoes attacking. It would be best to be polite and not afraid of this person; well, not too afraid at least. Besides, he looked to be around sixty years old, maybe slightly older. If it came down to it, she could overpower him… maybe. If she screamed really loud, that would help, too.

"I'll be right here. I've got some camping equipment. I thought it would be fun, you know, to sort of camp out here for the night before my furniture and stuff came. I mean, hopefully it won't be late or anything; you know you always hear horror stories about movers not showing up and all…" Her voice trailed away as she willed herself to stop talking.

Talking to fill the void of silence was not one of her better traits.

There was a moment of awkward silence before Jeff said, "So I hear you're going to teach at the college."

"Yes, like I told the realtor, I was offered a job in the anthropology department." This time, Ella was determined not to run her mouth off; she would answer his questions, but that was it.

Another minute ticked slowly by.

"I teach religion."

Jeff nodded slowly, as if digesting this information.

"Alternative religions." This bizarre, one-sided conversation was starting to wear on her.

Finally, Jeff spoke. "You mean like witches and stuff?"

"Well, yes; that, too—but also the rituals and customs of indigenous tribes."

Ella's lifelong quest for metaphysical answers had begun at a very early age. Curious about God and unwilling to take her local priest at face value, she read everything she could get her hands on, but especially loved the more exotic religious books. Hinduism, Buddhism, Kabala, Santeria… for the little Catholic girl, this was more than a glimpse into the forbidden; these books provided clues to the great mystery. Reading the philosophies of others was like finding a divining rod that might someday lead her straight into the grace of the Universe, and all this information helped filter her own experiences.

Jeff nodded once and turned to leave, apparently unimpressed by her career choice. He hesitated a moment, then turned back.

"Here's my number," he drawled, handing her a card. "I work nights, so I'm usually up around four or five in the afternoon. I sleep during the day. If you've got a problem, just call. I've got a machine."

"Thanks. I won't call at a time that wakes you, don't worry."

Once again, he nodded at her, then turned and left. As she leaned against the living room wall for support, Ella noticed that her knees were weak.

"Daisy, he spooked me. My heart's racing a mile a minute."

Daisy looked at her, ears perked. "I'm sure he didn't mean to do it. It's been a long day, he's a stranger. I got startled, that's all." Taking a shaky but deep breath, she headed toward the front door.

"We don't have time to sit around. We've got to unpack some of this stuff so we can go get a new tire. Oh—and call everyone back at home, too."

****

A few hours later, with everything unpacked, a fixed tire on the car (courtesy of Paterson Auto) and the spare back in the trunk, and food shopping done (including purchasing a good size canister of mosquito repellant), Ella and Daisy sat on a blanket in the living room to eat dinner. She'd contemplated opening a bottle of wine to celebrate her new home and arrival in a new town but decided that drinking alone would be depressing.

Depressing was a mood that she could live without, especially after the grief-filled year she'd just finished. It was time for something new: new friends, new career, new life.

In the weeks leading up to her departure, Ella had made sure to spend time visiting friends and saying goodbye. Everyone knew that e-mail and Facebook were poor substitutes for being there, but they would have to do for now.

Meg, who had grown up in the house next door to Ella and been her friend all through elementary and high school, spent more time than usual with her during that final week. "I have to get my 'best friend time' in; it's going to be a while before we see each other again," she told Ella. She surprised Ella by showing up all week to help her pack, as well as appearing with dinner on Ella's final night in her apartment.

"I know you've got everything packed already, so what were you planning on eating?" she said as Ella exclaimed in guilty pleasure at the Indian take-out. "It's our last night together here; let's open a bottle of wine and toast to new beginnings!"

They toasted to new beginnings, old friendships, friendships yet to come, people they remembered from years ago, and whatever else they could think of to toast. At the end of the night they sat surrounded by take-out wrappers, boxes, and the warmth of friendship. "When you least expect it..." Meg began, then started to giggle.

"What?"

"When you least expect it, I'm going to show up at your door and surprise you. So just, um, expect it."

Ella laughed. "You're drunk."

"Yep. I'm drunk, and I'm honest. But seriously, what's the hardest part of leaving? Are you worried about anything?"

Ella hesitated. "I have to say, besides the fact that I'm going to miss my friends, I'm kind of worried about leaving my dad. Lisa keeps saying this is probably not such a good move, and that I'm being selfish."

"Screw her. She doesn't really care about all that; she just wants you to stay so she has someone besides her kids to boss around."

"Probably. But still..."

"What?"

"I just feel bad. I feel like—I don't know, maybe Lisa's right."

Meg leaned forward. "Are you worried about your dad?"

Ella nodded. "I love that you know exactly what I'm thinking; I'm going to miss that. Anyway, yeah, that's part of it. I can't help but wonder if he's going to get lost in that house all by himself. What if he needs something? Who's he going to call?"

Meg laughed. "Besides Lisa or one of his many sisters, you mean? Ella, you can't be serious. Haven't you noticed what's going on in our old neighborhood?"

When Ella shook her head, Meg took another sip of wine. "Honey, your dad is going to be fine; in fact, more than fine. I noticed when I dropped off those books he asked for that there was no shortage of neighborhood ladies hanging around your father. I'm sure some of them are more than interested in changing his marital status."

"My father?" Ella said. "That's not right. I mean, my mom's been gone for a while now, but wow—I never thought he'd remarry."

"I didn't say he was going to remarry, but it's obvious that most of those ladies have their sights set on him, and you know what that means. They shower him with food, they show up to help him with the house, they invite him over. And now that you're leaving town, they have an even better excuse. Seriously, don't worry."

Ella laughed. "I guess you're right. I didn't realize it, but it kind of makes sense now that I think about it. Thanks, Meg."

At the end of the night, when Meg was sober enough to drive, they tearfully hugged each other. "You be careful, okay?" Meg said.

"I'll be fine. Visit me, please? I'm going to need all the support I can get. Anytime you want to come down, you can. There will always be room for you to stay with me."

Meg nodded. "I'll call you later tomorrow. And let me know when you get your internet installed."

Snapping back to the present, Ella remembered that she hadn't yet called anyone at home. She considered the dinner hour and wondered if it was a good time to call.

With a cheese-topped cracker in hand, Ella froze, listening. Music played in the distance, a lively tune that had an unfortunate, tinny sound, like an old recording. The song was almost familiar, but she couldn't quite place it.

"I hope the neighbors don't play music all the time. I'm going to have enough trouble sleeping in a new place." The thought of all the unpacking she faced forced a yawn. It had been a long drive, and Ella was certain she would sleep well—bed or no bed.

While cleaning the dinner debris, she called her father, sister, and Meg. Most of the conversations were spent reassuring each of them that yes, she was just fine, no, she had no problems, and yes, the house was great. By the end of her third phone call, Ella was overwhelmed from it all, not just the drive and the move, but also the emotion of the day and finding herself alone in a strange house.

"It's definitely time to get some sleep. Everything looks better once morning comes."

Setting up her sleeping bag in the upstairs bedroom, she cast a glance toward the door that led into the hallway, wondering exactly what it was that made Daisy growl earlier. At the moment, the dog was lying on the floor, resting her head on her paws. She was mild-tempered, small, sweet, and great company, and she normally didn't growl at anything.

The question, however, seemed to be not so much what it was that Daisy was growling at, but whether it was still there.

Chapter Three

LIGHT GIGGLES DANCED THROUGH THE air, happiness unhampered by the oppressive humidity that clung to all living things. A canopy of trees provided some relief from the sweltering sun but did nothing to ease the inhospitable mosquito attacks. She was floating, watching two girls: one dark-haired and one light-haired, sitting on a large tree stump, heads bent over a book. Their giggles were interspersed with the occasional swat at the lunging insects, but their focus was rapt.

"Listen to this," one of the girls whispered. "Indian summer is like a woman. Ripe, hotly passionate, but fickle..." I know those words, Ella thought as the girls dissolved into more giggles. They're reading Peyton Place. Ella tried to focus as they talked.

"I wish we could go down to Miss Hope's store." The petulant voice of the young girl floated through the dream.

"You know we can't! Who knows what would happen if we show up there together?" the second girl whispered, her voice reflecting a well-worn fear.

It never occurred to Ella to wonder if this were real or not; such is the stuff of dreams, our mind's acceptance of a universe alongside our own. As she drifted toward the morning light of consciousness, a wisp of thought penetrated the dream. Who are these girls, and why am I seeing them?

***

The day dawned with the clarity that happens only on certain August mornings, with a hint of a breeze and a sense of expectation. Because the windows were open, Ella could smell a strong scent of salt water, the smell of the beach. With no curtains on the windows, the sun washed uninhibited into the bedroom, illuminating the wood floor where her air mattress lay. Mourning doves cried into the beginning light as the first waves of heat began drifting through the open window.

Ella rolled over, hoping for a little more sleep, maybe even just ten minutes. It was 6:30 a.m., much too early to be getting out of her cocoon and starting the day. Yesterday had been long and wearing, and today she was faced with unpacking in triple-digit heat. She guessed it was already in the high seventies in her bedroom, but there wasn't much to do until the movers arrived.

Ella pushed a long, dark curl off her face as she remembered her dream, something about being in the woods. As she tried to dredge up the dream, another memory floated through her mind; it was the memory of a nickname her mother had given her years ago: "sort-of-psychic." Her mother used to call her "sort-of-psychic" to describe the dreams and intuitions that Ella sometimes had; sometimes the things she saw happened, sometimes they didn't. God, she hoped last night's dream wasn't a "sort-of-psychic" moment... she hated those almost as much as she hated seeing ghosts.

Her cell phone rang and Ella squinted to read the caller ID. *Who the heck is calling me so early?* She didn't recognize the number, but it had a Connecticut area code.

"Ella, I can't find your house!"

Sitting up, she struggled to place the voice.

"Ed?"

"Yeah, I know we're early, but we're lost—and you'd better help us out of here quick."

"Where are you?"

"We're sitting in the truck in the parking lot of some little coffee shop on Route 171. Maybe it's me, but I think it's gonna get ugly real soon."

"I know where you are; I drove past that place yesterday. I'll be right there. Don't worry, you're not far from me."

Ella quickly pulled on a pair of shorts and a T-shirt that read *Humpty Dumpty was Pushed.* Pulling her hair back into a clip as she searched for her flip flops, Ella wondered what could be happening at the little coffee shop. Ed and Pete were the movers, two friends she'd known from school—and they weren't guys who usually got themselves into trouble.

Both men were large, and both had been on the football team. She often thought of them as gentle giants, since they obviously had the ability to do damage but limited that to their time on the field. Completely opposite in coloring, together they were a striking pair: Pete was of Nordic lineage, with blond hair and pale skin, while Ed was a very dark-skinned African

American.

At least all her stuff was here, right on time.

Ella called Ed as she drove to the coffee shop. "I'm almost there. I'll see you soon." Less than a minute later, she turned into the parking lot and pulled next to the big white moving truck. Climbing out of her car, she couldn't stop her grin. "Hey, you guys! Glad you made it!"

A look of relief passed over Ed's face. "Sorry to call you out here this morning."

"Don't worry about it; the roads are confusing. You can follow me back to the house. I just want to run in and grab a cup of coffee first. Do you want anything?"

"No, let's get to your house," Pete was leaning across the seat as he spoke to Ella. "C'mon, we need to go."

Ella shook her head. "Give me a minute. It's early, and I really need a cup of coffee. I'll be right back."

Pulling her purse strap over her shoulder, Ella entered the coffee shop. The bell on the door chimed as everyone turned to look at her, staring.

Conversation stopped.

"Good morning." Ella nodded, determined not to be intimidated. As she stood at the counter waiting for service, she looked around—despite everyone watching her.

The restaurant, called "The Coffee Shop," seemed like a typical small town, out-of-date diner. The Formica-topped counters were old, and the leather and chrome stools showed signs of wear. Faded posters of vintage cars hung on the beige walls, while a large black and white numeral clock stared back at her. Ella wondered what was taking so long.

Finally, a man in a food-stained tank top approached the cash register where she was standing. Ella smiled at him and said, "Hi, I was wondering if I could get a couple of large coffees to go."

"For you?" the man asked.

"For me and my friends, the movers. They just got here with my stuff."

"You're new in town."

Ella nodded curtly. If he didn't want to be friendly, that was fine with her; she didn't have to be friendly, either.

"Hey, you're awfully pretty. Where you from?" The voice came from a group in the booth closest to the door consisting of five young men dressed in caps and T-shirts. For the first time, Ella felt the stirrings of genuine unease.

"Connecticut."

The man who spoke to her didn't smile. "Cun-et-ee-kut...you're a long way from home, girlie."

Ella wasn't sure what to say; she didn't want to antagonize these men, but she didn't want to appear weak, either. "It's not that far."

"Far enough," the man behind the cash register said as he dropped a cardboard coffee cup on the counter in front of her.

Ella looked down at the coffee cup, then up at the man. "Can I have three of these, please?"

"Nope. Only got enough for you."

Ella looked around. Something was off, and she wished she'd listened to her friends. The bell on the door chimed again, and Ella turned to see Pete walking toward her.

"We don't need any coffee; we're fine," he told her, trying to telegraph a message with his eyes.

"Y'all know your way out of here when you're done, right?" the man with the cap asked Pete. "Wouldn't want you and your friend out there to get lost."

"We're fine, thanks. C'mon, Ella. Let's go."

"Yeah, *Ella*, you should go. Have fun with your friends." Ella looked at the man smirking at her from the booth and felt a flare of anger as she spit her words out. "What's your problem?"

Pete pulled on her arm. "We're leaving now," he told the crowd.

When they reached the door, Ella turned. "I thought Southerners were supposed to be polite? Obviously, you didn't get the memo."

"And I thought Yankees were supposed to stay home, *Ella*." His hard eyes glittered as he looked her up and down.

"Jerk."

Outside, Ella told Pete, "Sorry. I don't know what got into me."

Pete nodded. "Let's just get to the house."

***

Ed and Pete amazed her. She hadn't expected such organization; in fact, she hadn't been sure what to expect. They were, after all, just a couple of old friends who'd started a moving business. She thought movers just dumped all of your stuff in one room and left; instead, they brought everything in, put boxes in the rooms she indicated, and even set her furniture up where she thought she might want it. Not that she had too much furniture; her apartment in Connecticut had been full, but that was only a small, one bedroom place.

"You sure have a lot more space here," Ed said during a break. "You get a whole house now. Moving up in the world, aren't you?"

Ella laughed. "I was just thinking about that. I'm probably going to need more furniture. I thought I had too much stuff, but not anymore. With things so much cheaper down here I can afford more space."

Ed looked at her. "Yeah, it's less expensive—but you wouldn't catch me living around these parts."

"Listen, Ed, about the coffee shop thing… I'm sorry. I should have listened to you when you told me we had to leave. I still don't know what their problem was."

Ed's voice was gentle. "Their problem was *me*. Didn't you figure that out?"

She dropped her head, knowing he was right. Ed was a black man obviously not welcome in that part of town. He put a finger under her chin so she'd look up at him. "You're not responsible for what those people say. But you've got to promise me you'll be careful. You're a beautiful woman, living alone. You got their attention today, and I don't think that's a good thing."

Ella shivered. "I'm sorry."

"It's not your fault. It's just the way it is —at least in some parts of the world. That's why I'll be glad to move on to our next delivery. You never know what can happen in a town like this. Strange accidents happen all the time. Especially to people like me."

"Maybe that used to be the case," she argued, "but it can't be like that anymore. I know that prejudice exists everywhere, and people say stupid things—but strange accidents? Do you really think those guys would hurt you?"

"Yes. I think they might hurt anyone they don't like. That's why I told you to be careful. Keep your doors locked, and maybe this'll blow over." He stood, ready to get back to work. "I better help Pete finish with those boxes. I think the temperature outside has gone up five degrees since we started this conversation."

As Ed went back to the truck, Ella sat in her new kitchen, lost in thought and nursing the remnants of a lukewarm coffee. Could the whole town really be prejudiced? Probably not; she imagined, however, that a couple loud-mouthed individuals could make it seem that way. It was always the loudest, most insensitive of a group that got the most attention, and that man at the coffee shop was definitely loud and insensitive.

She wasn't naïve enough to think that the world was one big happy family, but she always thought that the kind of prejudice he was talking about only happened in small pockets around the country. *I thought this happened in the deeper parts of the south. I didn't expect it here.* Apparently, it was anywhere.

Although she hated it, racial insensitivities were nothing new to her. Even the liberal Northeast had more than its fair share of racists. She could only live her life being good to others and hope that it somehow made a difference. Maybe Ed was wrong in thinking that she could be hurt by anyone from the diner this morning. Those men might be rude, but would they really try to harm her?

"Before we change the world, we've got work to do, Daisy," she said, standing. "Those boxes aren't going to unpack themselves." Daisy's tail gave an answering thump on the floor. "It's too bad you don't have opposable thumbs; you'd be a real help if you could open all the boxes for me, maybe hang a few pictures."

Once they finished, Ella gave Ed and Pete a good tip in appreciation of their work. "I can't believe you worked in this heat!"

Ed looked down at her. "You better get used to this heat. You live here now."

"I know," she said, pushing her rapidly curling hair out of her face. "I better get some good hair products, too!" She stepped forward, reached up, and gave both Ed and Pete a quick hug. "Take care of yourselves, and drive carefully."

Ed hugged her back. "You take care of yourself, too. Stay safe, and try not to get into trouble around here. You might want to keep some of those smart-ass T-shirts packed away. You're gonna scare the natives."

As they walked back to the moving truck, Ella could hear Ed humming a tune. She stopped, listening. *That's the same song I heard last night... what the heck is that tune?*

Waving goodbye, Ella wondered if it were possible for her to get into serious trouble living in a small town and teaching at a community college.

Chapter Four

IT WAS EARLY AFTERNOON, AND Ella was surrounded by boxes. Forgoing her usual shorts and T-shirt in favor of wearing something that might be slightly cooler, she'd changed into a bright-colored sundress. The turquoise dress made her normally green eyes appear blue, and she fanned her face with a copy of *Buddhism Today* magazine. Perhaps it was time to turn the air conditioning on.

"It's a good start. I just have to put everything away, find out how to recycle all these boxes, buy some things for the house, meet new people, get ready for my new job... before you know it, we'll start to feel like we're home." Daisy looked at her, raising a doggie eyebrow. "Right, we are home."

A rapid knock at the door interrupted her ramblings. "I hope it's not my new neighbors catching me talking to myself. I'll just say I was talking to the dog... no, that would be worse..."

It looked like the man at the door had on a utility worker type of uniform.

"Yes?" she asked, speaking loudly enough so he could hear her.

"Cable guy!" he yelled. "Gonna have to let me in if you want to watch TV tonight!"

He looks like the cable guy, with his clipboard and uniform, but I don't like the arrogant way he's standing at my door. Do people around here always just show up, expecting to be let in? How am I supposed to know who these people are?

Standing at the screen door, Ella asked, "Can I see some identification, please?"

She knew that the screen itself wasn't very solid and he could have pushed his way in if he wanted.

"Excuse me, ma'am?" he asked.

"Hasn't anyone ever asked to see your identification before?" Ella knew she was being obstinate, but she wasn't letting a stranger in.

"No," he said, looking pointedly at the large truck with the company logo on the side.

Ella took a deep breath. "Listen, mister, obviously I'm not from around here, and I don't know you. For all I know, you knocked the other cable guy over the head, grabbed his uniform and vehicle, and are making your way through neighborhoods robbing and killing people. So, let's see some identification."

Lisa would be proud of me.

He stared at her for a moment before smiling. "You must be from up North. Well, alrighty then, little lady. Hold on, I got it right here..." His voice trailed off as he searched through his wallet, triumphantly producing two laminated cards. "See, now, here's my union card, here's my company identification, and here's some pictures of my grandbabies. Ain't they somethin'?"

She looked closely at each item produced before letting him in. "I hope you're not insulted," she said, "but one can never be too careful, right?"

He nodded. "I know. I heard they got lots of crime up north there. But this is a nice little town. You're going to like it here. We're not like those big cities you're probably used to." They stared at each other for half a beat before he asked, "So, it looks like you're not married."

"What would make you think that?"

"Nothing on your finger, missy." Shaking his head, he added, "I'll just bet a pretty little thing like you will get snatched up right soon. You'll probably be giving your own Daddy some grandbabies, too."

Ella's jaw clenched as she stood in front of him, fuming.

Another moment of silence passed before he asked, "Where do you want your computer hooked up?"

Ella led the way as they climbed the stairs to where her office would be. "Do you know the difference between a Yankee and a damn Yankee?"

"Yes," Ella replied curtly, "and I understand that I would be a damn Yankee. The computer, as you can see, is in front of the window here." It was an old joke, one she'd heard on her previous visit to Virginia; she hadn't liked it any better then, either.

Ignoring her, he said, "Yep, a Yankee is someone from up north who comes to visit—and a damn Yankee is someone from up north who comes to visits and stays." Shaking his head and laughing, he crossed the room to the computer.

For the next hour, she followed him as he went about the business of hooking up her telephone, cable television, and internet service. At one point, he looked at her and said, "You've probably got lots to do, maybe get your kitchen all set up. I can finish on my own."

"No, that's all right," she said. *There's no way I'm leaving a stranger alone in any room of my house.* Especially this particular stranger, who annoyed the heck out of her, and especially after what happened in the coffee shop that morning. For all she knew, as soon as her back was turned he'd start rifling through her underwear drawer. "I'll just stick close by, in case you need anything. Do you need anything?"

"Well, bless your heart. I'm just fine. I'll probably have to get under the house in a little bit. I'm sure you don't want to follow me there, too, do you?"

Since she didn't have any personal things under the house, she thought that was unnecessary. "Nope, I'm sure you'll be just fine under there," she answered brightly. If she were bothering him, that was too bad.

An hour later, he was finished. After he made a great display of showing her how her voicemail and remote control worked, he was ready to leave. Not a moment too soon for Ella, either, since she'd had about all she could take of snide Yankee comments.

"Now you remember, little lady, you're in the South now. You're gonna want to learn to make biscuits and sweet tea," he said, chuckling a little.

Ella wasn't certain, but at that point she thought he must be kidding, but she couldn't help the flush that spread over her as she thought about it. Clearly the cable guy thought women were supposed to be married, pregnant, and in the kitchen. Was this what he really thought, or was he baiting her? Her exchange with the customers in the coffee shop flitted briefly through her mind. Maybe this small town had more than just racial prejudices... no, those people were not representatives for a whole town. Wasn't she thinking just a little while ago how one or two obnoxious people could make things seem worse than they were? Besides, maybe the cable guy thought he was being funny—or God forbid, cute.

"Ya'll have a nice day, ya hear?" she said as sweetly as she could as he was leaving. With a saucy little wave, she shut her front door, relieved to have her cable service installed and even more relieved to have the man out of her house. Southerners confused her. She wasn't sure if the man was joking with her or if he truly didn't like "those damn Yankees". She had a feeling it was the latter.

As she stomped around looking for the remote to change the television channel from the Shopping Network, the phone rang.

"Hello?"

"It works! Your phone works! So how is everything? Did Ed and Pete show up? Have you met anybody? What are you doing?"

"Hi, Meg." Ella aimed her remote at the television, wondering what was on her new channels. Same crap she'd gotten in Connecticut, probably. "Yes, Ed and Pete were here, and they had an interesting welcome to the town. I've met a few people. The first one I'm scared of—which is not good since he takes care of the house—and the cable guy I'm furious with for being way too chauvinistic and telling me I need to find myself a man and learn to make sweet tea and unpack my kitchen—of all the ridiculous things, Can you believe—"

"Whoa, wait, stop. Start at the beginning, you've already lost me."

Ella took a deep breath and told Meg about the scare she got when Jeff showed up at her door yesterday and her confrontation in the coffee shop.

"So, you really think you've landed in some kind of 'Deliverance' type of place?" Meg sounded doubtful.

"I don't know. I do know that the cable guy just left, and let me tell you, I think he's about as Neanderthal as they come. He kept calling me 'little lady' and 'damn Yankee,' can you believe that?"

Meg laughed. "Actually, yes, I can believe it. You probably intimidated him. You're an attractive, outspoken, liberal young woman. I have a feeling he doesn't see a whole lot of you around that part of the world."

Ella frowned. "I don't think that's necessarily true. Sometimes people are so set in their ways they don't even realize how they react to others. I mean, really Meg, he didn't have any idea he was being insulting. He kept saying 'bless your heart' and all this other southern nice stuff, only I'm not sure it really was nice."

It sounded like Meg was choking on the other end of the phone.

"What?" Ella said.

"I thought you of all people would get it."

"Get what? What's to get?"

"Don't you know what 'bless your heart' really means?"

"I assumed it was a nice way of saying 'bless your heart.' But I'm starting to think that Southerners have their very own language, and of course I have no idea what the rules are down here. If all Southerners are like this, then I say it's a good thing we won the stupid war!"

At that moment, there was a definitive noise: someone cleared their throat and knocked on the back door.

Chapter Five

"HELLO? ANYBODY HOME?" A SOFT but distinctly female voice called out.

"Damn," Ella whispered to Meg, "I've gotta go. Somebody's here. I hope they didn't hear me." She quickly disconnected.

This time, Ella knew she had no cause for alarm. First, it was obviously a female at her door—and right or wrong, she felt safer than she did with a strange male at the door. Second, Daisy was already sitting at the back door, tail wagging against the floor, an expectant look on her face. Daisy wouldn't look that way if a crazed serial killer was standing there.

"Hi!" Ella opened the door. "Come on in. My name's Ella," she said, extending her hand.

The woman entered carrying a bulging grocery bag. She looked to be about seventy years old, a petite figure with bright silver hair and sparkling blue eyes shining out from behind little round glasses. She was almost the same height as Ella, and she carried herself with perfect posture. Gingerly, she shook Ella's hand.

"Forgive me for intruding. I'm Alice, your new neighbor from down the street. I wanted to stop by and welcome you, and I've brought you some tomatoes from my garden." As she said this, she handed the bag to Ella, who couldn't help noticing that Alice wore a conservative summer skirt and jacket with Jimmy Choo shoes—or at least some damn good knock-offs.

"I love garden tomatoes, thank you so much! Can I get you anything? Something to drink? I have water, juice, or soda, or I could make some coffee... it's so hot out there, you must be thirsty."

The woman smiled at her. "Well, bless your heart dear, I don't want to take up any of your time. I know you must have lots to do," she said, looking around at the empty boxes. "It always takes a while to get settled, doesn't it? I wanted to introduce myself and let you know I'm in the yellow house across the way. We're not directly across from you, but we can get to each other if need be. There aren't a lot of houses on this street, so we do try to check in with each other when we can."

"Please, come in, make yourself comfortable," Ella said, gesturing to the table and chairs in the kitchen. "Do you live with your husband?" Ella could have bitten her tongue off as soon as she said the words.

Here I am, assuming she's married. That's almost as rude as the cable guy.

"Well, in a manner of speaking I do. My Albert passed away ten years ago, but I still feel like he's with me every day of the week. We were married for almost forty years, you know. I still talk to him as I putter around the house."

Ella wondered if Albert ever answered her, but she didn't dare ask. Instead, she said, "I'm sorry for your loss."

"Well, I was, too—at first. But it's funny, I kind of like it better this way. I still get to have Albert around, since he never really left and all, but I don't have to clean up after him. Isn't that about the best deal in town?" With that, Alice let loose with a large laugh, as if they'd shared a very funny private joke.

Ella smiled, delighted at this woman's personality but uncertain about what she was saying. She wondered if Alice was joking or if she really walked around the house talking to her dead husband every day. Either way, Ella wasn't sure she wanted to know. Alice's experience was a little too close to her own 'sort of psychic' self she was trying hard to avoid. And she did not want to see any ghosts.

"Thank you for the tomatoes. I'm sorry you can't stay for a drink or anything," Ella said, wondering if she might be able to sneak a cigarette once Alice left. After the day she had, she deserved it, lung cancer or not. Of course, since that was exactly what her mother was dead from, it was hard to have even one cigarette without all sorts of other feelings intruding. *Maybe I can get through one day without smoking.*

Alice cocked her head to the side, watching Ella. "You're from up North, aren't you?"

Ella suppressed a groan. She didn't want to have another round of "damn Yankee" jokes, and she wasn't up for discussing the relative merits of biscuits and sweet tea. But politeness dictated that she at least answer the woman.

"Yes, you could say that. I'm from Connecticut."

Alice fixed her with a firm stare. "Be careful around here, okay? Young girl like you needs to be careful, being all alone and everything."

Despite the heat, Ella shivered, wondering why the woman was telling her this. "I'm fine, really. I've got Daisy here," at the sound of her name, Daisy wagged her tail, "and I don't let anyone in the house that I don't know." *Except for people who barge in uninvited.* "Or at least I make them show me some identification."

Alice snorted. "Yeah, I heard all about that. Frank, the cable guy, had himself all worked up real good, telling everyone you asked to see his identification. First time anyone's ever asked him that. Of course, we all know him around here." Laughing, she added, "Next time I need my phone repaired, I'm going to ask him the same thing!" Taking a seat at the kitchen table, Alice looked very much like a woman in charge. "Have you met the owner of this house?"

Ella slid into the chair across from Alice, wondering how the older woman had heard about the incident with the cable guy. He'd just left her house.

"No, I haven't met anyone but Jeff, his son. The whole thing was handled through the real estate lady, so I never actually spoke to the owner. Does he live around here somewhere?"

Alice wrinkled her nose. "No, he doesn't, and you can be glad of that. You won't have to worry about him. I can't tell about his son, though..." Looking behind Ella as if to ensure they were alone, she added, "You be careful, that's all."

Ella nodded, wondering if she'd missed something. "I will, don't worry. Does the owner usually bother the tenants? He hasn't come over, and I wouldn't know him if I saw him."

"No." The end of Alice's long finger sparkled with bright pink polish as she tapped the side of her well-creased face. "I don't think he'd dare come around here. But I do think he has lots of influence on that son of his, and if he wants something done, then the son makes sure it happens. That family has always been kind of private; the mother left years ago, and the father never seemed to want to get rid of this house. I don't know why, considering..."

"Considering what?"

Alice shook her head. "Nothing... nothing at all. All right then, I'll be on my way. Remember, anytime you want to visit Albert and me, feel free to stop in. Just come on over to the yellow house across the way."

As Ella waved goodbye to her new neighbor, she felt a pang of sympathy for the woman. "She's older, and probably a little lonely. No wonder she still talks to Albert," she said to Daisy. "I'll make sure I check in on her. She might not have any family around here."

Ella looked at Daisy. "Plus, maybe she'll tell me where she goes shoe shopping. But I draw the line at sitting down and having sweet tea with her if Albert's in the room."

Ignoring the pile of boxes staring at her, Ella decided instead to eat a late lunch. *But where?* As she thought about going out to eat, recent conversations floated through her mind. Conversations that hinted at the darker side of humanity. A prejudiced town, a strange landlord... was there really any threat, or was she just feeling dramatic?

Maybe a tomato sandwich would suffice. It would save time, money, and the hassle of finding take-out. Reaching for the bread in the cabinet, she heard a big sigh, accompanied by a breeze that raised goose bumps on her arm. It must have been a blast from the air conditioning, but still she shivered, unnerved and not really sure why. It was only air conditioning.

"I remember my mother used to say this feeling comes when someone walks on your grave," she muttered to Daisy. But Daisy had left the room, leaving her alone in the cold draft.

***

Later that evening, Ella surveyed the beginnings of an organized home. Most of the boxes for the kitchen were unpacked, and she had run the dishwasher several times before putting things away. Of course, pictures still needed to be hung and items arranged, but at least the house had a small semblance of order. She was tired and knew it was time to quit working. Grinning, she thought of Alice and considered when she might visit. She liked her neighbor with the fun shoes.

She stopped short, grin fading. A coldness came from deep inside her body that had nothing to do with the air conditioning. *What the heck?* Shivering, she remembered Daisy's reaction to the kitchen upon their arrival.

Maybe Daisy had seen, smelled, or sensed something else. But that was silly—the dog had probably caught a whiff of some other animal that lived there. Ella looked at her dog. "C'mon, girl, let's get you dinner so I can stop thinking what I'm thinking."

Daisy sat at her feet, unblinking.

"Okay, fine, and we'll go for a walk after dinner. But I'm not sure how long a walk it'll be. I'm not all that comfortable in the neighborhood yet." She had an unsettled feeling about the area, the kind of feeling that made her stomach wavy.

Walking to the kitchen, she poured kibbles into a bowl for the dog. "I'm sure it's the adjustment to a new place."

Daisy's ears perked and tail wagged.

She was trying to remember where she'd put Daisy's leash when the phone rang.

"Ella, welcome! This is Lorraine Endelby calling. I just wanted to call to tell you how excited we are that you've decided to join us here in Virginia!"

Ella smiled. They had spoken a couple of times since Lorraine had offered Ella the job, and each time Ella found herself warming even more to the woman. At sixty-something years of age, Lorraine was a perfectly coiffed, well-mannered Southern lady, the epitome of good manners and grace. Ella had a feeling, however, that beneath all that polish was a core of steel—as she had seen firsthand the way Lorraine managed to maneuver people into doing what needed to be done. Ella's interview at the college, located in a neighboring city, had taken place over the course of several days. On more than one occasion, Ella witnessed Lorraine's management style, and it was impressive. The woman knew how to get things done.

"Lorraine, it's so nice to hear from you. Are you ready for the new semester?"

Lorraine laughed. "Oh, you know how it is this time of year. We have the schedules all finalized, but there's still so much to be done. Somehow or other, it all comes together, though. How was your trip? Are you settled in yet?"

"It was a long and boring ride, but thankfully I have all my things." Ella didn't think it would be wise to mention that she'd hallucinated while driving.

Lorraine sounded sympathetic. "My dear, I know how difficult it can be to move. So much to unpack, then finding exactly where everything goes. I wish you the best of luck. Now, there's a few things we need to discuss before you come in next week. I was wondering how you would feel about teaching just one more class than we had originally planned. This is a class on Rationalism versus Spiritualism. The intent of the course is to have the students examine diminishing rationalist thought in this country and compare it with fundamentalist and spiritual beliefs that are replacing that line of thinking. Perhaps you can even get some students to share their own personal beliefs and how it has affected their world views."

If I agree to do this, it will show that I can be a valuable part of the team. I still have a few weeks before classes start to get organized.

"If this is new, is there a syllabus or anything in place already?" Ella wondered how much work would need to be done. "Do you have an idea of how many students you think will sign up for it?"

"Although we're offering this relatively late, we think this class will quickly fill and become popular. I have a syllabus prepared, and I've outlined the academic expectations, but it would be mostly up to you to choose supporting materials. You should remember, though, this part of the country is the beginning of the so-called 'Bible Belt,' which means that you may have to employ a great deal of tact with this subject. Do you think you're up for it?"

Ella was surprised. She knew that at some point she would be asked to take on more than just the three classes she'd been assigned to teach, but she didn't think it would happen quite so soon. But the subject matter sounded interesting, and this was, after all, her new life. She agreed to teach the new class.

"Excellent!" Lorraine sounded pleased. "I've emailed you the outline we have for the course, and when you come in next week we can go over it in more detail, as well as discuss your ideas for the class. But we can talk more about this next week. Is your computer up and running?"

Ella smiled. She'd caught the fact that Lorraine had already emailed her the course outline before she'd accepted the class. "Yes, my computer is all set. I look forward to seeing what you've put together."

"Good. Now, just one more thing before I let you get back to unpacking: what is your new address? We need to update our records for you, and I don't think I even asked where you found a new home."

"I'm in Paterson. I really like the idea of living in a small town, since that's where I came from. Somehow, the sprawl of the city didn't seem right for me, even though that's where the college is and that's where I stayed when I was here. I took a chance on a place I hadn't seen before."

"How lovely. I think you'll like it there. My husband and I like to go to Paterson for the Fourth of July fireworks. The only thing to watch for is the mosquitoes. You have to be careful, they're almost large enough to take down a small animal."

Ella laughed. "I noticed. I had some sort of illusion that I'd be able to sit on the back porch to grade papers—but that idea went right out the window pretty much the moment I got out of the car."

"Don't worry, dear, it's always worse at this time of year. In the spring and fall it's much more bearable."

Ella noticed that Lorraine didn't say that the mosquitoes went away, she just said that they became more bearable.

"And your address is...?"

"It's 313 Burnt Ridge Way, Paterson. Was there anything else I forgot to give you?"

The silence on the other end lasted for so long that Ella thought the connection had been lost.

"Lorraine? Lorraine? Are you still there?"

Lorraine cleared her throat. "Yes, dear, I'm still here. But…did you say 'Burnt Ridge Way?' Are you at the old Bartok house?"

Ella thought for a moment. "I guess I must be because the man I met that said his dad owned this house is named Jeff Bartok. Do you know the house?"

This time, Lorraine answered immediately. "I certainly do. I had no idea that's where you were moving to… my goodness… I'm so sorry, Ella dear."

Ella frowned. Lorraine sounded genuinely agitated, something that she hadn't expected from the older woman who seemed so poised.

"Lorraine, what's wrong?"

Ella could hear Lorraine taking a deep breath before answering. "My dear, I wish I had helped you find a place to live. I have friends I could have spoken with, or perhaps I could have contacted an agent for you." She stopped for a moment, then in one big rush said, "Quite frankly, if I'd had any idea that you would end up in *that* house, I never would have allowed it!"

Chapter Six

"EXCUSE ME?" *WHAT ON EARTH was this woman talking about?* Ella's first reaction was confusion. Her second reaction, indignation, she controlled. Did Lorraine really believe that she could tell Ella where she could or could not live? She didn't say anything because she knew that at heart Lorraine was a kind woman. Maybe Lorraine knew something that Ella didn't.

A long moment of silence stretched between them.

"Is there a problem with the house? Because everything seems fine to me. It's been freshly painted, with new appliances, and it's clean... well, there's that whole mosquito thing, but there's not much I can do about that, is there?"

Ella could almost hear Lorraine thinking before she answered. "I'm sorry, Ella," she said. "Perhaps I spoke too harshly. It's just that the house you're living in has had so many people passing through. It seems as if anyone who moves in never seems to stay for very long. Why, it's usually just a month or two before it's up for rent again. And I've heard... well... oh, never mind, I'm not going to get into any kind of gossip. Are you okay living there? Have there been any problems?"

Ella answered carefully. "What kind of problems do you mean?"

Lorraine laughed a high, slight giggle that sounded out of place. "I'm just a silly old woman, that's all. I feel responsible for you, since you moved all the way down here on your own and you're living without your family."

"Lorraine, thank you. I'm fine, and everything at the house has been fine. You seem really upset by the fact that I'm living here. Is there something I should know?"

Lorraine sighed. "No, dear, I don't think there's anything you need to know. Let's just say that since there's been such a high turnover of people renting that house, I assumed there must be something horribly wrong with it. I was hoping you would be able to settle in comfortably so that you could focus on your new job. I'm sorry to have distressed you."

Ella wasn't sure that Lorraine was telling her everything, but she decided to accept her at face value. "I appreciate your concern. There's so much to do to get ready before I start teaching this fall, there's not much that can distract me. I'm looking forward to seeing all the staff again, as well."

"Oh, dear, I almost forgot; when you said you were looking forward to seeing everyone, it reminded me. Do you remember Katie and Roland?"

Ella smiled. Katie Hollister and Roland Lagasse were the top two people on her list of folks to call.

"Of course! They were wonderful when I came down to interview with you. I even had dinner at Katie's house in Yorktown. I wanted to call them, but I can't seem to find my address book. I know it's in one of these boxes, I just haven't gotten to it yet."

She wasn't about to tell her new boss that she actually hadn't seen the address book in quite some time. Ella often lost things; it was almost a part of her daily routine. Usually, the lost item turned up in the next few days, and the odd thing was that she usually found whatever she'd lost in the spot where it was supposed to be. At this point, it was just another accepted fact of her life: things went away, and then they came back.

Lorraine answered. "Both Katie and Roland asked me about visiting you tomorrow. If that works for you, why don't I call them after we get off the phone and give them your address?"

"Perfect! Any time after twelve would be great. We could have lunch here." She hesitated for a beat, then added, "You know that you're welcome to come over as well. I'd love to see you."

Lorraine was silent for so long, Ella wondered if she was still there. "Sorry dear, I was just thinking of my schedule. Thank you for the offer, but I'm afraid I won't be able to. Perhaps some other time."

After disconnecting, Ella thought about what Lorraine had said. Maybe the reason nobody stayed in that house was because the landlord was creepy, although, to be fair, he'd come over for a perfectly good reason. Maybe it was the cable guy, chauvinistic jerk...

She went back to the couch with a new book she wanted to read but was too agitated to focus. "I will *not* let Lorraine's comments bother me. Come on Daisy, let's go." Daisy's ears perked up, but she sat unmoving on the floor. "We're not going to let anyone get to us. I know this is a new neighborhood, and I said we were going to do this, so let's go for a walk." Ella picked up the dog's leash and started walking toward the door. Daisy immediately got the message and sprinted in front of her. Laughing, Ella said, "That's the spirit! We moved to a small town for a reason: it's quiet here at night, and it's supposed to be safe. Let's explore the evening."

After carefully spraying herself with bug repellent, they set off. The first thing Ella noticed was the abundance of stars. "Daisy, isn't this beautiful? We don't have any street lights, we can see the entire night sky." She took a breath, gazing at the display strewn above her. Instead of making her feel small or insignificant, stargazing always made Ella feel as if she were part of something bigger, something comforting.

Ella and Daisy were careful on their walk. She took note of which way they went to avoid getting lost. She also avoided the ditches on the side of the road. Used for rainwater management, they were a hazard for walkers. Taking their time, Ella and Daisy meandered up and around the streets of the neighborhood. Other than a barking dog and a motorcycle revving in the distance, there was nothing in the stillness to bother either of them. The sounds of night insects were all around, and the warmth of the day still clung to the evening. Because of the humidity the air felt soft, like an embrace.

"See? I just needed to get out. I don't know why I let myself get so spooked."

She slowed as she walked past Alice's house, trying to get a glimpse of where the interesting old woman lived. It looked like a cozy little house, and she thought she could see a bit of a well-tended garden. There was an upstairs light on, but Ella didn't want to linger. "I don't want to startle her, she might think we're up to no good."

Renewed, Ella traipsed back to the house. "Just like I thought, there's nothing to be afraid of here. Lorraine is worried because she feels responsible for me." Standing in the yard, Ella fumbled in her pocket for her keys. Suddenly, Daisy stopped in front of the porch, hackles raised and growling. Looking up, Ella sucked in her breath. The front porch light illuminated large, angry red letters that had been sprayed onto the house.

YANKEE WHORE

GO HOME

For a moment, Ella couldn't think. The words on her house made no sense. Then, an image of the men in the coffee shop flashed through her mind. With trembling hands, she pulled her cell phone out of her pocket. Dialing 911, she shivered. The deep shadows surrounding the house could provide cover for anyone who wanted to hide. Was it possible that whoever had done this was still there, waiting for her?

***

It didn't take long for the police to arrive and gather evidence. Maybe it didn't take long because the evidence gathering part was limited to the officers looking at the spray painted letters and shaking their heads. Apparently, the Paterson police department was not going to dust for fingerprints, scrape for DNA, or examine the yard for foot imprints. It was definitely not what the folks on the CSI show would have done, but Ella didn't feel like she was in any position to complain.

After the officers left, Ella called and left a message on Jeff Bartok's answering machine. Hopefully, it wouldn't be long before he could have the letters washed off or painted over or whatever needed to be done. She shivered every time she looked at the pulsing red words.

Determined to put the incident out of her mind, Ella marched into the kitchen. Daisy sat just outside the doorway, an expectant look on her face. "Come on, girl, come get your treats," Ella called to her, holding out dog biscuits. Daisy didn't budge. She sat there, looking at Ella, waiting. "Come on! I'm not going to stand here all night." Again, the dog wouldn't move.

The musical strains of Ella's cell phone rang from the living room table. "Okay, fine. Here's your treats," she said, putting them on the floor as she walked past the dog to reach the phone.

Glancing at her phone, Ella felt that familiar urge for a cigarette. Damn lung cancer. It had been a long night, but she really should answer the call.

"Hello?"

"Is everything okay down there?"

"Of course it is, Lisa. Why should anything have changed since we spoke last night?" There was no way she was going to tell her sister what had happened. Telling Lisa about the vandalism would only prolong the conversation, and Ella was tired.

"You didn't call, and I had no idea if your moving buddies had shown up or not, or how your first night was in the new house. What if you'd been attacked overnight and we had no idea what became of you?"

Ella closed her eyes, wondering if Lisa's sisterly intuition made her call. "I'm fine. The movers got here this morning, and it's been a long day."

There was a short silence before Lisa answered. "Oh. Okay. I just wanted to call and make sure everything worked out for you. I'm sure you're pretty tired after unpacking and all, so I guess I'll talk to you later."

Something was wrong, but Ella couldn't figure out what. It was unlike Lisa to give in so easily. "What's going on? Is everything okay? Is Dad okay?"

"Everything's fine. I just thought I'd call, that's all."

Realization struck Ella. "Where's Dan?"

Sometimes Lisa's husband, Dan, went out with his friends at night. Lisa hated being in the house alone and would usually have Ella come over or spend time on the phone with others after her daughters went to bed.

"I'm not sure," Lisa answered softly.

"What do you mean you're not sure? Where did he say he was going?"

"He said he was going to George's house to play cards with the guys tonight, but I saw George's wife in the grocery store a little while ago."

"No card game?"

"No card game."

Ella thought for a moment, her tiredness gone. "You know, Lisa, this is really not like him. He doesn't usually lie to you—"

"That I know of."

"True, but maybe you should give him some slack on this. Maybe he's afraid to tell you what he's really doing."

"Maybe he *should* be afraid to tell me."

"No, really, he's been a good husband to you, and he's a good father. If you're thinking he's cheating on you, I have to say that just doesn't seem like him. I can't imagine he'd risk losing you and the girls for some sort of fling."

"What if it's more than a fling? What if he's found someone else?"

Ella wasn't sure what to say to her sister. While she was fairly certain her brother-in-law wasn't the type to cheat on his wife, these things happened. And after all, what did she really know about him? He spent lots of time working at the office as a high-powered financial executive, making gobs of money so they could live in a nice house and the kids could go to good schools. Maybe he was having an affair, but that was definitely not something she could say to her sister, not without knowing the truth.

"Lisa, Dan loves you. He loves the kids. Try to remember that before you decide he's guilty of something you have no evidence of. Maybe he's planning a surprise for you, and you're going to ruin it all by screaming at him when he comes home. Just be gentle, and try to remember he's innocent until proven guilty."

Lisa let out what sounded like a short sob. "You're right. I shouldn't let my imagination run away with me. I started thinking all these horrible thoughts, and then I didn't know what to think."

"Be there for him when he gets home, and talk to him. Don't yell. If he's lying, I'm sure you'll know."

Lisa gave a half-hearted laugh. "That's true. He's a terrible liar, I can always tell. Thanks, El. Sorry I bothered you."

"It's not a bother. Now go make yourself pretty for when your husband gets home."

Ella ended the call, hoping that she'd done the right thing. What if Dan *was* having an affair? "I doubt Lisa will let him survive long enough to get divorced," she muttered, climbing the stairs to her bedroom.

As she walked up the stairs, book in hand, Daisy raced to her side. Ella smiled. "You are a silly dog sometimes, you know that?" As Daisy jumped up on the bed, Ella settled herself in with her book.

The book couldn't hold her interest. The image of the words sprayed on the front of the house kept haunting her. Obviously, the only people she'd met and annoyed so far were from the coffee shop. She was worried. *What if it wasn't the guys from the coffee shop? What if it was someone else who hates me enough to vandalize the house?*

Whoever it was, she wouldn't let them scare her away.

***

Lorraine waited impatiently while the phone rang on the other end of the line. Finally, it was answered.

"Hello, Roland, this is Lorraine. I'm sorry to be calling you so late."

"That's all right. I was just organizing my stuff. I can't find my syllabus from last year, and I've spent the past hour looking for it on my computer. Have you had a chance to talk to Ella yet?"

"Actually, yes, that's why I'm calling. Ella has invited you and Katie over for lunch tomorrow afternoon. She told me to let you know she was going to call as soon as she found her address book. Please, Roland, you must go. I know you wanted to get together as friends anyway, and I think it's imperative that you go to her new house."

"Why? Is something wrong?"

Lorraine took a long time answering, leaving silence hanging between them. "Lorraine, what is it? Has something happened to Ella? Is she in a bad neighborhood?"

"No," Lorraine answered. "It's not that. She's living in Paterson. She's rented out the old Bartok place."

There was a hesitation on the other end of the line. "Lorraine, don't worry. Katie and I will go over there tomorrow and make sure everything's okay. I'll talk to you afterward and let you know how it goes."

Ending the call, Lorraine prayed she'd done the right thing.

Chapter Seven

IT FELT LIKE LATE AFTERNOON. Perhaps it was the slant of the sun, the oppressiveness of the humidity, or the overriding listlessness of everything, even the bird songs. Ella recognized the woods, as well as the two girls that sat together on the tree stump.

"This is just nasty if you ask me."

"But Hattie, all the movie stars look so glamorous when they do it. Maybe it will make us more sophisticated."

The girl called Hattie laughed. "What do we care about that? Being sophisticated in a town like this still ain't gonna get us nowhere."

The other girl was quiet for a moment. "But we don't have to live here forever. Someday we'll be able to go wherever we want."

Hattie's lips thinned as she slowly shook her head. "No, my friend, I think some of us are meant to stay here for always."

Another moment passed with only the background drone of insects. Hattie sighed and reached her hand out. "Okay, fine. Give me one more cigarette. Let's see if I can do this without coughing this time."

***

The following day was exactly as the forecasters had predicted: hot, humid, and sunny. Summer in Virginia generally contained a combination of those three ingredients, and Ella was happy about that. She loved the warmer weather and despised the cold. Her bones would literally ache during the fierce New England winters, which could last for months on end. She was curious as to how severe the winter would be this far south. Hopefully, snow shoveling was a thing of the past.

Ella spent the entire morning preparing the house as best she could for her expected guests. Jeff had stopped by earlier with a power washer and cleaner, and it wasn't long before the offensive words were erased.

With a nod and a gruff holler through the screen door to be careful, Jeff was gone. Although Ella thought it was strange he didn't come in to ask questions, she was relieved. The last thing she wanted was to explain how she'd attracted the attention of some nut, especially when she wasn't sure how it had happened.

After racing through the house to clean, she shoved what she couldn't organize into the closets. Her stuff could be arranged later, but for now she needed to get to the grocery store. "If there's one thing I know how to do, it's feed people," she said to Daisy, who perked her ears at the mention of food. She came home laden with hamburgers, hot dogs, corn on the cob, chicken, salad, green beans, and drinks. Also, just in case, she decided to make a pan of lasagna. "We can always have leftovers if we have too much food," she told her dog, who she swore sighed in contentment, "but there's nothing worse than not having enough."

The morning passed in a frenzy of food preparation. Every now and then, Ella found herself humming a tune with the radio or doing a little dance around her kitchen as she cooked. The house was starting to feel like a home, and having friends visit emphasized that feeling.

She chose a bright pink sundress to wear and paired it with strappy black sandals. It was a great color for her complexion, and it matched her cheerful mood.

A little after one in the afternoon the doorbell rang, followed immediately by sharp knocking.

"Hello!" a voice called out through the screen. "Welcome to Virginia! It's the Welcome Wagon!"

Ella hurried into the living room. "The door is open. C'mon in."

Katie bounced in, carrying a huge bouquet of flowers and a bottle of wine, with a genuine smile on her face and obvious delight at seeing Ella again. "You made it!" she said, squealing as she gave Ella a big hug. "I'm so glad to see you. We were hoping you'd take the job and join us in our little corner of the world. Here, I brought you some flowers and wine as a housewarming gift."

Roland was right behind her, his arms full. "And I come bearing food as well: brownies, cookies, muffins, and a container of genuine Southern chicken salad, all for our celebration today. Welcome! We're glad you're here!"

Ella laughed, warmed by her new friends' spontaneity, delighted that they were there and suddenly feeling as if she'd made a very good decision with her life—vandals or no vandals.

"It's great to see you guys, and thank you for the gifts. Katie, you look gorgeous as usual, and Roland, you're as handsome as ever. Come in, let me give you a tour."

Katie laughed. "Not only do you refer to us as 'gorgeous' and 'handsome,' but is that lasagna I see in the kitchen back there? Homemade lasagna? Compliments *and* food? You'll never get rid of us!"

"Lasagna?" Roland echoed. Ella smiled. He reminded her of Daisy: at the mention of food, she expected to see his ears lift up. As she looked at her two new friends, Ella was struck by how well they balanced each other. Katie Hollister, petite, blonde, and blue-eyed, was the perfect complement to Roland Lagasse, who was the archetype for tall, dark, and handsome. While Katie's looks hinted at innocence, with her long loose curls and propensity to dress in flowing garments, Roland was tall with a craggy worldliness to him, deep brown eyes, and dark hair that tended toward unruly.

As far as Ella could tell, the two were just good friends and acted more like brother and sister than anything else. When she'd initially met them during her interview and they'd later gone out for drinks, both had proclaimed themselves to be single, and happily so. Still, Ella wondered why two good looking people who got along so well never became a couple, but that was a conversation left for when she got to know them better. She fussed over the flowers from Katie, which were a vibrant display of color: bright yellows, deep oranges, and startling reds. Ella inhaled, appreciating the earthy, floral scent before she put them in a vase.

Finished with the flowers, she turned to her friends. "What would you like first, drinks, food, or tour?"

Roland cleared his throat. "Before we do that, there's something I need to tell you. Lorraine called me last night."

"She was really upset that I rented this house. Do you know why?"

"Because she feels responsible for you," Katie answered.

"It's more than that," Roland said, looking sideways at Katie. "First, I told her I'd make sure everything was okay here. When you show me around, I'm going to check the house—if that's all right with you. Then later, maybe after a glass or two of something, Katie and I can tell you a little history of this area."

"Not that there's anything to tell that you should worry about," Katie said. "You haven't made a poor choice or anything. It's just..."

"We heard about last night," Roland finished for her. He looked concerned.

"Lorraine didn't know anything about the vandalism when I talked to her, and I didn't tell her. Are you okay?"

Ella nodded, wondering how they'd found out about her house. "I'm fine. I'm sure it was just kids goofing around."

"Are you scared to stay here now?" Katie looked concerned.

"No, not really. I'm sure it won't be a recurring event." She wasn't sure at all of that, but she felt like it was the right thing to say.

"You poor thing." Katie draped an arm across Ella's shoulder. "You're probably right, I'm sure it was kids. If you need anything, let us know. We want to help you get settled and get to know your new town."

"I've met a couple of people already. My neighbor across the way is very sweet, and she's got great shoes, but I wonder if she's getting a bit senile. She lives in the house with her dead husband."

Katie's eyes became huge at this comment, so Ella hurried to add, "I don't mean literally, she claims his ghost is there."

At that, Katie nodded. "That would be Albert," she told Ella. "Alice is a unique and gifted woman."

"You know her?"

"We know everyone," claimed Roland, putting his arm around Katie. "We've lived in this area our whole lives, and it really is a small town. Come on, let's get started. I need to be able to tell Lorraine that I checked under all your beds and in the closets but couldn't find any boogeyman before we tackle that lasagna."

They laughed, but as Ella gave the tour of her new home, she noticed that Roland did indeed open all the closet doors, as well as look behind the shower curtains. To his credit, he also checked the plumbing and air conditioning unit, ensuring that everything was in good working order.

"Did you really think you were going to find something?" she asked.

He shrugged. "No, I didn't, but it makes sense for me to look, just like it makes sense for me to test your locks downstairs. It's not that I think anything is wrong, but you're a single woman living on your own and it pays to be cautious."

Ella folded her arms over her chest. Something else was going on, and she wanted answers. "Then why is Lorraine so upset? You said she didn't know anything about the vandalism."

Roland and Katie exchanged a look before Roland answered. "First, let's get ourselves a drink, and we'll tell you what we know."

Minutes later, Roland and Katie were seated comfortably at the kitchen table while Ella prepared the chicken for grilling. "Okay, people, spill it. What's up with the house? Is it because that Jeff guy is so creepy? Is he some kind of criminal or something?"

"Not that we know of," Katie answered. "I'm sure Roland will correct me if I make a mistake, but this is what I know." She looked at Roland, who nodded at her to continue. "Years ago, Lorraine used to live in Paterson. In this neighborhood, actually. You have to remember, it was a different time for us, culturally. At that time, our country—and this area—was struggling with the beginnings of the Civil Rights Movement."

Roland interrupted her. "In some places, the Civil Rights Movement didn't exist or was blatantly ignored. We all know that some parts of the South were more resistant than others. Even today, this town can be somewhat insular. There are wonderful people here, but if you go out shopping on a Saturday and look around, you'll see mostly people who resemble each other racially."

"You mean white people," Ella said.

Katie nodded. "There's a rumor that there used to be a sign at the edges of town that read, 'Turn back if you're black.'" She paused, shivering. "I don't understand that type of attitude, but unfortunately, it exists. Some of the good old boys around here scare the living daylights out of me. That type of prejudice—back then and today—can be dangerous."

Roland agreed with her. "Please, Ella, don't argue with folks when it comes to that kind of stuff. I don't want you to become a target for anything."

"You think I'm in some kind of danger?" Ella was incredulous. Her mind flashed to the confrontation at the coffee shop.

"No, I don't, not really," Roland said. "It's just that you're a Northerner, and people sort of expect you to already be kind of... liberal, I guess."

"You bet they think that. You should have heard my conversation with the cable guy," she said, still upset by the man's patronizing attitude the previous day. She avoided mentioning the altercation in the coffee house, saving that information for later. "Okay, I get it. You don't want me to mouth off and get myself persecuted, or ostracized, or have eggs thrown at the house, or whatever. But what does that have to do with Lorraine?"

"As I said, she lived in this neighborhood years ago," Katie continued. "In the late fifties, I think. If you thought the cable guy was bad, you would have hated it here then. People were much less tolerant, and it was a generally accepted attitude. Anyway, despite all that, Lorraine had a very dear friend. Her name was Hattie, and she happened to be black. They were the same age, sixteen or seventeen, and used to hang out together. I don't know where they would go, though." She turned to look at Roland, a question in her eyes. "It's not like they could go out in public and have a soda."

Roland nodded. "That's true. Remember, this was the time of segregation, with separate bathrooms and water fountains. I think they used to read books together or do homework or whatever. Lorraine told me a little about her friend, saying that she was a very insightful girl, smart and funny. When she had time off from her job, Hattie and Lorraine used to sneak out to the woods to smoke cigarettes and talk about Jane Eyre or whatever they were reading at the time."

A memory was nudging at Ella, but she forced herself to listen to what Katie was saying.

"It's very sad. I think Hattie was the first true friend Lorraine ever had, and I get the feeling there was a genuine respect between them. Every time Lorraine mentions her, you can tell she misses her terribly, even after all these years. I guess some childhood friendships don't ever fade."

"What happened?" Ella stood at the sink, raw chicken in her hand. Part of her didn't want to hear the story; she didn't have to be psychic to know that whatever they were going to tell her was going to be bad.

Chapter Eight

ROLAND SHIFTED IN HIS CHAIR. "We're not sure what happened, even now. One day, according to Lorraine, Hattie just disappeared. There had been some kind of storm, maybe a hurricane. Nobody knew where she went, but even worse, nobody tried to find her. It was as if Lorraine was the only person who cared about what happened to her friend."

Ella shook her head. "Didn't the police try to find her? She couldn't have just vanished."

Katie gave a ladylike snort while Roland went on to explain. "Again, it was a different era. From what I heard, the police did a report, but they never spent any time investigating. Hattie had no close relatives that put up a fuss, and there were no search parties. After all, this was a young Black woman who was working as a domestic servant. She was, for all intents and purposes, a nobody."

Ella took a deep breath. She'd imagined that moving to a small town would add an element of peacefulness to her life, away from the chaos of an urban environment. Apparently, she was wrong. "My God, that's terrible. Someone, somewhere, must have missed her and mourned her?"

"Yes, someone did," Katie said. "Lorraine."

Ella thought for a moment, her brow wrinkled. "I understand that this neighborhood holds some sad associations for Lorraine, but she had such a strong reaction when I told her I was living in this house. Was this where Lorraine lived?"

"No, this is where Hattie worked," Roland said. "She worked for the Bartok family."

A chill settled inside Ella, and all she could manage was a whispered, "Oh."

"So now you know." Katie stood and crossed the kitchen to where Ella stood, still holding the chicken over the sink. "And you can think about this terribly morbid story on some dark and stormy night. For now, it's a beautiful day, we've got lots of food and drinks, and we're all together. Let's set up outside and enjoy ourselves."

Ella smiled ruefully, putting the chicken on a platter and washing her hands. "We can certainly try, Katie. But I cannot guarantee that the same thing won't happen to us. In fact, I think I may know what happened to Hattie."

"What?"

"She was carried away by the killer mosquitoes outside. I've never seen anything like them in all my life."

Roland stood to help with preparations. "Don't worry, we've come up with a method. First, the anti-mosquito lotion. Then the bug spray. The combination of the two works like a charm. Citronella candles and some type of witch's incantation are a big help, too."

The three of them applied lotion and bug spray before carrying the food and condiments outside. On the back deck, Ella had a round outdoor table and green plastic chairs she'd washed that morning. They were old but serviceable, dragged all the way down in the movers' van to be put to use for as long as they would last.

"Okay, ladies," Roland said, seating himself comfortably. "You may commence cooking my meal."

The two women looked at him, then at each other. Ella pointed at him. "You did *not* just say what I think you said?"

Katie winked at her. "Leave this to me," she whispered, sashaying over to the grill. "Roland, sugar, I can't remember how to get the grill started. Can you help me, just this little bit?"

Ella held back her laughter as Roland jumped up to help Katie. "Of course, step aside. I'll do the man's work around here."

Ella knew Roland was joking around, but she still found it hilarious that it took him a while to realize that Katie was getting him to do all the work. When the burgers and chicken were almost entirely grilled, he turned to them and said, "Hey, since when did I become the cook?"

"Right after we made you carry everything out—and don't forget, this is right before you become the maid," Katie said, taking a swig of beer. She showed him her empty bottle. "Oh, and I'd like another, please."

Roland took a pretend swipe at Katie, but he got her the drink anyway.

The rest of the afternoon passed pleasantly, with all of them talking, laughing, eating, and drinking.

At one point, Ella paused, looking around her. Katie and Roland were talking about the latest movie they'd seen. The air had cooled just enough so it wasn't too hot. It was a perfect day with her new friends, and thoughts of vandalism and missing persons had faded. *Maybe small town life in the South won't be so bad after all.*

It was early evening when Katie and Roland decided to leave. But first, they helped Ella put all the food away and clean up the remnants of the backyard picnic. In the kitchen, Ella turned to her friends. "I've wrapped two separate plates for each of you to take home."

Roland smiled at her. "I will *never* refuse food. In fact, I'm a little like Daisy: if you keep feeding me, I'll keep coming back." When he got to the front door, Roland hesitated, turning back to Ella.

"Listen, I know that was a kind of heavy story we told you today. What's in the past is in the past, and I don't think there's much we can do about it. Lorraine has her own reasons for worrying about you, but I think that her reasons have more to do with the past than anything in the present. But you're a single woman living on your own, and while Alice is great to have for a neighbor, she won't be able to offer you much in the form of protection. You've already had one problem here. Make sure you lock up at night, and be careful in general, okay?"

"That's our Southern hospitality kicking in," Katie told her. "We like to make sure everyone is safe and sound and locked up good."

"Thanks, I'll remember that." Ella laughed, waving a final goodbye. Shutting the front door, she hesitated for a moment before turning the deadbolt. "He's right, Daisy, you know? Besides, everyone else is telling us the same thing: be careful. Maybe they're onto something."

Daisy looked at her, head cocked to the side as if she were trying to say something.

"What is it, girl?"

The dog glanced over to the closet where her leash lay, then gave a soft whimper.

Ella hesitated. It was great having her friends over that day, but with them gone she felt a little uneasy. The last time she went out for a walk, she came home to spiteful words on the house. Would that happen again? But she couldn't stay in the house forever. Maybe she could take a plate of food to Alice.

Reaching into an overhead cabinet, Ella got a large plastic container and filled it with lasagna and grilled chicken. In another container, she put salad, then placed them both in a bag to carry to Alice's house. Grabbing the leash from the closet, she remembered to turn on lights before they left. The light outside was fading fast, and Ella didn't want to walk into a dark house when she got back.

They walked into the twilit night, that in-between time when the harsh edges of day fade and all things have potential again. The soft air carried a hint of possibility, and a faint breeze stirred, light as a feather on her face. The street was deserted with only the sound of a mourning dove to keep them company. Before long, they were standing in front of Alice's door, ringing her bell.

Ella had barely moved her hand away from the doorbell before the door opened. Alice stood before her, a bright smile on her face. "Come in!" she said. "I've been waiting for you. Albert told me you'd be visiting tonight."

Chapter Nine

"I JUST FINISHED MAKING A pie. Would you like some?"

Ella smiled in response. "Actually, this time I've come bearing gifts for you. I had friends over today, and we had so much food I thought you might enjoy some. The lasagna is homemade, as well as the sauce."

Alice made her way through the crowded living room into the kitchen. "Can you bring those packages back here for me, dear? Thank you."

As Ella walked through, she noticed that although the room was crowded with furniture, pictures, and figurines, the house felt like a home. A well-loved home. It was clean, and the furniture was older but well-kept. The walls were painted a creamy color, with chair rails in dark blue. A couple of pieces of art were on the walls, mostly paintings of seascapes and lighthouses, as well as what looked like old family pictures. It felt like her grandmother's house, with different stuff but the same atmosphere.

Carrying the food into the kitchen, she told Alice, "I won't stay long. I wanted to stop by and give you this and let you know how much I appreciate you coming over yesterday with the tomatoes. They were delicious."

Alice nodded and waved her hand in the air. "My pleasure, dear. There will be plenty more of those as the summer winds down. My garden has been rather prolific these days. Now, tell me, did you have Katie and Roland over to your house today?"

Ella nodded, wondering how Alice could possibly have known about her guests. "How did you know that?" *How do people in this town get their information?*

"Lorraine called earlier. About once a month, she comes to check on me, and in-between that she calls. We've known her for quite a while now, ever since she was young. She mentioned that she recently hired a new woman-professor to teach all those interesting courses, and I realized it was you when I met you. Of course, I haven't told her about you being my new neighbor."

Ella sighed. "I did. She didn't take it very well."

"No, I can't imagine she did at all."

There was a brief silence before Ella hesitantly asked, "Did you know Hattie?"

Alice sat up straight. "Yes, I did—and that's all I'll say about that. It was a tragedy, but we don't need to discuss that right now. The moon is about to rise, you know, and you must be careful what you say and when you say it. Folks listen, and spirits can hear. Sometimes we call them to us without even realizing it, so you must be careful."

Ella nodded, confused. What spirits was Alice talking about? Was she trying to say that Ella was calling these spirits to her already, or was she simply warning her not to do so? And if that was the case, how on earth was she supposed to know how *not* to call spirits? She might have been a college professor, but Ella didn't have the first clue about anything that had to do with real life spirits. The closest she came to that was watching ghost hunters on television.

"If I'm not trying to call them, then the spirits won't be called, right? Don't you have to issue a sort of invitation?"

Alice snorted. "Sometimes they're just like us, honey. Have you ever seen a woman get all dressed up, short skirt, low cut blouse, makeup, just to go out on the town?" Ella nodded, so Alice continued. "As soon as a woman dresses like that, what does a man think? He thinks that it's some kind of invitation, that's what. Not all men, mind you, just the foolish ones. But they're out there, you and I both know that. Same goes for the spirit world. Some of them can deliberately misunderstand something you're doing just so they can pretend it's an invitation. Be careful. Let's talk about something else. Will you grow a garden this year? You might still have time to put up a few plants, maybe grow some rosemary or dill in the kitchen."

Ella willingly went along with the subject change. "If you keep giving me things from your garden, I won't have to plant anything, but I think I'll wait until next year. Lorraine has surprised me with an extra class to teach this semester, and preparing for that will take up most of my free time. Then it takes more time to grade all the papers and tests. I'll let myself settle in first, maybe try a garden next year once I feel more like a native."

Alice laughed, shaking her head. "I'm not sure when you'll start feeling like a native, but you're welcome to my garden vegetables anytime."

"Thanks, Alice. I should go. I promised Daisy a good walk, so we need to get started before it gets too late. I hope you enjoy the lasagna."

Alice walked her to the door, asking if she needed a flashlight.

"No thanks," Ella answered, "I've got my cell phone."

"If you need anything, come on over. If something serious happens, I'm sure my Albert will let me know."

Ella smiled and said goodbye, wondering about what Alice had told her. Despite her occasional batty behavior and talk of ghosts, she liked the older woman.

Ella and Daisy walked the same route they'd taken the night before. "It's starting to feel familiar, isn't it Daisy?" she asked the dog, who was busy sniffing the ground. "I have to say," she continued, talking to the dog, "I know Alice has that whole thing about her husband's ghost living in the house with her, but she reminds me of a grandma. Kind, self-sufficient, and maybe a little eccentric. I hope I have that same attitude when I'm older."

Daisy answered with a small 'whuff.'

They walked for almost an hour, giving Daisy a chance to smell new smells and Ella a chance to think about her new job. Her plan was to get started on her course outlines the next day. She made a mental to-do list, including reviewing the materials Lorraine had sent.

The rhythm of her thoughts shifted to her mother, particularly the fact that her mom would have been proud to see all her schooling actually pay off. She would have been proud of her daughter just because she was her daughter. Before she knew it, tears filled her eyes. Ella tried to focus on something else. She didn't want to wallow in her grief, she just wanted to move on.

Ella was glad she'd remembered to leave the outside lights on. Nobody had spray painted the house, but the long shadows stretched toward her. She stared, thinking that it looked like the house was staring back at her. Shaking her head, she unlocked the door and went inside. It was time to get a good night's sleep, especially with her imagination working overtime again.

Settling on the couch with her laptop, Ella did a few minutes of work before spending the next hour on Facebook and email. Finally, realizing the time, she stretched and went upstairs.

Climbing into bed, she reflected on how much she missed her family and friends in Connecticut. *This is the first time I've lived in a place that my mother has not seen.* In fact, it was strange that she couldn't just pick up the phone and call her mom. But it would do her no good to dwell on the grief, so she focused instead on immersing herself in a book.

***

Soon after, the book slowly falls from her hands as her eyes close. In sleep, Ella was peaceful. The light from the lamp on the bedside table illuminated her face, her breathing even as she succumbed to the fatigue from the day. A few minutes later, the light clicked off.

***

Ella is floating again. She recognizes the scene below her as the same wooded area she was in previously. This time, the hot, wet air wraps around her like a bandage. On the path ahead is a young, dark-skinned girl, laughing and skipping. Her happiness is obvious in the way she moves, a glow from within lighting her entire being. She calls over her shoulder, "I'm in love! Ain't love grand?" As the girl laughs, the wind picks up and carries the sound of her laughter away, creating a tomb-like silence. As she glances over her shoulder again, a crease of worry appears on the girl's face. "I'm in love," she says, this time with a hint of stubbornness. Instead of skipping, she changes to a jog, looking backward once in a while. The sunlight that had dappled the forest floor is gone, and the trees overhead become looming and oppressive while darkness beckons from the shadows. Ella can hear the girl's labored breathing as she breaks into a run, her braids flying behind her. She doesn't want to get caught. "No, no, I'm in love!"

***

The night air was still, it wasn't a breeze that had woken her. No sounds came through the open window, no peepers, no frogs, no barking dogs. There was only her breathing, gasping as if she were underwater. The room was dark, with a hint of moonlight from the window.

The dream was different this time. None of the other dreams about those girls felt like this. This was creepy.

Then she heard it: a steady thumping noise, as if someone were beating a drum. A low growl emanated from Daisy. Placing a hand on her dog, Ella could feel the raised hackles.

"Come on, girl," she whispered, "let's see what's going on." Grabbing her phone and pepper spray from the nightstand next to her, she tried to creep quietly down the stairs. Daisy remained glued to her side.

The thumping grew louder, as did Daisy's growl. The noise was coming from the kitchen. She was shaking. Despite the heat of the night, Ella felt cold all over.

She knew if someone were in there, she'd have to call the police, but she wondered if it was only kids trying to scare the Northern girl. Her determination hardened. They were *so* not going to get away with this—

they were going to regret messing with her. Phone at the ready, she pushed 9 then 1, and held her finger over the final 1, ready to tackle whatever was making the racket in the kitchen.

She made her way across the darkened living room and stood at the entrance to the kitchen. The temperature in the room had plummeted drastically, and Ella imagined that her breath was creating frost in the air around her. This was her house, and she would *not* let some locals looking for a laugh scare her away. She was surprised the intruder couldn't hear her rapidly-beating heart. Taking a deep breath, she tried to stop the violent shivering that had overtaken her. Before she could think about what she was doing, Ella reached for the wall switch and flipped it up. As the overhead light brightened the room, Ella blinked, wondering if she were still dreaming.

Things were floating in the air, pans and glasses and dishes spinning wildly out of control. All the cabinet doors stood wide open. She stared in disbelief and aimed the phone as if it were a weapon at the scene in front of her. At her side, Daisy half-whimpered and half-growled, cowering behind Ella but unwilling to leave her side.

The thumping noise, whatever it was, had thankfully stopped, then everything was suspended for another brief moment before crashing to the ground. At the deafening noise, Ella shut her eyes, unable to move and wondering if perhaps she were hallucinating—or maybe just crazy.

The silence that followed was complete.

Still shaking, unable to stop herself, Ella opened her eyes. Standing in the corner was a young woman, arms outstretched toward Ella and mouth moving. There was no sound, nothing but what looked like a desperate plea emanating from the image before her.

Chapter Ten

ELLA TRIED TO SCREAM, BUT the only noise that came out was a very loud whimper. Immediately, the woman vanished.

She felt as if she'd just run a marathon, her heart beating wildly and her lungs desperately needing air. The floor was littered with kitchen debris, and she couldn't stop shivering from the chill all around. Daisy stood beside her, shaking and whining.

Trembling, she pushed the final number 1 on her cell phone.

Rooted to the spot, Ella raised the phone to her ear: there was silence. In desperation, she wondered if she had any service, until she realized that the call had been dropped. Pressing the 'End' button, she dialed again.

"911, please state your emergency."

"I think there's an intruder in the house, but they may have left, I'm not sure." Ella thought she may have been babbling, but she couldn't stop talking. "I mean, it almost looked like a ghost, but it wasn't, it couldn't be, so someone was here, right?"

"What is your address, ma'am?"

"313 Burnt Ridge Way. Paterson. I'm in Paterson."

"Is there anyone in the house with you right now?"

"Uh, no."

"Please hold."

Never having been put on hold by the police before, Ella wondered how long she'd have to wait. At least they had her address.

Quickly, Ella turned and scanned the room behind her. It might have been a joke, but there might be someone in the house. Despite her years of studying strange religions and exotic customs, her mind wouldn't accept an alternative to pranksters. It was time to take a look around, since the police were probably on their way.

"If this was a bad horror movie, I'd roll my eyes and think the woman was an idiot for not waiting for the police," she said to Daisy, talking out loud to dispel the fear still coursing through her. "But I don't want to wait. I won't let some yahoo scare me out of my own home. I'm sure this is the work of some jackass who thinks it's funny to go around scaring women."

An image of what she'd seen flashed through her mind. A woman, arms outstretched, silently screaming...another violent shiver passed through her.

Was it possible? Could it have been something else? Daisy, still next to her, was shaking but no longer whining. "It's okay, baby." Ella knelt down and held the dog. "Nothing's here, don't worry. Nothing. I'll put some nice music on, and we can both calm down while we wait for the police."

Upon hearing the first strains of a Bach violin concerto, Ella took a deep breath. She wasn't sure she believed what she'd just said to her dog. She couldn't be certain nothing was in the house—but if there was, she had no idea what to do about it.

***

As the early dawn light began to seep into the cracks of the morning, Ella sat at her kitchen table with sore muscles and gritty eyes, a coffee mug in hand and baseball bat by her side. She'd pulled the baseball bat out of her closet earlier that morning, only because the heft of it made her feel better. Ella wasn't sure if she could actually use it as a weapon.

The police response had been anticlimactic, again. They searched the house because it was required, handed her a business card, and left. At the time, Ella was indignant. "I don't think they really cared," she told Daisy as she swept debris from the floor. This incident was different than the last one, even though the police told her a mess in the kitchen was not evidence of a crime occurring. Maybe a 911 call reporting a ghost wasn't high on their list of criminal priorities, but what if she'd been in real danger?

Logically, Ella knew that if the woman in her kitchen wasn't an intruder and if kids weren't playing pranks, then she had seen something else. Her mind struggled to put it all together, wondering if she might have caught the hallucinating virus from Alice.

Maybe I'm going crazy from the strain of the move.

Pulling herself out of her circular thoughts, Ella walked through the house, turning off lamps and overhead lights. Weary, she dropped onto the living room couch. Maybe Lisa was right. Ella cringed as she remembered the conversation they'd had about this move.

"Of course, you're going to take the job closer to home," Lisa had declared when Ella told her about the job offer. "It would be stupid and thoughtless to go all the way to Virginia. Besides, you need your family around to watch out for you. Frankly, your whole life I've watched you make the worst possible decisions."

Ella's temper flared. "You're not listening to me. The job in Connecticut is okay, but it's not what I want. It's an adjunct position, and there's no chance of tenure."

"Right, of course Miss Pee Ayych Dee must do what's right for her. Don't worry about your family—or the fact that you're leaving your father behind."

"What do you mean the worst possible decisions? What have I done with my life that was so bad?"

"Remember your date for the senior prom? I told you not to go with that creep. Look what happened."

Ella couldn't believe her sister was bringing up this old argument again. It was always the same conversation, and Ella knew exactly what her sister was going to say next, as if they'd both studied their lines.

"He left you standing all by yourself in the middle of the gymnasium—and then he went on to a long and illustrious life as a sex offender. I've got to say, I think you got off easy with that one. Then there was the talent show—"

"Are we going in chronological or alphabetical order?" Ella demanded.

"Chronological, I can categorize better that way."

"Stop, okay? Just stop. All I want right now is to be normal and have a normal life. Mom's sickness was... long. I need my life to start now. There's a reason I turned down all those late nights in the back seat of that basketball player's car in high school, you know."

Lisa smirked. "Yeah, you don't know what you were missing."

Ella fought the urge to scream. "I know what I *wasn't* missing: I wasn't missing studying or passing my exams or getting into college."

"Funny, isn't it, that with all that school work you had to do, I'm still the one with the husband, big house, and two kids."

"I don't want a husband right now."

"Mmmhmmm... listen, you should think hard about this. Make sure it's the right decision, because it's a big one. You know I love you, and I only want what's best for you, right?" Lisa shook her head. "Ella, sometimes you can be so naïve."

Maybe calling her family right now wasn't the best option. Lisa might have been right, but Ella didn't want them to think she couldn't handle things, or worse, had cracked under the strain of the move. It was better to go forward with her original plan as best she could.

Slouched on the couch, Ella half wished she hadn't thrown away her last pack of cigarettes.

The weight of the bat was heavy in her hand. Although she was scared enough to stay up all night, the lack of sleep was catching up with her.

"Maybe we should take a nap," she whispered to Daisy. "Just for a little while. We can eat later."

Rising from the table, she dragged her body up the stairs and into the bedroom. Despite all that coffee, sleep was instant.

Chapter Eleven

A WEIGHT WAS PRESSING ON Ella's chest, a heaviness bearing down making it difficult to breathe. Climbing from the depths of her consciousness, Ella opened one eye, only to find another eye staring back at her.

"Get off me, Daisy," she croaked. When the dog didn't move, she rolled over and dislodged the ball of fur from her chest. The clock on the bedside table read 10:30, and the sunlight streaming in told her it was still morning.

"Daisy, I don't know what the hell happened down there last night, but I don't think it was the spray painter. I think it was something else. The problem is, I don't know what to do. But you know what, Daisy?"

The dog wagged her tail as Ella spoke. It was easy to talk to Daisy. She didn't talk back and never once told Ella she was crazy.

"I'm going to find out what I can. I just have to be logical and methodical. I'll do my research like I would with any other project and see what kind of information I can find about house ghosts. Then I'm going to find out how to get rid of them. The police might never find who sprayed that stuff on the house, but I can handle one little ghost. Besides, with this kind of interruption every night, we're going to be exhausted."

An idea struck Ella. "You know, this is probably why nobody stays in this house. That was pretty scary, and who knows how many people had that happen. But we're not going to let this frighten us, are we? Not like it scared everyone else away. We're going to get rid of that thing and live here peacefully."

In the light of day with the sun streaming through the window it was easy to say these things. *How will I feel once the sun sets tonight?*

Sitting up in bed, her chest tightened as her eyes filled with tears. "Mom, I miss you. But I don't get it. How come I only see you in places like the highway, and you haven't been here?"

She took a breath to try to clear her head and ran her fingers through her hair. This was not the time to wallow in depression. "We might as well get up. It's no use dwelling on what we can't change."

After a quick shower, Ella chose khaki shorts and a fitted T-shirt that read 'Alcohol and calculus don't mix. Don't drink and derive.' Despite all the caffeine she'd consumed the night before, she made more coffee. Waiting anxiously for the pot to fill, she looked for her phone. She may as well get it over with and call home. She decided not to mention last night's incident, but she still felt a need to connect with her family. After all, it wouldn't be unusual for her to check in with everyone.

Talking with two of her aunts, Lila and Calla, Ella was comforted by their questions and news about home. Everyone was well. Lila was baking cookies for her niece's birthday party next week, Calla had brought her car in for a tune up, and they were going to church that evening. Even her father sounded cheerful when she called, filling her in on the latest happenings in his neighborhood and the coffee shop he frequented. Ella was careful not to mention anything about her experience the previous evening.

Listening to her father's voice, she realized that going home was not an option. She reasoned that it didn't matter, that she was fine and had always been able to take care of herself. This situation was no exception; it was just a little different. She was a researcher, and with the right kind of inquiries she could figure out anything. Besides, it had been so difficult to leave Connecticut in the first place that she had to see this through, if only to prove she could.

As they spoke, Ella's thoughts strayed back to the morning she left Connecticut.

Paul Giancetti doted on his daughters. Ella remembered her childhood, with his strong hands holding her afloat as she learned to swim, the hours he spent patiently teaching her to ride a bike, and the many school functions he attended, ill-at-ease and alone, her mother too sick to be there.

She remembered his simple question when she told him about the job in Virginia. "Are you sure?"

"I'm sure."

"Like you were sure about saving the bird last year?"

"He fell out of the nest. I had to do something, or Mrs. Kaplansky's cat would have gotten him. Just because he pecked me, or bit me, or whatever, doesn't mean I didn't save him."

"No, you saved him, but then we had to get you to the doctor to treat that broken skin. All I'm saying is you need to think things through, think about all the things that can happen."

"Daddy, this is different. I'm an adult, and this is about taking a job. A real, paying job."

Paul nodded. "Tell me what you need."

That pretty much summed up her father's approach to parenting. *Tell me what you need.* He did his best to make sure his girls had it, whether it was help with homework or finding the right dress for a dance. Even if money was tight and the dress wasn't a designer label, Paul did what he could for his girls. It was what he assumed any father would do.

The morning of moving day was worse than Ella imagined it would be. After everything was loaded onto the truck and it was time to say goodbye, she stood with her family, frozen and lost. Her father, sister, and aunts had gathered at her small apartment to wish her well. As a family that relied heavily on food for all their gatherings, there was plenty of coffee and donuts. She'd planned to be on the road by six a.m., but at six-thirty she was still standing around with a chocolate glazed donut in her hand, wondering how she could swallow anything with the lump in her throat.

"Why don't we all go outside and get some air?" her Aunt Calla had finally suggested.

Once outside, Ella knew it was time to say goodbye. Her father placed his worn, calloused hands on her shoulders.

"Don't worry about nothing," he said gruffly. "If you don't like it, you can always come home."

"I'll call you," she hiccupped. "And I'll email pictures, too." Throwing her arms around her father, she whispered, "I'll miss you, Daddy."

He pat her on the back as he used to do when she was a child. "I'll miss you, too, sweetheart. Remember, I'm coming down for Thanksgiving, okay? And you'll be here for Christmas." With a final hug, he told her it was time. "It's going to be okay. This is what your mother would have wanted. Now get going so you can avoid traffic."

Here she was starting her so-called new life, trying not to think about mistakes, or fear—or ghosts. Especially ghosts. Dialing Meg's number, she thought it was better not to dwell on how much she missed her family since she had no intention of moving back. Her call went straight to voicemail, where she left a message. With that done, she went to her computer. It was time to do a little research.

First, Ella typed the word 'ghosts' into a search engine. There were over 33 million results, most of which were personal reports of ghostly encounters. She sighed in frustration as she read some of the entries related to ghosts and haunting. There were generalities in each story: moving lights, rumors of a haunting, and ghostly figures in the window.

Annoyed, Ella wondered if she'd find anything of substance. Rumor and supposition were everywhere, but that kind of research did nothing for her.

Realizing she needed a different approach for better results, Ella changed her search parameters to include only well known universities. What she found surprised her. Within the websites of Ivy League colleges was a surprising amount of information concerning the paranormal. Her experience within a university setting had been confined to the anthropological aspects of the afterlife, yet she found that both Harvard and Cornell Universities had conducted experiments in extra sensory perception and paranormal activity. Yale University had once invited a prominent detective who referred to himself as a real life ghostbuster to speak at the university. Ella focused on this article, for this man had not only spent his life tracking down ghosts, but he also had impressive credentials.

The quote from the detective read, "To investigate the paranormal, do not make assumptions. Begin with the evidence in front of you and go from there." She read that statement twice, thinking about how that applied to her situation.

Ella looked up at the ceiling. The detective was right: she couldn't start by assuming she knew the answer when she didn't really know what she had seen. Maybe she'd eaten some bad mushrooms or something.

Ella sat back and thought about her experience. Reaching for a notebook, she began listing the details. First, she heard a thumping noise then found all those pans were twirling in the air. Then there was the woman, standing with her arms out, trying to communicate something. She paused, squinting as she tried to reconstruct the scene in her head. After a moment, she added '*very cold*.' Even with her limited knowledge of ghosts, she knew that cold air signified a presence. Everyone knew that.

She'd have to wait and see if anything happened again. If it did, then she would compare the two experiences to find any correlations. Easy enough.

Perhaps her experience was related to the vandalism. Any number of people could have been responsible for that, from strangers to her new landlord. It was also possible that Jeff, the landlord's son, was really some kind of sick freak who liked scaring people.

Ella squared her shoulders and decided no matter what, the next time there was any type of occurrence she would call the police again. Even if they laughed at her or put her on hold, they still had to come to the house. There was no point in taking chances.

She got up and stretched, feeling more relaxed now that she had a plan of action. It was time for lunch, but after that she'd go right back to the computer. She was far from finished in her quest for information.

***

A couple of hours later, Ella sat back and stared at her computer screen. When she had been unable to find conclusive information about the existence of ghosts and haunted houses, she decided to take another approach. She wondered briefly why she was even looking for the information, but she knew deep down that the real reason was fear; she was nervous about the possibility of a ghost, but she was more afraid of the people that tried to scare her.

Tapping her pencil on the side of the desk, she thought about the experience. *Did I see a real ghost?* Ella didn't think anyone would be able to pull off that kind of a stunt without some seriously sophisticated equipment. The evidence in front of her indicated that something was in the house, so maybe it was okay to start with the assumption that this was a ghost. In that case, she needed to consider who it was and what it wanted.

Leaning back in her chair, Ella considered the possibilities. All she knew about the house was what Katie and Roland had told her. Lorraine's friend named Hattie disappeared after a hurricane in the sixties and was never found. Could it be her? If she could find a picture of Hattie she would know for certain that it was her ghost.

Tapping on her keyboard, Ella tried everything she could think of, from accessing back issues of local newspapers to researching genealogy websites, but there was not one single piece of information about Lorraine's friend Hattie. There was no mention of a disappearance, no mention of a lost girl, nothing. It was as if the young woman had never existed.

Standing, she reached for her big red exercise ball and stretched backward over it. While the blood rushed to her head, Ella studied the ceiling and mentally reviewed what she knew about Hattie. Not much, she concluded.

With her thoughts chasing one another in a circle, Ella realized she needed a break. "C'mon, Daisy, it's time for lunch." After devouring a hastily made ham sandwich and washing it down with lemonade, Ella made a decision.

She needed more information to understand what was happening now and what had happened in the past in that house. Seeing a ghost bothered her more than she would have imagined possible, and combined with the nastiness of the spray painted messages, it was very disturbing. Not for the first time that morning, Ella found herself on the verge of tears, wondering who that person or thing was and why it was the only one she saw. Why couldn't people see the ghosts they really wanted to see?

A light breeze blew through the room, dislodging a scrap of paper that fluttered to the floor and landed next to a stack of boxes. It was a paper she'd put on her desk yesterday after everyone left. With unsteady hands, she dialed the number. After only two rings, it was answered.

Chapter Twelve

"KATIE, IT'S ELLA."

"Ella! I was just thinking of you. I'm having some of your delicious lasagna. Thanks again, it's great."

Ella smiled, hoping that action would mask the uneasiness she felt and make her voice sound more cheerful. "You're welcome. I love cooking for people. I'm glad you came over yesterday, especially since we'll all be busy soon with teaching and grading papers."

Katie sighed. "That's true. I've been teaching computer programming for five years now, and it seems that this year I've lost my enthusiasm for it."

"I hope you're not thinking of leaving the college?"

"No, nothing as drastic as that. It seems each year I get the same kind of students. None of them are very attentive, or they're trying to get an easy grade. Or even worse, they think they already know everything there is to know, so they don't really pay attention until they get their first failing grade. But don't listen to me. I'm getting boring and old, and I'm starting to feel stuck."

Ella twirled a curl of hair around her finger. Leaning back in her chair, she noticed the abundance of dust dancing in the sunlight beam. How did dust accumulate so quickly in a house she'd just moved into? She would have to make sure she did a thorough cleaning before her family came to visit, which gave her a few months. She might be able to have the place acceptable by then, ghost-free and all. "First of all, Katie, you're not much older than me. Second of all, don't worry about feeling stuck. We all feel that way sometimes."

"I know, life is never what you expected, is it? I'm sorry, Ella. I'm not usually into all this philosophizing, that's Roland's job. I don't know what got into me today."

"Like I said, don't worry about it." Ella hesitated, not sure how to proceed. More dust settled on the computer screen, momentarily distracting her.

After a short silence, Katie asked, "Was there something in particular you called about?"

"Um, yes. I was wondering if you had any more information about Lorraine's friend, Hattie. Do you know her last name, or anything about her disappearance?"

There was a hesitation on the other end of the phone. "Why the sudden interest? You're not going to go looking for her, are you?"

Ella crossed her fingers. "Looking for her? I wouldn't know anything about that. Where would I find her? No, I was curious. I mean, it's a terribly sad story, and you mentioned she didn't have family. I wondered if they ever put up a memorial or anything."

Katie's smile reached through the phone. "I almost forgot, this story is new to you, isn't it? Anyone who's lived around here forever—like me—has heard this so many times, we don't think about it. I could see how it might interest you. If I remember correctly, Hattie was supposed to be eighteen years old, and Lorraine was seventeen. Her last name was Smith. Summer had ended, and Hattie disappeared during the hurricane."

Ella's heart sank. With a last name like Smith, she was almost guaranteed to spend an extra day or two wading through names that would have nothing to do with her Hattie. Maybe there was some other way. "Hurricane? Was it a bad one?"

"Yes. Hurricane Donna killed quite a few people."

Ella wrote the information down and thought for a moment. "Do you think it's possible that Hattie was a victim of the hurricane?"

"No, I don't see how that would be possible. Her body would have been found eventually."

Ella wasn't ready to let go of the idea. "I guess, unless she was washed out to sea or something."

"Sorry, I don't mean to be dismissive, but why on earth would a housekeeper be washed out to sea? She didn't live on the beach, and I don't think she would have gone there on her time off. I could be wrong, but I'm fairly certain that African Americans were not allowed on the beaches in Paterson. They had to go to the neighboring town if they wanted beach access."

Ella sighed. Katie was right: who would travel to a beach during a hurricane? The only thing she couldn't get past was the idea that people lived in such a divided society. "I hear stories from that era, and I have trouble imagining it. The concept of segregation is so bizarre to me. When I see those old photos of black-only drinking fountains and white-only restrooms, it gives me the creeps."

"I know. It's definitely not something most of us Southerners are proud of. We had a rough time with desegregation in the south. In some places the issue shut down offices and schools."

Ella thought back to a history class she had in college. "I think I heard something about this."

"Again, not our proudest moment," Katie said. "Virginia led a campaign called massive resistance, and in places like Prince Edward County, northwest of here, schools were closed for five years."

Ella was stunned, trying to absorb this fact. "Five years?"

"Yes. From 1959 to 1964 Prince Edward County flat-out refused to fund the county school system, which closed the doors to all students. They didn't want to desegregate, period. It was sometime during this time period that Hattie disappeared. With all the racial tension floating around there really wasn't much effort put into locating her. Because, let's face it, who do you think was on the police force?"

"White men," Ella answered, feeling a new sadness, not just for Hattie, but for a nation that struggled with hatred and hostility. "Thanks, Katie. I was curious, since I'm living here and all." She paused, wondering how to phrase her next question. "Do you see any leftover hostility, or have folks around here gotten over it and moved on?"

Katie hesitated. "Some things have changed, some things haven't. There's always going to be people filled with hate for whatever reason, you saw that with the vandalism on your house. I'm sure you have that kind of attitude up North, too, right?"

"That's true." Ella thought of the recent tension in a small Connecticut town between a group of Italians and Hispanics. Prejudice, it seemed, was everywhere. "I guess I understand a little more of what Roland was trying to say to me yesterday."

"He can be very protective in a big brother sort of way. You seem like a woman who's able to take care of herself. From what I can tell, you call it like you see it, and that's great. We need a little of that here, especially at the college."

Ella wasn't so sure she was what the town or college needed, but she kept that thought to herself. It seemed her determination to have a new beginning in life had led directly to a confrontation with ongoing hostilities.

It was just her luck to find herself attracting the attention of people who didn't know the Civil War had ended. "Thanks. I appreciate the insight, and I'll give you a call in a few days. Maybe we can get together again."

"I'd love that, Ella. I'm sure I'll see you at work soon anyway. We're getting ready to have our annual round of pre-semester meetings, so I'll be dragging myself through the hallways next week."

As she ended the call, Ella tried to assimilate everything she'd learned. Virginia had struggled with desegregation, but so had most of the South. Just because it was an issue in 1960 didn't mean it was an issue now, right? Or was it? The spray painted letters on her house and the attitude of the cable guy indicated an ongoing fascination people in this area had with Northern and Southern distinctions.

Katie had mentioned Hurricane Donna, as well as Hattie's last name. She could start by researching the storm.

Ella snorted, thinking that if Katie had seen how scared she was last night, she wouldn't think she was quite so capable of taking care of herself.

As she walked downstairs to refill her coffee mug, the phone rang. This time it was Meg.

"Ella!" Meg's enthusiastic voice shot through the phone. "How are you?"

"I'm fine. What are you up to today?"

"Okay, what's wrong?"

Ella sighed. Obviously, her friend heard something in her voice, a shift in tenor or something that betrayed her distress. *I love Meg, but I don't have the energy to tell her everything.* Ella didn't want to discuss police, vandalism, or ghosts, so she stuck to telling her the truth without the details.

"Nothing. I've been doing research all day. I just came up for air and food, so my head is still a little foggy. How about you? Anything new since yesterday?"

Her answer had apparently satisfied Meg, as she proceeded to give Ella an update on her latest date disaster. "Good golly, I counted six gold chains around his hairy neck, with a shirt unbuttoned down to his navel. Eewww..."

At the end of the conversation, however, Meg asked again, "El, are you sure you're okay? Nothing happened, did it? Do you want me to come down?"

"No, I'm fine. Like I said, I'm a little tired. I had some new friends over yesterday, and I've been working all day today. But you're always welcome to visit, you know that."

"Tell me about your new friends. Are they nice? What do they do? Where did you meet them?"

Ella laughed. "Slow down! Their names are Katie and Roland, and they both work at the college. Katie teaches computer programming, and Roland is a philosophy professor. I think you'll like them when you get to meet them."

"Are they a couple, as in boyfriend and girlfriend or husband and wife?"

"No, they're not. I think they'd be great together, but Katie told me when I first met her that Roland was more like a brother to her and it would be too weird for them to be together. They're both super nice and easy to be with, and they have a good sense of humor."

"Hmmm... well, if he's good looking, are you interested in dating him?"

Ella didn't have to think about the answer. Handsome as Roland was, that *thing* was not there for her, the thing that made her heart race and her knees weak. It had been a while since she'd met anyone she was attracted to, but she was a patient woman. She could probably wait all summer for the right man. "He's not for me. I've got too much work to do, and he's not really my type."

"Okay, but don't become so much of a bookworm that you get all pale and never see the light of day again. Listen, I've got to go, but call me sometime next week and tell me more about your new life."

"My glamorous new life with my new executive office suite and villa on the water?"

"Yup, that's the one. Let me know when you get a boat, and I'll come down to visit. Bye!"

As she ended the call, a smile tugged at the corner of Ella's mouth. Meg never failed to cheer her, even when Meg didn't know that Ella needed cheering.

Ella didn't know if she wanted a man in her life right now. Though it would be kind of nice to have someone help her carry the groceries inside and snuggle next to at night, she couldn't picture someone fitting into her bizarre world of possible ghosts and a suffocating sister.

Chapter Thirteen

SITTING AT HER COMPUTER, ELLA typed *Hurricane Donna, Virginia.* The information she found was interesting, considering she now lived in an area likely to get hit by another major storm. According to a NOAA website, thirty-six hurricanes made landfall in Virginia between 1951 and 1999. Hurricane Donna, one of the more damaging storms, caused fifty deaths in the United States. A hurricane history of Virginia told the story of Hurricane Donna starting on the west coast of Africa and blowing through the entire length of the Atlantic coast. It struck Virginia on September 12, 1960, as a Category Three hurricane.

She now had the date that Hattie disappeared, which should narrow her search considerably, but a couple of hours later she had to stop. There was absolutely no information to be found on the internet regarding the disappearance of Hattie Smith. *This is a waste of my time.* Perhaps she could get information some other way, like checking the local historical society.

As Ella thought about it, her anger and resolve to find out what happened grew. It was almost criminal that someone disappeared and it hadn't been mentioned for decades, not even a 'remember when' in the newspaper. How could a town forget something like that?

Ella stilled as a sickening thought occurred to her. Was it possible that the whole town was in on the secret of what happened to Hattie Smith? Could this have anything to do with the message left on her house? She shook her head. There was no way that Lorraine would let something like that happen to her friend. Lorraine was not the kind of person to be pushed around easily, and she wouldn't stand by and allow some kind of massive cover-up take place.

The phone rang again, pulling her out of her thoughts. "I guess I'm the popular girl today."

"Ella? It's Alice from across the road. I'm calling because Albert mentioned that you need to speak with me. Is everything all right over there?"

Ella drew in a breath in surprise. Albert was either a very intuitive ghost or a nosy one. Then again, maybe ghosts talked with each other. Perhaps the visitor Ella had last night had gone to see Albert next. Could ghosts communicate with each other? Ella sighed and rubbed her forehead. This was starting to get very weird, and she wasn't sure what to say to Alice.

"Everything's fine over here. What have you been doing with yourself today?"

Ella listened with delight as Alice proceeded to tell her about a movie she'd seen that day. It was obvious that Alice liked action movies with police chases and car crashes.

"And they had a butt shot, too, so it was well worth the price of the matinee ticket."

Ella wasn't sure she'd heard Alice correctly. "Butt shot?"

"Yes, dear, you know, a naked man's butt in the shower. I love those scenes. It was a nice butt, too."

Ella gave in and burst out laughing. This had to be the best thing she'd heard all day.

"Are you feeling better?" Alice's voice was gentle.

"Oh, yes, thank you Alice. I'm not laughing at you. You just surprised me."

"I know. Albert is standing in front of me, waving his arms around. He says there's something you want to talk to me about."

Ella sobered quickly. She didn't want to share her experience yet, not even with Alice—or Albert. What she really wanted was a cigarette, but that wasn't going to happen.

"You mentioned last night that we shouldn't be talking about the spirits or we might attract them. At least, that's kind of what I thought you said."

"Yes. But sometimes even when you don't talk about them, they still hang around. Certain places hold certain energies, and they become trapped there until they're ready to move on or justice is done."

"Alice, it sounds like you might be referring to Hattie, am I right?"

"Frankly, I'm not sure that she's the one that's in that house, dear," Alice answered gently. "It might be Hattie, and it might not. I've never encountered any spirits in that place, but I know that others have. That's why they all moved, you know."

"I guessed as much," Ella mumbled, thinking of her lost night's sleep. "Do you have any idea what happened to Hattie?"

"I wish I did. She was such a kind girl. And smart, my goodness, she was smart as a whip. She and Lorraine used to read all kinds of books and have wonderful conversations about everything from religion to politics to the meaning of life. They were quite close."

Something occurred to Ella as Alice spoke, and she voiced her thoughts. "They spent a lot of time at your house, didn't they?"

"Yes." Alice was somber. "I couldn't have them going off into the woods all the time; I didn't think it was safe. They certainly couldn't go into town together. All that nonsense about people using separate facilities, separate beaches—why, that was a load of you-know-what. They used to sit right here in my living room and have tea together and study and talk, talk, talk. This was when my own two children were still barely able to walk."

Alice sighed, a sigh born of the weariness that comes with having seen too much. "Sometimes I think I can still hear them late at night, giggling away at some silly thing or other." Her voice became stronger. "But I'll tell you one thing that I know for a fact. Hattie would never have up and left without telling Lorraine where she was going. After that nasty hurricane came through, it took us a day or so to figure out she was gone. There was so much damage and so many people trying to put the pieces of their homes together, with no electricity or anything. I always thought that if we reported it sooner we might have had a better chance at finding her."

"You can't know that for certain. If there was foul play, then there's nothing you could have done to help her anyway."

"I know. It's a regret I carry. She was a wonderful girl, and I always thought she had so much promise. Even if she had to work for that Bartok man." Alice said this last part with such obvious venom that Ella decided the Bartok family was a subject better left for another day.

"Alice, there is one more thing. I know you have Albert with you, and he's a ghost, but before that—did you always believe in ghosts?"

There was a moment's pause before Alice answered. She sounded thoughtful. "I'm not sure I ever considered it when I was younger. Of course, I'd heard ghost stories and such, but there was always daily life to contend with and not much time for fanciful thinking. But yes, there came a point when I realized that not only did I believe in ghosts, I had one in the house."

"You mean after Albert died?"

"Oh, no, dear." The whistle of a teakettle could be heard as Alice answered. "We had a ghost in one of the first houses we ever lived in. Albert was alive and well back then."

Chapter Fourteen

ELLA WONDERED IF THINGS COULD get any more bizarre.

"We were living in an old farmhouse in a tiny town called Dendron, over in Surry County. That's across the river, west of here. We'd only been married for a few years, and Albert got a job with his cousin at a feed store. We might have had plenty of love between us, but not a lot of money, so he had to take what jobs he could get in those days. We couldn't believe our luck when we found that house. It was lovely and not very far from where Albert worked. And it was cheap. Of course, in hindsight we realized the reason for that."

Alice let out a small harumph. "Nobody told us about all the other folks that couldn't—or wouldn't—live there. We even had trouble getting our milk delivered. Now that I think about it, it's a wonder we didn't realize something was wrong sooner. Folks were nice to us, and we received plenty of invitations to go to other homes and do things, but no one would ever come to our house. It used to frustrate me, made me wonder if my cooking or housekeeping was all that bad."

Ella tried to offer some comfort. "I probably would have felt the same way. At least you weren't completely ostracized."

Alice sighed. "No, it wasn't as bad as that. Folks avoided the house, not us. Anyway, strange things were happening during the day. If I put something on the counter, it would disappear, then turn up two minutes later on the kitchen table. It was as if someone were playing small jokes on me. Albert and I found it charming, at first."

"But then?" Ella prompted, wondering if she really wanted to hear the rest. She hoped this ghost story would have a happy ending—if that were even possible.

"It became malicious. Whoever—or whatever—was playing tricks on us started to get nasty. My dishes and glasses would break, or something would fly through the air and hit us over the head. The day I got pushed down the stairs was the day Albert packed our bags and we left. Neither of us knew why this presence started behaving badly, but we did know that living there was going to cause one of us serious harm. We came back to this side of the river, and I've been here ever since."

"Do you think it was testing you in some way?" Ella asked, thinking about some of the legends she'd read of in other cultures.

"I'm not certain. Maybe more than one presence was in the house. All I know for sure is that I didn't like being pushed around, not by humans and not by ghosts. Does it really matter all that much why they do it?"

"Maybe."

"No, dear, it doesn't," Alice said softly. "We cannot save the world, not the world of humans and certainly not the world of spirits. Unresolved emotions need to be worked out, true, but it must happen because we want it to happen, not because someone else insists on it. Do you understand what I'm saying?"

Ella nodded, even though Alice couldn't see her. "Yes, I do. But I think everyone needs a little help now and then, dead or alive."

Alice chuckled. "Well, my Albert is nodding at me, so we must be done with what we were supposed to talk about. You can call me anytime, dear."

"All right..." Ella answered feebly, uncertain as to why Albert was nodding or what Alice could do for her if the apparition appeared again.

Getting ready for bed that night, Ella's entire body was wrapped in fatigue. Even Daisy looked tired. Yawning as she climbed into bed, Ella realized she hadn't left lights on downstairs. Her last thoughts before drifting off to sleep were that it didn't matter. No matter how much noise anyone or anything made that night, she wasn't going downstairs. They could paint the whole house red, but she was too tired to care.

***

Again, she floated. She knew the dream this time, knew that she'd be seeing one or both of the girls. They were sitting on the old tree stump. Their pleated skirts covered their knees, which were drawn up to their chins. Their white blouses were plain, with Peter Pan collars. Ella was surprised at the beauty of the darker-skinned girl; she hadn't noticed this in the previous dreams. With large, melted chocolate eyes and high cheekbones, her face looked as if it had been exquisitely sculpted. Both girls were thin, and their expressions were solemn. The air was hot, heavy, and still as their whispers drifted up to Ella.

"It's a secret, so you can't tell anyone. Swear to me that you'll never tell."

The fair-skinned girl had light brown hair and a round, serious face. She appeared to be younger than her friend because of her air of naïveté.

"Never?" she asked.

"Never," her friend said. Weariness echoed in her voice. "You can never, ever tell. Swear to me, please?"

"Okay, I promise. I'll never tell, not ever. What is it? What's the secret?"

And just like that, there was a magical transformation in the eyes, face, and posture of the dark-skinned girl. She glowed from within, smiling enough to light a thousand worlds. "I'm in love," she announced to her friend. After several squeals, the younger friend asked, "Why can't I tell?"

There was a moment's pause as the two girls looked at each other. "Oh," she said quietly. "I see. I didn't think—never mind. Are you happy?"

The dark-skinned girl nodded. "Very."

"But, what's going to happen next?"

"One step at a time," she answered, as if all the wisdom of the centuries were contained in the depths of her soul.

Ella snorted. At least she thought she snorted; it was hard to tell since this was a dream. Love is nothing but trouble, Ella thought, and that young girl will find that out soon enough. It's too bad they can't hear me, or I'd tell them to stay far away from men who make promises. Maybe they can hear me; after all, this is my dream.

Ella took a breath and yelled, "Make sure he treats you right! Don't let him take advantage of you, no matter what."

Both girls looked up. "Did you hear that, Hattie?"

"Lorraine, you're always worrying. That was nothing but the wind."

Still, both girls looked around, almost fearfully, as the wind stirred through the trees.

"Storm's coming," the girl called Hattie noticed. "We'd better get going. Your mama's going to be looking for you soon, and I've got to get back to work."

"Work," Lorraine said scornfully. "You mean —"

"Sssssshhhhh…there's eyes and ears all around us."

Both girls stared into the woods before scrutinizing the sky above, seeming to look straight at Ella. Simultaneously, they stood and walked quickly down the path, away from Ella.

"Wait!" Ella cried. "Wait! I have to know what happens! Don't leave!" The treetops swayed as the wind increased in intensity, swirling the dried leaves on the path.

Hattie turned and looked directly at Ella. "You know, Lorraine, sometimes

it seems…"
  "That there's ghosts in these woods, Hattie."
  Arms linked, they disappeared from Ella's view.

***

Ella woke with a start, wondering why her face was wet. Daisy watched her with concern. Placing a hand to her own cheek, Ella was startled to realize that she'd been crying.

"That idiotic young girl was in love," she told her dog. "Oh my God, that changes everything. Obviously, this wasn't good." When Daisy perked her ears, Ella explained. "Whoever Hattie was in love with must have killed her. The husband or lover is always the killer. Everyone knows that."

Her gaze wandered from the clock on the side of the bed to the window. Not surprising that at 7:15a.m. it was already hot.

"We made it through the night!" As Daisy perked up her ears, Ella said, "Nothing happened. No visitations, no ghosts, only a full, solid night of sleep. And one little dream." Details of the dream drifted through her mind, leaving her feeling slightly off-center.

"I assumed these dreams were real," she whispered. "I thought I was seeing Hattie and Lorraine." Ella shook her head at her dog. "I need to get out more." Could the dreams have been factual? The details had appeared to her as if she were watching the history of the girls, but it was more likely that she was trying to work it all out in her head. Maybe her subconscious was seeking an explanation for Hattie's disappearance, which made more sense than having dreams where she could see the past.

She needed a break from thinking about ghosts, Hattie, and the house. Her research from the day before must have sparked her imagination, causing weird dreams. It was time to take a break from everything, explore, and get to know the area a little better. Maybe Officer Drake would be out patrolling, and she'd see him again. It was good to have friends, she reasoned. And he looked like he'd be a very nice friend to have.

With that decision made, she swung her legs out of bed, intent on getting downstairs to the coffeepot. She could work on her course outline later, after she took a day for herself, and maybe even after this whole ghost business—or whatever it was—was resolved. After all, there was still a week or so before she had to meet with Lorraine about the new class. "Plenty of time."

Daisy started to whine and a gentle breeze swept through the room, dislodging the papers on her nightstand. Squinting at the papers that fluttered to the floor, she announced, "I have every intention of finding out what's going on here. One way or another."

Chapter Fifteen

IT DIDN'T TAKE ELLA LONG to pack a cooler with sandwiches, dog biscuits, juice, and water. She'd dressed comfortably in a short denim skirt and a T-shirt that read '*Earth is Full. Go Home.*'

"Come on, Daisy!" she called, anxious to leave. One way or another, she was going to have fun today, and vandals, ghosts, and missing girls could damn well go away. Or wait for her to come back, which she admitted was probably what was going to happen anyway.

Keys in hand, Ella saw it on the front porch when she turned to lock the front door. The red letters were painted over the door. Backing off the porch and down the steps, Ella swore softly as she read the words GO HOME BITCH.

Dumping the cooler on the ground, she pulled out her cell phone. Impatient, she jabbed at the numbers, her breath coming in short gasps. "Hi, Jeff, this is your tenant, Ella. Again. There's more graffiti on the house this morning. Please have it cleaned off." Her jaw hurt as she clenched her teeth. "Thank you."

Grabbing the cooler, she stomped to the car. This was ridiculous. Whoever was trying to scare her was not going to succeed. And she sure wasn't going to call the police and hang around and wait for them. They didn't help her last time, anyway. She knew Officer Drake would have helped, but she wasn't lucky enough to have him show up; instead, she got Mr. Cranky-Pants in a uniform, who probably wouldn't care if the perp was standing on the front lawn with a can of spray paint in his hand.

Now Ella was most definitely in a bad mood.

Sitting in the car, she took a deep breath. As mad as it made her, she couldn't do anything about the situation unless she caught the vandals in the act. Shivering, Ella thought about the fact that she'd slept undisturbed through the night. There had been no ghosts, only spray painters. Even Daisy hadn't barked, which was odd. Then again, maybe the vandals hadn't been there at night. They could have done their damage in the morning, while Ella was showering. If this kept up, it was possible they might try something else, like entering the house to cause damage.

It did her no good to speculate or stay angry, and she wasn't going to let whoever was harassing her ruin her day. Ella rummaged through her purse, looking for the scrap of paper where she'd written the address of the local museum. "You won't be able to come inside," she told her dog, "but there's a nature trail around the marsh. We'll take a walk there." And maybe by the time they got back, Jeff would have cleaned the paint from the house.

The town of Paterson had an interesting mix of architecture. Huge, new boxy houses sat side by side with small, rundown buildings. The newer homes were built on raised platforms or stilts to protect from flooding. Some of the older homes had also been raised. Flooding, it appeared, was a real issue.

Glancing at the directions she'd written, Ella saw that her route to the museum took her through the heart of town, which consisted of a small rectangle of grass in the center of the road and a street lined with crepe myrtle trees. Like the houses, the stores were a mixture of old and new, with historic buildings next to a strip mall shopping center containing the grocery store, dry cleaners, and pizza restaurant. It was a small, well-trafficked area. Five minutes later, Ella gave a small cheer, put her signal on, and turned into a driveway. She was proud of herself for being able to find her way around town after having been here for such a short period of time. Putting the car in park, Ella stared at the structure in front of her.

The sign over the front porch announced "Paterson Museum." The building was one story, with white trim prominent against the butter yellow wood shingles. The wide front porch boasted broad columns and a railing, while several empty rocking chairs waited. Like a negative superimposed over the scene before her, Ella could see that this porch was once home to old men who watched and women who gossiped. Myriad people had come and gone through the front door, while a few dark-skinned customers used the smaller door on the right side of the building. The sign over that door read "Colored Entrance."

Pulling herself out of the scene before her, Ella thought about the difference between then and now. Truthfully, it wasn't that long ago that this town, this store, was a very different world.

Knowing that her dog would not be welcomed inside the museum, she tied Daisy's leash to a tree and left her a small bowl of water. The scent in the building was familiar rather than unpleasant, the smell of antiques and old homes, well-polished wood passed through the centuries and long-forgotten memories stirring in the lazy beams of afternoon sunlight. Only the regular ticking of a clock could be heard. Ella walked slowly, looking at displays and absorbing the atmosphere and information.

The museum was filled with historical artifacts such as handmade quilts, farming tools, and photos of early settlers. Scanning the photos, Ella wondered if she might see any of Hattie. Disappointed but not surprised, all the photos were of white farmers and fishermen. Walking to the back of the store, Ella noticed a woman behind a counter holding a magnifying loupe and studying what looked like an old piece of fabric.

The woman straightened and smiled. "Hi, I'm Deborah, the historian here. If you have any questions, don't hesitate to ask."

Ella was relieved to hear the woman speak without a twang. Perhaps she could get an unbiased view of the town from another outsider. "Can you tell me about this building and the people who lived here?"

Deborah launched into an account of the history of the building. "This used to be called Miss Hope's Store and was the general store for the area. Like most general stores, they sold groceries and goods, and it was a social center. You could usually find men hanging out on the front porch, and if anyone wanted to know what was going on, this was the place to be. Of course, there was a separate side entrance for blacks, which was used quite frequently as most people in this area had domestic help. Sometime in the late 1960s, the family who owned it died out, and in the mid-1970s the building was abandoned. It wasn't until 1983 that the townspeople got together and decided it was time to preserve this part of their history. They created a nonprofit organization, did a little fundraising, and here we are. Fortunately, we have the space to store a large number of old documents, and the Historical Society meets in the back room on the third Wednesday of every month."

The historian's description of what the building had been used for sounded very close to Ella's parking lot imaginings, but it wasn't as if she'd imagined something extraordinarily farfetched, like circus animals coming through. "I'm sure it took more than a little fundraising."

Deborah sighed. "Okay, a lot. But it also took some convincing on the part of the restoration group to get the full backing of the town for this project. There were many people against refurbishing this building, despite its historic significance. They thought the town could make better use of it by selling it off to developers and using the money for other projects, like expanding the business district or attracting more development. I heard it got to the point where it was almost violent."

Ella liked the idea of preserving history. There were enough shopping centers already, who needed another pharmacy or dollar store?

"I just moved here and am still finding my way around." Ella hesitated, debating the wisdom of asking about the haunted history of the area. Deborah might think she was crazy, but at this point Ella didn't care. She wanted answers. "I'm curious... are there any ghost stories attached to this building?"

Deborah put her magnifying loupe down. "No, none that I can think of. Some places around here have ghost stories, but I think that's mostly in Yorktown, the next town over. You'll probably find a ton of old houses with that kind of thing there. But..."

"But?"

Deborah fiddled with the pencil in her hand before walking around the counter to stand in front of Ella. "Where did you say you were from?"

"I didn't. I'm from Connecticut." Ella waited as Deborah seemed to gather her courage to speak.

The historian cleared her throat before speaking. "I have to tell you I never heard any ghost stories, but scary things happen in this town."

Ella was impatient to know what the woman was getting at. "What do you mean by 'scary things'?"

Deborah shook her head, then put the pencil on the counter and started twisting the string of black beads that lay against her blue blouse. "Just stuff I've heard. Sometimes it's hard for an outsider to live here, even if you've been here for years."

Trying not to let her frustration show, Ella looked over at the pictures again. "I would think that if the people here are so happy with their little town, it wouldn't have been hard to get the museum going."

Deborah nodded. "I thought the same thing. It was actually the folks who moved here, the ones the locals call the 'come-heres,' who wanted to preserve the place."

Ella was confused. "'Come-heres?'"

For the first time, Deborah smiled. "It's a colloquialism. 'Come-heres' are people like you and me that move here from somewhere else. 'Been-heres' are the people that have always lived here."

The dinging of the bell over the front door interrupted Deborah. Ella spoke quickly, aware that someone else had entered the museum.

"If you happen to find any information about the hurricane that came through in 1960, I'd love to hear about it." 'Ella wasn't sure how much she could ask, and the hurricane seemed like the logical place to start. Asking about weather wasn't likely to get nasty words spray painted on her house, but then again, what did a 'come here' like her know?

"Is there anything specific you're looking for?"

"Anything about what the people went through, the damage, anyone that might have been injured... general history stuff." Digging through her purse, Ella found a pen, wrote her email and cell phone number on the back of a grocery store receipt, then handed it to Deborah. "Don't go out of your way, but if you come across anything I'd love to know the details."

"Don't worry, I'm a historian. I love looking up old things. If you're finished in the museum, feel free to take our nature walk through the marsh on the boardwalk. In fact," she said, looking out the window, "I think your dog is waiting for you."

Ella looked out the window and grinned. Sure enough, there was Daisy, watching the museum with her head cocked and her ears up, as if expecting Ella to come out any moment.

"Thanks for the info. I better get going."

There was no breeze as Ella and Daisy followed the boardwalk around the marsh, with only the cattail and cord grass still and silent witnesses. A great blue heron stretched his wings, and Daisy snapped at the dragonflies as they meandered along. An occasional turtle ducked into the water while the call of a red-winged blackbird sounded. As the clouds slid over the sun, Ella caught a glimpse of a man ahead of them, walking at a brisk pace. Squinting, she thought he looked like Jeff, the landlord's son, but it was hard to tell. He wore a baseball cap, obscuring some of his face. Ella thought it was strange that Jeff would be walking through there, as she assumed he'd be sleeping at that hour. Her phone call had probably woken him, though, meaning he should be supervising the clean up at the house. She shrugged. It was none of her business what Jeff did, as long as he took care of the spray paint.

Back at the parking lot, Ella paused while deciding what to do next. "What do you think, Daisy? It's not quite lunch time, should we go somewhere else?"

"I know exactly what you can do."

Her breath caught in her throat as Ella turned to see who was standing behind her.

Chapter Sixteen

"LORRAINE!" SHE EXCLAIMED, RELIEVED TO see the older woman. "Do you always sneak up on people?"

Lorraine bent down to pat Daisy on the head. "Your dog knew I was here. Did you enjoy the museum?"

Ella thought about her strange conversation with Deborah. Based on Lorraine's reaction to her new address, maybe it would be better not to mention what the historian had said. "Yes, it was great. I love poking around old historic places and seeing how people used to live. Are you here to visit the museum?"

"Goodness, no. I must know that building like the back of my hand. In fact, I used to come here when I was a child. It was Miss Hope's back then, a kind of general store that was our grocery store. Not like today, with super stores open every hour of the day. I'm a volunteer here at the gift shop."

"I really enjoyed this place," Ella said, "and honestly, it's great that you have such a gifted historian working here. She's very knowledgeable."

Lorraine nodded. "I had a feeling you would like her. I was going to introduce you eventually, but now I don't have to. Deborah, like you, is from up north. You may find you have more in common with her than you realize."

"Oh?" Ella wasn't sure where this was going. Lorraine's face looked funny, like she was trying not to laugh.

"Yes. When Deborah first moved here, she simply decided to forego having her cable installed. It seems that the cable repair person said something to her...”

After a moment of silence, Ella shook her head. “You’re kidding, right?”

The corners of Lorraine’s mouth quirked up. “Heavens no, I am not kidding. You two really do have something in common. A mutual dislike for cable television installers.” Giving in to a wide smile, Lorraine added, “That had to be the funniest story I’ve heard since... well... since Deborah moved here.”

Smiling in response, Ella answered, “I’m glad I’m not the only person who had that reaction to him. I guess this means that the whole town knows the story?”

Lorraine pretended to think for a moment. “No, not everybody. I don’t think the Carver twins over on the south side of town heard about this. Of course, they are only six months old, but still...”

Ella threw her hands in the air. “I don’t know how you all do that. Really, how does everybody around here know everything almost as soon as it happens?”

Lorraine raised one eyebrow. “That’s the beauty of small town life. Anyway, how are you settling in? Is everything satisfactory? Have you spoken with your family?”

Instead of feeling like Lorraine was being pushy, Ella appreciated the questions. She assumed it was obvious she was going to miss her family, as this move was a first for her. All her years of college were spent no more than an hour away from home, an easy commute for visiting and laundry. “I’ve talked to my sister and my father several times. My father is being well taken care of by the neighborhood widows, and my sister is overseeing everything these days.”

Ella wondered if she should mention anything and decided to gauge Lorraine’s reaction. “You know, when I was walking along the boardwalk, I could have sworn I saw Jeff Bartok. Does he come here often?”

Lorraine nodded. “He’s usually here on his days off. Did he speak to you?”

“No, I’m not even sure he saw me.” Maybe he didn’t want to tell her that he hadn’t cleaned the latest message off the house yet. That was fine, she wasn’t at the house. Hopefully he’d get to it before she got back, since she had no desire to chat with him or anyone else about the matter. The thought of those hateful words caused her stomach to burn, but for now, she was determined to enjoy the day.

“That’s Jeff. Sometimes he’s in his own little world. Have you driven over to Yorktown yet? It’s a great day for the beach over there.”

Ella was uncertain. While she was just getting to know Paterson, maybe it would be better to stay in one town. She couldn't find her GPS that morning, and the thought of getting lost in a new place gave her pause.

"Why not try exploring Yorktown?" Lorraine continued. "The historic district and battlefields are near the beach. It's adorable, and you might be intrigued by all the history there."

Her hesitation was short. This was, after all, her day to get out and enjoy herself. If she got all agoraphobic about leaving town, it was like giving in to the fear that had been creeping around the edges of her consciousness. "Thanks, maybe I'll try that." She wrapped Daisy's leash around her hand, considering what Deborah had said to her. "I was asking Deborah if there were any ghosts here in this old museum, and she said no, but she thought maybe I could find some in Yorktown. What do you think? Are there any around here?"

Lorraine's gaze was steady as she answered. "What kind of ghosts were you looking for, Ella?"

Ella wondered if she'd gone too far. She wasn't certain how much she could push the subject with Lorraine, regardless of how friendly she seemed. "Well, you know me, always interested in the weird stuff. I like checking out areas that are considered 'haunted' by others."

Lorraine's gaze softened as she looked at a spot just beyond Ella. "Are you really asking me about ghosts, Ella, or are you asking something else?"

"Both, I guess."

Birdsong punctuated a moment of silence. As she was assaulted by the smell of fresh cut grass, Ella suppressed a sneeze. A decision made, Lorraine's attention focused sharply on Ella. "Okay, here's what I know. There are places in Paterson and Yorktown that are alleged to be haunted. I cannot verify that, but I can tell you that if you have any questions about Hattie, you should just ask me."

There was a heavy silence, into which Ella spoke. "I'm sorry. I know this is a painful subject for you. It seems almost personal, somehow, because I'm living in the house where she was last seen."

Lorraine agreed. "Yes, it is personal. I suppose you were bound to get involved almost as soon as you moved in. What was your question about Hattie?"

Her mouth suddenly dry, Ella tried to swallow. "I was wondering if she had any relatives."

Lorraine's eyebrows raised fractionally as she studied Ella. "Yes, I believe she did have a relative. She lived with a family on the other side of town, some sort of cousin of hers. This cousin was married with a family of his own, and he resented her living with them. I don't know if this was because they were poor or if they didn't get along. And that sums up all I know of her family."

Ella knew she shouldn't ask—really, she shouldn't—but she couldn't help it. "Didn't you want to know? About her family, I mean. Isn't that part of what friends talk about and complain about with each other?"

Lorraine might have been standing in front of Ella, but Ella knew that in her mind she was very far away. "Yes, I suppose that is what friends talk about, but Hattie and I were different. We used to read books together and discuss them. We talked about the classics, then talked about them again if they were made into movies. We loved reading books we weren't supposed to, like *Peyton Place* —"

"What did you say?" Ella interrupted.

"I said we loved reading, why?"

"No, what did you say that you read? *Peyton Place*?"

"Yes. Is that still such a shocking book, Ella? Do you disapprove?" Lorraine looked at her with mild amusement.

"No, it's not that. I thought... never mind. I don't know what I thought." There was no way Ella was ready to share her suspicions with Lorraine, not yet. And she was certainly not ready to share that she'd been having dreams, a whole series of them, that seemed to involve Hattie and Lorraine. No, she thought, that kind of information could wait until maybe she was tenured. Or even after that, if ever. Until then, she should probably keep it to herself.

"Thanks, Lorraine." Ella cleared her throat, knowing she'd come to the end of her questions with Lorraine. "Um...I think I will go visit Yorktown. How do I get there?"

After getting directions, Ella and Daisy set off, following Route 17 all the way into the heart of Yorktown. From Route 17, she took a right onto Cook Road, following this to the end, where she followed the signs for the beach area.

Yorktown had a colonial ambiance, created by the architecture and historic buildings. Some of the tiny houses with subdued colors and black shutters had a plaque affixed near the front door, announcing the original families, as well as the year the home was built. Others were two-storied, made from brick, a material easily found in Virginia. Even with cars rolling through the streets, the overall sense was of having stepped back in time.

With blanket and food in hand, Ella and Daisy found a spot by the York River. The beach was busy, full of families swimming and teenagers giggling in groups on the sand. Ella closed her eyes for a moment, savoring the sunlight. She was a long way from ghosts and vandals, probably exactly what she needed. In this beach setting, surrounded by bright sunshine, people talking and laughing, dogs barking, and cars driving by, it was easy to question the previous night's experience.

She knew one thing for certain: the previous night's experience may or may not have been supernatural, but the spray paint on her house was very real.

Ella dropped her head onto her arms as she sat with her legs folded against her body. Obviously, sitting on a blanket on the beach was not clearing her mind. Maybe going for a walk would help.

Brushing herself off, Ella wondered for a moment what to do with her blanket and picnic items. *That's the thing about beaches, you never really know if it's okay to leave your stuff on the sand or not.* Deciding she had nothing of value, she tucked her cell phone into her pocket and deserted her things to the blanket.

Crossing the main beach road, Water Street, Ella did a double take. Before her was a gated cave. This was unique. Most of the caves she'd been in were gate-free. The sign read "York Under Siege, 1781" and stated that General Cornwallis, America's original bad guy, might have hidden in that cave. Although it was an interesting story, Ella thought any cave with an iron gate set into a rock outcropping with empty beer cans and debris littering the floor was creepy.

"I'm assuming this is a local party spot, but I can't imagine how kids get in there."

"They squeeze through the bars. After all, they're only kids." Ella jumped at the unexpected sound of a voice next to her. She was going to have to stop talking to herself, especially if she wanted to appear reasonably sane. A man of about her age stood there, with blond hair in a crew cut and deep blue eyes that she wanted to climb into.

Ella couldn't help staring at his well-toned body any more than she could stop the blush that crept into her face. "I didn't realize I said that out loud."

He laughed. "It's okay. I talk to myself all the time. Did you get a new tire for your car?"

Ella was tongue-tied. Here he was, and she was about to sound like the world's biggest moron. "Yes, thank you for your help." There was a moment's pause before she added, "I recently moved to Paterson."

"Nice town. That's where I work. But you already knew that." He leaned over to scratch Daisy behind the ears.

Brushing her hair back with one hand, Ella looked at him carefully. He was handsome, sure, but she didn't usually stand around having fantasies about kissing strange men. Ella wondered if she'd be having this reaction if it were, say, next month and she was feeling more settled.

Ella tore her eyes away, not wanting to stare like she was some weird stalker-lady. But gol-ly, he was good looking. Trying to focus on a point just behind him, Ella's breath caught. Staring right at her was a man in a dirty T-shirt, cap askew on his head. It was the man from the coffee shop, the one she had had words with. She wondered if he was going to confront her and wished she had her big friends by her side again.

"Do you know him?" Officer Drake asked.

"Not really. Well, I had a thing with him." Wincing, she realized after the words were out how it sounded. "Not a good thing. I mean, not a thing with us, like, together. We argued."

Nodding, he told her, "Be careful. He argues with a lot of people. And he's not very nice about it."

Before she could answer, a strident voice sounded from the pocket of the man's shorts. "*What we have here is a failure to communicate... what we have here is a failure to communicate...*"

Ella looked at him in surprise. "'Cool Hand Luke,' right? The warden?"

He smiled at her, making her insides more jumpy than they'd been a minute ago. "Not many people know that." Glancing at his cell phone, he frowned. "Excuse me. I've got to take this. Have fun."

As he walked away, a pang of disappointment shot through her. *It's probably his wife calling to remind him to pick up milk or something.*

Trying not to stare as he walked in the opposite direction, Ella led Daisy across a brick sidewalk and toward a shopping area. There were a number of finely decorated shops here, all of them selling things Ella knew she either didn't want or couldn't afford. This section of Yorktown was very well designed, and everything blended harmoniously to create an atmosphere of history and fun. She thought about the pronounced difference between this town and Paterson. Yorktown was gorgeous, and the 'birthplace' of America, but Ella didn't think she would be able to live in a town with a constant stream of tourists. She was glad she'd chosen Paterson, despite recent house events. *Maybe Jeff has cleaned those awful words and nothing weird will happen again.*

Lost in thoughts of ghosts, she didn't notice the revving noise on the street. As the drone grew louder, Ella looked up to see a motorcycle careening toward her. Jumping back, she raised her hands in front of her as the driver jumped the curb, blocking the sidewalk. The rider was dressed entirely in black, with a dark visor on the helmet, making it impossible to identify him. With the bike blocking her path, Ella froze, wondering if now was a good time to turn and run.

Chapter Seventeen

REMOVING THE DUSTY SHELL HELMET, the figure in black smiled at her. He wore black jeans, a black T-shirt, and scuffed black boots. Ella let out her breath and smacked him in the arm. "You scared me to death, you know!"

Roland smiled. "Couldn't you tell it was me?"

"Not in your Johnny Cash outfit, no, I could not. What are you doing here? And where did you get the motorcycle? That's pretty impressive."

Ella looked carefully at the bike Roland was riding. Consisting of chrome and fringed leather, the motorcycle was surprisingly not the requisite black; instead, it was tan, ivory, and pale yellow. There was an Indian head painted on the front gas tank and galloping horses on the fenders.

"Motorcycles are a hobby of mine. I've been riding since I was a kid. If it's a nice day, I like to go out for a ride."

Ella looked over his shoulder at a group of bikers gathered across the street. They were a mix of men and women, ranging in age from young to old, scruffy to clean shaven. Ella wondered if they were all locals, or if any of them were from Paterson. In a close knit community, it made sense that everyone knew the history of the area. Was it possible that any of them had information about the recent vandalism at her house? As soon as she had the thought, she dismissed it. If any of those people knew about the vandalism, Roland would be sure to tell her.

She eyed the motorcycles. "You and your friends all have Harleys. Interesting."

"Yeah, how can you tell they're Harleys?" Roland asked, nodding at the group standing on the other side of the road.

"Easy," Ella replied. "Square rocker boxes, two external push rods... plus, they say Harley Davidson on the side."

Roland was at a loss for words. Ella took pity on him as he sat there, mouth hanging open. "Close your mouth, you'll catch flies," she snapped. "I used to date a guy who drove one of those things, that's how I know. It's not such a big deal."

A slow smile played at the corner of his mouth. "No, it's not such a big deal. Hey, I drove by your house earlier, thought you might want to take a ride with us."

Ella wondered if he'd seen anything. Probably not, since he hadn't mentioned the most recent vandalism.

"I guess I'd already left," she answered.

"Yeah. There was some guy walking down your driveway, though."

Was it possible that Roland had seen the person responsible for spray painting the house? "What time were you there?"

"About an hour ago," he answered.

An hour ago she had already left to go to the Paterson Museum, so he must have driven by her house after the vandalism took place. But if he were there after the fact, who was at her house?

"Did you recognize him?" she asked.

Roland shook his head. "Nope, never seen the guy before."

It must be the person Jeff sent over to clean the house, Ella reasoned. Nobody else would be there, and she'd already seen her arch nemesis from the coffee shop a few minutes ago.

"We were getting ready to head over to the Yorktown Pub for a bite to eat. Why don't you join us?"

"Thanks, maybe some other time. I still have work to get done. Shelves to hang and furniture to rearrange."

"If you need some muscle, let me know." Roland straightened as he spoke.

Ella raised her eyebrows, looking him over. "Oh, and why is that?"

"I'll call Katie for you," Roland replied with a grin. "Seriously, why don't you let us come over tomorrow and help you out? We can help hang shelves and decorate and stuff."

"Thanks, but I don't think —"

"That's what friends are for. Besides, it's easier to move furniture when you have help. Don't worry, we won't knock holes in the walls or do anything that'll get you in trouble with your landlord."

Ella watched as a family walked behind him. Gulls screeched overhead, waiting for food people might drop. "My landlord is different. I've only met his son. I never met the man that owns the house, but Jeff made me sort of uncomfortable. He seemed a little... creepy. Do you know Jeff Bartok?"

Roland stared at the York River, squinting. "Yes, I know him. Everybody around here knows him. He's quiet, and I can see how he might make someone uncomfortable. But don't worry, he would never hurt anyone. I felt really bad for him when I was growing up."

Roland looked like he was reliving memories. "Why?"

"He was older than me, and from what I knew he never had a mother. When he was a little kid, she took off, never came back."

Ella's attention sharpened. "Doesn't that make two women who disappeared from that house?"

Roland let out a big sigh as he turned back from watching the river. "Not really. Jeff's mother, she was a real piece of work. I think some people around here were glad she left. She didn't disappear into thin air; she let everyone know she was leaving town and that she wasn't leaving by herself. She loved to drink and party. Of course, these were all stories I heard from other people who knew her, but I don't think anyone except Jeff really missed her. He was young, about three years old."

"But you two aren't close in age at all. What made you feel sorry for him? It's not like you went to school together."

Roland shrugged, seeming embarrassed for the first time since Ella had met him. "I don't know. I guess it's that I heard all the stories when I was growing up, and I couldn't imagine not having a mother. My mom and I, we've always had this really great relationship. I think I would have been totally lost without my mom."

He may have been embarrassed, but he was sincere, Ella decided. "That's really sweet, you know," she told him, realizing as she said it that his motorcycle friends were walking toward them.

"Yeah, that's me all right," he muttered.

Ella started to edge away from the group, telling Roland, "I'll see you later, okay?"

"Hey, where ya going?" one of the bikers yelled at her.

"I have to go. My dog and I already had lunch, and I have work I really need to finish," Ella told them. She wasn't sure why, but she was feeling distrustful of all strangers. It was time for her to scurry back to the safety of her home—even if her home had distinctly non-safe moments.

Roland gave a little wave. "See you tomorrow, maybe around one o'clock? I'll call Katie and let her know we're helping you." Ella started to protest, but Roland cut her off. "You need help, so we'll be there. Don't worry about it."

"Thank you. I appreciate that. I'll have lunch ready when you get there."

Roland's eyes twinkled. "I was counting on it."

Ella was still smiling when she got back to the beach. Her phone rang as she was gathering her blanket and bag.

Lisa's voice was shrill. "He won't tell me. Can you believe that? He won't tell me!"

For a moment, Ella was confused. Then she remembered Dan being out the other night. "Maybe it's something embarrassing."

"And maybe I'll have to follow him next time."

"You're going to follow him?"

"Why not? I can play detective if I want to."

Ella said nothing, thinking that was exactly what she was doing here in Virginia. Except there was no cheating spouse, only a presumed dead girl. Maybe she and Lisa had both inherited the Nancy Drew gene.

"Lisa, be careful, okay? I'm not saying don't do it, just be careful."

"Thanks," Lisa sniffed. "I appreciate it. I'll talk to you later."

Ella hung up, wishing she could do more for her sister, but she was confident that Lisa and Dan would work it out.

The ride back to Paterson was uneventful as Ella passed what were starting to become familiar landmarks. Pulling into her driveway, she noted that the spray paint was no longer visible.

Although the day had been hot, the interior of the house was cool. She went into the kitchen to get a drink and downed it in one gulp. Refilling her glass, she carried it upstairs, thinking that she really needed to get started on those course outlines.

Feeling drowsy, Ella flopped onto her bed and closed her eyes to rest for a bit. Work could wait.

***

We always know what is familiar to us, even when it is changed within the dreamscape. The store held a peculiar quality to the light, making it sepia toned. In the corner of her mind, Ella thought, "I'm back, but I'm someplace else. I know this place." She drifted through the front door, noting the sign that read "General Store." The store contained exactly what was expected of such a place: canned foods, dried peppers, cigarettes, and candy. The back corner held rolls of fabric as well as a variety of tools.

Ella's attention focused on the two girls in the far corner. Drifting toward them, she tried to listen in on their conversation.

"Lorraine, it'll be okay. I promise," the darker-skinned girl said. Knowing this was Hattie, Ella moved closer to hear every word.

"It will not be okay. Remember the Lovings? Do you remember what

happened to them? They can't even come home or they'll be put in jail. All I'm saying is I hope you're sure about this, because I don't want to have to break you out of jail."

Hattie stood as tall as she possibly could and glowered at her friend. "You, of all people, I expected more from you. Are you trying to tell me that you agree with those laws and think that people of two different races shouldn't be married or together? What do you really think, Lorraine?"

Lorraine sighed, a deep sigh of weariness that was unexpected from one so young. "You know that's not what I think. I think those laws are nonsense, and I think you have a perfect right to be together. I want you to be sure of his love for you and not be taken advantage of. Trust me, if the authorities find out about this, they will do the same thing to you that they did to Mildred and Richard Loving. Only this could be worse, much, much worse."

Hattie deflated. "I know. It doesn't seem right, does it? How can the state tell us who to love? I mean, I didn't plan to fall in love with a white man. It just happened. But why is it so wrong?"

Lorraine looked directly at Ella, as if she could see the visitor. "There's nothing wrong with what you're doing, but there is something wrong with the way people will look at it. You could get hurt, Hattie, and I don't mean your heart. People around here, they'll come after you."

"But why? Why is it so wrong?" Hattie repeated, her voice fading. In the distance, a muffled rumble sounded. "Why is it so wrong..."

***

The rumble continued, then turned into a low, throaty bark. Ella opened her eyes, confused. As she transitioned into wakefulness, it took her a moment to remember where she was. The slant of the afternoon sun told her it was later in the day, probably around five o'clock. The bark had come from Daisy, who was parked at the end of the bed.

"Mom?" Ella whispered without thinking.

She sat up and pushed the hair off her face. Her mouth was dry, and her body still felt heavy from sleep. She looked at Daisy, wondering why the dog's hackles were up.

The first strains of music drifted into the room on a breeze, reminiscent of gospel. *Some glad mornin' when this life is over...*

Letting out a breath, Ella started to relax. "The neighbors are playing that music again, that's all."

From nowhere, a deep, loud moan and a scream ripped the air and tore through Ella's stomach. In that instant, Ella was gripped by an echo of loss and desperation.

With a short bark, Daisy leapt off the bed and ran for the stairs.

"Daisy, no, wait!"

She stopped herself from running out the door toward Daisy. Terror shot into her body, and she couldn't get enough air in her lungs. "It's in the house. Whatever it is, it's in the house."

A shriek, followed by barking, snapped Ella out of her trance. This time, she knew exactly what to do.

Chapter Eighteen

GRABBING THE PHONE FROM A table, Ella punched the numbers 911. Her breathing was harsh and ragged when the operator answered her call.

"911, please state your emergency."

Don't mention the ghost or they won't show up. "I think someone is in the house with me," Ella half-whispered into the phone. She was sucking in air, unable to catch her breath.

"Where are you, ma'am?"

"I'm upstairs. At my house." *Oh God oh God oh God. This is starting to feel like one of those dreams, but it's real.*

"Are you located at 313 Burnt Ridge Way, Paterson?"

"Yes," she whispered. "Please hurry. I don't know what's happening down there."

"Hold for one moment, ma'am. Don't put the phone down, okay?"

"Right, sure." As if she'd put the phone down to find something better to do.

"Ma'am? A patrol car is on the way. Can you hear an intruder in the house right now?"

It had grown eerily quiet in the house. There was no noise, but Ella felt as if she were being watched. She turned and looked behind her.

"No, I don't hear it anymore, but I was taking a nap and there was this screaming coming from downstairs…"

"You're going to be fine, just fine," the operator soothed. "Tell me your name."

"Ella Giancetti."

"All right, Ella Giancetti, what's your phone number?"

Ella held the phone away from her for a moment, confused. "Don't you have that? Doesn't my number come up on your screen?"

"Yes, ma'am, but I need you to confirm your telephone number for me."

Ella sighed. The last dispatcher had not been nearly this thorough. At this rate, she could be hacked into tiny pieces, or taken hostage, or almost anything. There was no limit to what could have happened in the—looking at her clock, she realized it had been less than a minute that she was on the phone.

"Um...my number is...oh God...I don't remember. I just moved here—"

"Does it start with a 5?" the operator asked gently.

"Yes! It's 555-3629."

"How long have you been living in the house?"

"I moved here a couple of days ago. From somewhere else. I'm not from here." Desperation bubbled up inside her. If she didn't stop talking, she was afraid she'd soon sound like a complete idiot.

"The officers should be there soon. They will not have their sirens on when they arrive. Are you okay, Ella?"

Help is on the way, she thought, *and not a moment too soon*. This was getting a little ridiculous. Something had to be done. This time, she'd demand that the officers do some sort of investigating.

"Yes, I'm fine. I'll be fine now, thank you for your help," she told the operator.

"Wait, don't—" the voice on the other end was cut off as Ella disconnected the call.

Phone in hand, she made her way down the stairs, muttering as a dark determination settled in. "This is my house now, and I am *not* going to be frightened away. My name might not be on the deed, but I live here." As she carefully made her way down the stairs, her thoughts mirrored her resolve to hold her fear at bay. Would she see what she'd seen the other night? Would there be a ghost waiting to tackle her in the kitchen, or would she see a group of teenagers laughing as they ran from the house?

She stomped through the living room and into the kitchen.

Dismay swept through her as she surveyed the kitchen. She probably should have expected this. She started shivering, wishing she had a sweater. The temperature had dropped significantly, and she felt as if it were about thirty degrees Fahrenheit in the room. But the cold air and the oppressive silence surrounding her were nothing compared to the disarray.

Ella had worked diligently to clean the mess made from what she now thought of as "the incident." When she'd left the house earlier, her kitchen had been spotless and every pan, plate, fork, and knife had been put away in its place.

Her breathing was ragged as she stared at her kitchen. Once again, her pots and pans were scattered across the kitchen floor. All the cabinet doors and drawers stood open, and broken glass littered the center of the floor. The refrigerator door stood open, with food dumped onto the floor.

Her kitchen was a mess. A complete disaster of a mess. At least the refrigerator had been left intact last time.

Ella jumped when the phone in her hand rang. It was the emergency operator. "Ella, are you okay? Are there intruders with you right now?"

"No, I'm fine. Nobody's with me."

"Ella, do not hang up the phone again. The police are in your yard now and are visually inspecting the outside. What is your location in the house?"

The entire situation felt surreal. Could this really be happening? "I'm in the kitchen, looking at the damage that was done here."

"I'm going to tell the officers that you're in the kitchen and holding the phone. What are you wearing?"

Ella looked down. She had changed into light Capri sweat pants and a tank top when she got home. "Gray pants and a lavender tank top."

"That's great. You're doing great, Ella. Now let's see if the officer can identify the color lavender."

Ella gave a short laugh as there was a knock at the door. The operator on the phone said, "That's Officer Drake. Go ahead and let him in."

Ella peeked out the back door, and sure enough there was a police officer standing there, patiently waiting. Her heart sped up at the sight of him.

"Officer Drake?" Ella was breathless again.

"Yes, ma'am. You can tell the operator you're speaking to us now, and we'll take it from here."

"He's here. Thank you," Ella told the operator before disconnecting the call again. She had sort of regained control of her breathing and felt infinitely better knowing the police were at her house. Instinctively, she knew that this time she'd see some real results; Officer Drake at least acted like he cared, which was more than the others had done.

With an air of authority, he stepped inside the house and placed his hand on Ella's arm. "We meet again. You'll have to come with me, okay?"

"Sure, why? Where are we going?" It flitted through her mind that she'd probably go anywhere with this guy.

"We want you to step outside for a moment. We need to search the house."

He escorted Ella to a police cruiser, where a young woman was standing, obviously waiting for them. "This is Officer Sellers," he told her. "She's going to stay with you while we go through the house to make sure nobody's in there. Do not leave her side, okay?"

Ella nodded. "No problem. I'll be right here." She had no desire to get in the middle of their search. Ella was sincerely hoping they found something, some piece of evidence to suggest someone was there. What was scarier, a real person in your house or a ghost? *The ghost, definitely. It can't be caught and put in jail.*

Ella shifted from one foot to the other, trying for patience. She knew she needed to let him do his job, then she could talk to him about what was happening. *I wonder if he's married?* After all, the important stuff needed to be researched.

Ella glanced at the police officer standing ramrod straight next to her. With long, dark hair gathered in a ponytail, she kept her eyes focused on the house in front of them. Her nametag read "J. Sellers." From her silence, Ella wondered if she was new to the police force. The silence stretched, and once again Ella fought the desperate urge for a cigarette.

If ever Ella had a reason to take up smoking again, this would be it.

Maybe I can get some information. She cleared her throat before asking, "We're not in a high-crime area, so I guess this is a little unusual, right?"

"Not too unusual. Not here," J. Sellers responded, not looking at Ella.

"What do you mean, not here?"

"Nothing, really. We get a fair amount of these types of disturbance calls out here, that's all." As she was answering, Ella noticed that the officer seemed almost nervous, staring intently at the house in front of them. Ella wondered what the officer was afraid of.

"Do you get these types of calls all over town, or only here at this particular house?"

"I cannot state crime statistics with absolute certainty, ma'am."

Ella had never liked being brushed off by anyone, but she knew then that J. Sellers was not going to hand her any information.

It puzzled her. Why was the officer being deliberately obtuse? And why wouldn't she look at Ella? There wasn't any time to dwell on that thought, as Officer Drake strode out of the house directly toward them.

"The house is all clear, Ms. Giancetti. We found no sign of anyone on the premises." His earnest demeanor carried a sense of compassion, and his blue eyes were solemn as he looked at Ella.

Maybe it was the kindness he exuded, but Ella speculated that Officer Drake was new to his job. Or maybe it was just his helpful attitude, a direct contradiction to his co-workers' bored demeanors. J. Sellers was not the only police officer that seemed uninterested. Others were gathered around a different patrol car, talking and laughing.

"It's nice to see you again. I'm sorry it had to be in an emergency situation. I hope you had a good time at the beach today." His direct manner and warm smile made her heart beat a little faster.

She tried to focus on her current situation. "So, what happened here? Did you find any indication that someone broke in?"

Officer Drake shook his head. "I'm sorry, ma'am, there seems to be no sign of forced entry. Did you lock your doors when you came into the house?"

Ella looked at the sky. She had a feeling he wasn't going to like her answer, him being a police officer and everything. "I'm not sure. I really don't remember. Sometimes I lock my doors, and I usually lock them at night...why would someone walk into my house and destroy the kitchen? What is that about?"

Officer Drake shrugged. "Do you think there's anyone who might be trying to scare you?"

Ella shook her head. "No, I just moved here. I haven't had enough time to meet anyone yet." *Except for one coffee shop altercation, a cable man, and a surly landlord*, she thought, keeping those comments to herself.

"Well, you did the right thing to call the police," Officer Drake said. "But next time, don't go toward the disturbance, all right? Why did you go into the kitchen?"

Ella knew she was going to have to give him a really good answer for that particular question, since it was something she was wondering herself right now.

Chapter Nineteen

"BECAUSE THIS IS MY HOME, and I can't stand the thought of someone trying to scare me. I decided enough was enough, and I was going to let whoever it was know that they can't get away with this any longer."

Officer Drake's expression was grave. "Has this sort of thing happened before?"

Ella blinked. *He really is taking me seriously.* He wasn't going to look around for a minute and leave, which pretty much described her last experiences with the police.

Maybe it would be better if she talked about what happened. If the police knew the whole story, they might be able to protect her.

Drawing in a breath and hoping not to be labeled as crazy, she looked down and began to tell him about the other events in the house. He listened carefully, asked questions, and asked about the details of that night. She deliberately left out the part about the pans floating in the air before they crashed to the ground. Instead, she told him that her kitchen was a mess that time, as it was this night. He took notes and asked even more questions. It was more than an hour before they finished, after which he asked her if she'd like to file a report.

"I'm not certain, I didn't do that before," Ella replied slowly. "What would that entail?"

Officer Drake explained that she could file a damaged property report if anything of value in the house was ruined. Since they were unable to find signs of an intruder, they would not file a breaking and entering incident report.

"I think it's nothing more than a big mess," Ella told him. Her glassware wasn't valuable, it was easily replaced.

"Okay. It looks like everything is in order, and it's safe for you to enter your house." He wrote for a moment, then handed her a business card. "Here's my information if you have any questions. If you see or hear anything unusual, anything at all, don't hesitate to call 911. You never know, it might have been someone playing a joke, or it might have been someone who truly meant to harm you. Make sure you always lock your doors when you're in the house, even if it's daytime. Criminals are unpredictable."

Ella smiled weakly at him. "So, you're telling me that you have no idea what happened in there?"

He slowly shook his head. "I'm sorry. I can't find evidence of anything other than your kitchen being messed up."

Ella looked around and noticed that the other police cars had left, with only Officer Drake remaining. She shuddered. He was going to leave, too, and she'd have to go back into the house by herself.

Ella looked directly at Officer Drake. "What about the screaming? Why would somebody go into my kitchen and make noises like that?"

He hesitated for a moment. "I would like to say that it was probably kids playing a joke since you're new in town, but I don't want you to let your guard down. Try not to be afraid, and always be aware of your surroundings. When you drive someplace, check your mirror to see if someone is following you. Before you get out of the car, make sure you look around to see if there's anyone hanging out in the yard. Stay focused and aware and you should be okay. Don't forget to carry your cell phone with you, and make sure it's fully charged when you go out."

Ella looked him directly in the eyes. "Officer, you seem like a really nice person. I'm sure you're good at your job, and my dog likes you, which tells me more than enough about you as a person." They both looked down to see Daisy, relaxed, lying at his feet. Ella continued. "How long have you worked here?"

He blushed when answering. "Only about six months now. I finished my stint in the military, then went to the police academy when I got home. I'm originally from New Jersey, but I really like this area, so I decided to come back for a new start."

Ella smiled. "I think you made a good choice. I understand the winters here are much better than Jersey. I'm from Connecticut and moved here to take a job. But I have to tell you, something seems a little strange to me."

"What's that?"

"I don't want you to take this the wrong way," Ella started slowly, hoping she wouldn't sound offensive, "but I was wondering, is this a high crime town?"

Officer Drake laughed before he could stop himself. "I'm sorry," he said, trying not to smile. "To me, this town seems like Mayberry, USA. Not much happens here beyond the usual drunk driving and occasional shoplifting sort of thing. Why?"

"I noticed that your co-workers, the other police officers, weren't as diligent as you tonight."

Officer Drake frowned, and Ella hurriedly said, "It's not that I think they're not good at their job or anything. I just find it kind of strange that you were the only one taking this seriously. I mean, what if someone was in there with a gun or something? The last time I called, the officers were here and gone within fifteen minutes."

"I don't know about last night, but tonight…I noticed that, too," he said soberly. "Like I said, I haven't been here that long, but I wondered why they weren't more —" He stopped before he could finish the sentence. "Anyway, I'll ask around. Maybe they know something I don't know. The new person is always the last to know anything."

Ella smiled. "Especially when the new person is a Yankee."

At that, Officer Drake laughed again. "Have you tried the sweet tea yet?"

Ella pulled a face. "Don't even mention that stuff to me. How on earth can anyone consume so much sugar in one glass?"

"Don't worry, you'll adapt. Eventually. You might not ever drink the tea, but before you know it your voice will start to carry a slight drawl and you'll be reaching for a sweater when the thermometer dips below sixty degrees."

When he smiled at her, Ella couldn't help the fluttering in her stomach again. Officer Drake was a very handsome man, and Ella tried to look innocent as she glanced at his left hand. Unfortunately, he wore gloves.

For the moment, they stood in comfortable silence, gazing at the house as if it would offer up an answer to the events of the day. It was early evening, and the sun was dropping closer to the horizon. The last rays of light bounced off the windows, creating an orange glare that started to hurt Ella's eyes and prevented them from seeing directly into the house. The effect was supernatural, making it look as if there were a world within the dwelling that was closed to ordinary humans, a place subject to uncomfortable disturbances from another existence. Frankly, the house looked haunted.

Chapter Twenty

"DO YOU WANT ME TO go back in there and check it one more time?" Officer Drake asked in a subdued voice.

"No, thanks." Ella was quiet for a moment. "I have a feeling I'll be fine." Without consciously realizing it, Ella had come to a decision: she was going to figure this out. Since she was certain it was related to Hattie, she first needed to find out what happened to the young girl. She had to do this if she were to continue living in Paterson.

She turned to him. "I don't even know your first name."

"Kevin."

She held out her hand. "Kevin, thank you very much for protecting me tonight. I truly appreciate the effort you've put into making my home safe." She smiled, trying to appear confident. Confident women always got men, everyone knew that. As they shook hands, Kevin blushed and let go after several moments.

"Um…listen, there is one more thing…" he began.

"Yes?" Ella prompted, holding her breath.

Kevin seemed at a momentary loss for words. Pushing his police hat back on his head, hand on hip, he looked at the ground. Finally, he muttered, "It's your shed."

"My shed?" Confusion was evident in Ella's voice.

He looked up at her and said, "Your shed in the backyard. Do you use it at all?"

Ella shook her head. "No, I haven't even gone in there. I think it has a lock. Besides, I don't need to store a lawnmower or anything like that. The yard is taken care of by a service."

"Okay, good. That's good. I mean, it's good you don't have to go in there. That shed looks like it's about to fall down. It could be a safety hazard. If there are people, kids, messing around on the property, I wouldn't want you to get in trouble if someone got hurt in there."

They both stared at the ground for a second before Ella said, "Thanks."

"You should talk to your landlord, you know. Tell him he needs to fix that thing. What if it falls apart and damages your property, like your car or a guest's car?"

Ella's face softened. "Thank you for your concern. I'll mention it to the person that takes care of the house." Never mind the fact that the shed was about one hundred yards from her car, it was sweet of him to think of her well-being.

Kevin looked up at her. "So, do you have a boyfriend around that you could call to come stay with you? Someone to protect you?"

Ella shook her head, happy that he was being so obvious. It made life easier when you knew what people's intentions were. "Nope, no boyfriend. There hasn't been time for that. I've been busy finishing my dissertation, then looking for a job, then moving. Anyway, I've got my dog to protect me."

Kevin smiled at her. He didn't only smile with his mouth, he smiled with his eyes. She sent a silent plea to the Universe that he not be married or have a girlfriend.

"Yeah, I noticed that dog's a real killer."

They both looked at Daisy, who was lying on her side, asleep.

"Listen, you have my cell phone number on the card I gave you. You can call me whenever you like." Kevin's face sobered. "For now, though, with your situation you might want to consider some extra security."

Ella was hesitant. She had a new job, which was great, but she wasn't sure about having the added monthly bill of a security system. Things might be less expensive in the South, but she was still on a budget. "I don't know. I have my dog, who's really very good at letting me know when strangers are near, and there are locks on the doors and windows. I can't really afford a security system right now."

Kevin shook his head. "You don't need a security system. But this is a rental house. Who knows how many tenants have lived here, and if there are any extra keys floating around?"

Ella was speechless. She hadn't considered that possibility, but the more she thought about it the more it made sense.

Kevin continued, "Usually, landlords don't bother to change the locks when the tenants leave, unless they have to forcibly evict them. As far as you know, the entire town could have keys. You should change the locks and install a chain on the door as well."

Ella closed her eyes against the image of a man in a dirty t-shirt smirking at her. "Right. A chain. Different locks. I'll do that."

Kevin hesitated. "You should do it sooner rather than later. If someone is getting into your house, you don't want to give them another opportunity to harass you. People like that can be dangerous. I mean, maybe it wasn't a person, maybe it was something else that caused the mess in your house. Maybe it was your dog, or the house shifted and the cabinet doors opened…"

Ella gave Kevin a look that made him stop talking. After a beat, he said, "Okay, I admit I can't figure out what else could have caused that big mess in your kitchen if it wasn't a person. That's why I think you should get those locks taken care of right away."

"I know, but I don't know if I have the tools right now. I think I know where my screwdriver is, but I haven't seen my drill since…" She thought for a moment. "Oh, shoot, I know where my drill is."

"From the look on your face, I'm guessing it's not in the shed. Where is your drill?"

"Vermont."

"Vermont," Kevin repeated.

"Yes. My aunt has a vacation home up in Vermont, and I brought my drill up there one week to help her hang some shelves. I think I left it there." Ella was mentally kicking herself, since now she'd have to buy a new drill. Or wait for it to be mailed to her, which, knowing her aunt, might be quite some time.

Kevin cleared his throat. "If you want, I could come back after my shift ends and install those things for you. It won't take very long, and I won't stay or anything. You really shouldn't go another night without better security on your doors."

Here was her opportunity. "Won't your wife or girlfriend have a problem with that?"

Looking directly into her eyes, he answered. "Same as you, I haven't had a whole lot of time for that sort of thing. There's nobody at home waiting for me."

Ella let out a breath she didn't know she'd been holding and sent a silent thanks to the Universe. Once in a while, her requests were granted. "Thank you. I'm not sure I'd get any sleep tonight thinking about who had a key to the house. I'd probably move all my furniture in front of the door."

Kevin looked horrified. "Don't do that," he cautioned. "If there's a fire, you won't be able to… oh, you were kidding."

Ella smiled. He was cute, in that protective-cop kind of way. "Yes, I was kidding, but thanks for being conscious of my safety. What time should I expect you, and how much do you want for this?"

"I get off duty at seven-thirty. I'll go straight to the hardware store, so I'll probably get here sometime around eight. I don't know how much the locks and stuff will cost, so you can pay me when I get here. Do you need any flashlights or batteries while I'm at the store?"

Ella shook her head, confused by the last question. "No, I have a flashlight in the kitchen."

"Then I'll be back soon. In the meantime, lock your doors."

Walking to the street, he waited a moment before getting into the patrol car, almost as if he had something else to say. Finally, with a wave, he left.

Ella waved goodbye as the police cruiser pulled away. "Well, what do you know? I think he was flirting with me. I wonder if he'll ask me out later. I hope I can remember how this works."

The first thing she did upon entering the house was run upstairs to get changed. "In case Kevin comes back early," she told Daisy, who was looking at her quizzically. "I don't want to be dressed in the same old sweats I'm wearing now." She chose a pair of black shorts and a grey t-shirt that read, "*Jesus loves you but everyone else thinks you're a weirdo.*" The clothes were comfortable but fit well enough to show off a few curves.

"Come on, Daisy. I'll get you something to eat while I clean up that mess in the kitchen."

Pouring kibbles into a bowl for Daisy was easy, cleaning the kitchen was not. But really, what choice did she have? Who wants to eat food off creepy plates that have been tossed around the kitchen?

The light over the sink provided soft illumination while Celtic music played quietly in the background. While her hands were immersed in the warm, soapy water, the beginnings of a plan began to form in her mind. Determination drove her thoughts as she tried to outline a course of action that would remedy this bizarre situation. Lost in thought, it took her a few moments to realize that Daisy was growling at something in the living room.

"Oh, for God's sake, enough already."

Ella turned and stalked out of the kitchen into the living room. She stopped, unable to move any further. Dusk had crept in, allowing Ella to see the barest outline of a figure standing behind the screen door. Damn, Kevin was right. She should have locked the door.

Despite herself, she jumped as the raspy voice barked, "What the hell is going on around here?"

Chapter Twenty-One

THE DOOR SWUNG OPEN WITHOUT a sound. Ella held her breath, unable to move. The only thing in her hands was a dish towel—not a very effective weapon against intruders. Daisy stood quivering by her side, ready to defend her home.

As the shadowy figure stepped into the living room light, a small gasp escaped from Ella. Recognition was immediate, followed by fury.

"What do you think you're doing? You scared the living daylights out of me. You should know better than to creep around the house like some kind of criminal. What if I didn't recognize you and ended up hurting you?" she asked indignantly.

"With a dish towel?" he asked.

"That's not the point," she spat back. "You could have called or something." As he stood awkwardly in the living room, Ella relented a little. "I'm sorry I snapped at you, but you scared me."

"I didn't mean to scare you. I wanted to make sure you were all right. I try to take care of this place for my dad, and besides, I'd feel bad if anything happened to you."

Ella looked up at Jeff Bartok. He did seem repentant, and she felt another surge of sympathy for him as she remembered the story about his mother. "Don't worry about it. I'm a little on edge right now," she admitted, not willing to say more than that. Sensing no immediate danger, Daisy turned and walked to her dog bed in the corner, flopping down with a sigh.

"Can I come in?" His tone was contrite.

"Why ask now? You're already in," Ella observed drily. "Don't mind me, I get cranky when I'm scared. Do you want something to eat or drink?"

Jeff shook his head. "No, I want to know what happened." He paused for a moment, reading her t-shirt. Shaking his head, he looked at her and asked, "Why were the police here?"

Ella let out a frustrated sigh. "How do you do that? How do people in this town know everything as soon as it happens?"

He smiled at her, the first real smile she'd ever seen on his face. He didn't look mean when he smiled, and Ella thought he should try to do that more often. It made him look like the harmless guy-next-door. His smile gave him life and made Ella feel like she was talking to a sympathetic neighbor.

"I was down at the Shack when you called the police. One of the guys in there heard it on his scanner and told me something was going on at the house—again." He sat on the couch. Seeing the look on her face, he said, "The Shack is a local hangout. They serve really good seafood, and there's a bar with a big screen television where I like to watch sports and have a beer. But you still didn't answer my question. What happened?"

Ella hesitated. She didn't want to tell him about her suspicions, but he did have a right to know what was going on. And he did seem genuinely concerned, so maybe he wasn't such a creep after all. She decided to tell him a simplified version of the truth.

"First, let me tell you that it turned out to be nothing after all. When I came home this afternoon, I went upstairs to take a quick nap. When I woke up I thought I heard someone downstairs, so I called the police. They came and searched the place, but it looks like nobody was here." She crossed her fingers behind her back, a reflexive action born of guilt. Hopefully, he wouldn't ask too many questions.

Jeff looked at her for several moments. "And you're certain you didn't get hurt, and there's nothing more to this story that I'm going to find out at a later date?"

Ella lifted her chin. How dare he think she wasn't telling the truth? Even if she weren't telling the truth, he had no right to think that, she told herself unreasonably. "I'm fine," she said.

He nodded. "Good. When I heard that the police were out here again, I wondered…"

Ella watched him, waiting for him to finish his sentence. "What did you wonder?" she asked when it appeared he wasn't going to say anything more.

"I wondered what was going on. We've had some strange tenants in the past, and I was hoping you weren't going to turn out to be like them."

It was an odd thing for him to say, but Ella refrained from comment. "Thanks for having the outside cleaned up again." She wasn't sure what else to add to that and expected him to ask questions about the vandalism.

Instead, he nodded. "Yep, looks like you made an enemy. You know who it is?"

Ella shook her head. She had an idea of who it might be but was reluctant to point fingers without any proof.

"Well, when they catch him, make sure you press charges. That's a hate crime."

Ella was astonished. Sometimes Jeff scared her, and other times, like now, he acted decent. Not wanting to talk about the vandal, she changed the topic. "The police officer mentioned something I wanted to speak with you about." Almost imperceptibly, Jeff tensed. Ella noticed this because she was watching for it, wondering how much he really knew about the house. "He mentioned that there might be people out there who have extra keys to the house, old tenants and people like that. Do you change the locks when tenants move?"

His forehead wrinkled as he thought. "No, I don't think I've ever changed the locks in this house. That's a good point. Do you want me to have someone come over tomorrow and take care of that?"

Ella blushed. "Actually, I'm going to do it myself. I hope you don't mind. I have a friend on his way over in a little while to help me. I didn't want to sleep in the house tonight thinking people could get in here at any time." She held her breath, wondering if the town grapevine extended to knowing her social life as well. Given her previous history with men—or lack thereof—this was one area of her life she'd rather not have an audience.

Jeff nodded. "I don't blame you, I would have done the same thing. Make sure I get a copy of the keys. You should probably put a chain on the door as well. You can't be too careful, you know. Also, make sure you have your storm supplies ready. You don't want to get caught out here without supplies, right?"

Ella nodded, wondering why he was telling her about storm supplies. Jeff continued. "Is everything else okay? Are you happy with the house? I hope you're not planning on moving anytime soon with all the crap that's going on."

Ella wasn't sure if he were kidding or serious. "After all those boxes I unpacked? I may never move," she joked.

"Good. It would be nice to have someone stable in here." Ella wondered exactly how unstable the previous tenants were. Jeff made it sound like some very strange people had lived there.

He stood to leave. "Remember, give me a call when your lock is installed, and I'll stop by to pick up the new key."

Ella smiled. "Thanks, Jeff. I appreciate your concern—even if I yelled at you." As he was opening the front door, Ella stopped him.

"Jeff? There was something else the police said."

His face darkened, all remnants of the former smile gone. "Now what have they gone and told you?"

Chapter Twenty-Two

ELLA SWALLOWED. THE WORDS WERE hanging in the air between them, but from the dark look on his face, she wished she had not spoken.

"They said that I should tell you the backyard shed is in pretty bad shape. That's all. They didn't want anyone getting hurt over there. Maybe someone should take a look at it, make sure it's structurally sound."

His eyes darkened. "Have you been in there?"

"No," she protested.

"Good, because I told you before you moved in that the shed was off limits. You have absolutely no reason to be in there. Don't go nosing around, if you know what's good for you." He turned away from her, muttering something that Ella couldn't hear.

Ella's temper flared. "For your information, mister, you might have said something to that real estate lady you hired, but you never once told me I wasn't allowed in the shed. It wasn't on the lease I signed."

"Yes, it is," he growled, looking back at her. "Look at the third paragraph on the second page, under the heading 'Exceptions.' It's all there in black and white, so you better make sure you pay attention." With that, he left, letting the storm door slam behind him.

Ella was furious. How dare he come over and pretend to be worried about her when he was probably worried about something happening to the house? "What a rotten, stinky jerk. I knew there was something off about him. Who does he think he is anyway, telling me what I can and can't do? I'll show him…I'll…I'll…go in the shed!" The more she thought about it, the more sense it made, in a twisted kind of way. Maybe something in the shed would help her figure out what was going on in the house. Why else would Jeff act so weird about the whole thing?

It was risky, she knew. Prior to that day, she could simply claim ignorance, but after Jeff's tirade there was no way she could make that claim. She couldn't get caught going in there, but it would be totally worth it to see if he were hiding anything.

But what if Jeff *was* hiding something—what if it was illegal? She was friends with the police now, or one police officer, which might help. Although, if he had something to hide, maybe that was the reason strange things kept happening. Maybe someone was trying to get her to move or trying to find whatever was hidden in the shed. He might have a stash of drugs out there, or stolen items... Ella tried to reign in her imagination, knowing that the possibilities she could come up with were, in all likelihood, far worse than the truth.

Enough. She needed to start cleaning. There was a little time before Kevin arrived to install the new locks, and she wanted everything to look good. It took longer than she expected to sweep the broken glass and replace the items in the refrigerator. Immersed in thought, Ella jumped when the phone rang.

The voice on the other end sounded slightly nervous and edgy. "Ella, how are you? I was calling to make sure everything was well out there."

Ella smiled to herself, wondering if Lorraine had been in the Shack with Jeff Bartok when news of her 'disturbance' raced through town. "Lorraine, thank you for calling. Everything's fine. It was great to see you at the museum today. How was the rest of your day?"

Lorraine sighed on the other end. "Oh, the usual; catching up on paperwork and scheduling meetings. Actually, that's the other reason for my phone call. Unfortunately, we're scheduled to have a department meeting Thursday afternoon at one o'clock in my office. Of course, I'll call you if that needs to change. It'll be a short meeting, but we have to go over some important topics before classes begin."

"No problem. Let me write that in my calendar," Ella muttered as she scribbled the date and time on the back of a takeout menu before putting it under a magnet on the refrigerator.

"How have your course plans been coming along? Do you feel prepared for the semester?"

Ella cringed. Lorraine had no way of knowing what Ella had been up to, and she hoped her supervisor wouldn't guess that she'd done no preparations. None at all. "I think I'm ready. I might still have some work to do, but I have some materials together. I had a few questions about grading and policy, but I'll wait until the meeting for that."

"Perfect," Lorraine answered. "We've made a few adjustments to the system, and I'll review our grading policy in detail for everyone. Remember, if you have any questions at all, please don't hesitate to ask. I want this to go as smoothly as possible for you."

"Thanks, Lorraine. I appreciate your help and your vote of confidence. I'm excited about teaching here, especially the new class you gave me."

There was a small hesitation before Lorraine asked again, "You're very welcome, dear. We're glad to have you with us. I wanted to make certain, are you sure everything is okay at your house? I heard you had a little disturbance earlier."

Ella inwardly groaned. Clearly, there were no secrets in this town. "No, everything is fine, really. It was a slight misunderstanding. I thought I heard something, so I called the police. They came out and checked everything but there was no sign of an intruder."

There was another pause, this one longer than the first. "Just because they didn't find anything doesn't mean there was nothing there."

Ella snorted. "Thanks, that will help me sleep tonight. But don't worry, one of the police officers is coming back tonight to install new locks and a chain on the door. Between that and my dog, I should be safe."

"I'm not trying to scare you. It's just that I've heard so many different things through the years..."

As Ella tied up a garbage bag to take outside, she crushed the phone against her shoulder. "What have you heard?"

Lorraine's voice sounded strained. "I think what I've heard is speculation and rumors. It's not anything to concern yourself with, and I'm sorry I brought it up."

Ella laughed. "That's fine by me. I wouldn't be surprised if my family hasn't already contacted you to keep an eye on me. Sometimes they worry a bit, too."

"No, nobody in your family has called me—yet. Perhaps they don't have my phone number. I did, however, have an interesting conversation with your neighbor, Alice."

Ella carried the garbage bag to the can outside. "She's a sweet woman. She told me she's known you for quite a while." Ella thought that her phrasing was very discreet, but Lorraine decided to ignore discretion.

"Yes, Hattie and I used to go to her house to hang out together. It was a safe place to hide out. Of course, I realize now that the whole town knew we were friends. I suppose it was easier for everyone to ignore since we spent as little time as possible out in public together. We used to do our homework at Alice's house… well, I did my homework, and Hattie helped me. Sometimes, we'd watch the children when Alice needed to go to the store in the afternoons. They were still quite small back then, as I remember."

Ella had trouble picturing an entire town frowning upon a friendship. Hatred bred strange behavior, but it wasn't as if these girls were out doing drugs or causing property damage. For God's sake, they were kids doing schoolwork.

After a pause, Lorraine continued in a quiet voice. "Hattie was such a smart girl. She had a way of seeing the world that was fresh and sharp. I learned a lot from her."

"I'm so sorry for your loss. That must have been difficult, not knowing what happened to your friend." Ella knew she was taking a chance by saying this to Lorraine; it was possible that Lorraine would simply close up and not speak about Hattie at all.

But Lorraine surprised Ella by responding, "You know, I haven't thought about the details of that summer for a long time. At some point I put away the memories and emotions of our friendship in the closet in my mind. But with you living in that house, it's starting to come back to me, and I'm able to think about my old friend without so much grief. Once in a while, I even smile when I remember something."

Ella was silent for a moment, trying to imagine grief compounded by a disappearance. Walking back inside, she began cleaning her counters with disinfectant wipes. "I know what it's like to lose someone you love. It's never easy, no matter who it is. People think that losing a friend should somehow be easier than losing, say, a spouse—but that's not true, is it? Pain is pain, and grief is grief. All we can do is somehow get through it."

"You're right. I didn't mean to make you uncomfortable. I simply wanted to mention that Alice and I had a rather interesting conversation. I understand she's been speaking to you about ghosts?"

Ella paused. She wasn't sure where Lorraine was headed with this conversation, so she decided to be noncommittal.

"Yes, apparently Alice's husband is a steady presence for her."

Lorraine laughed. "Oh, Albert's been hanging around for years. If I were you, I wouldn't discount anything he says. He's been known to be frighteningly accurate most of the time."

Chapter Twenty-Three

A PICTURE OF ALICE IN her designer shoes flashed through Ella's mind. "I'll try to remember that. I really like Alice, and she has a wonderful vegetable garden."

The kitchen was finally clean, with pans washed and items in the dishwasher. Satisfied, Ella was leaving the kitchen when a sharp knock sounded at the door.

"Lorraine, someone's here. I should go."

"Is it someone you know? Do you want me to wait on the phone while you check the door?"

"No, I'm fine. It's the police officer I mentioned. He's here to install new locks." Ella definitely didn't want to be on the phone with Lorraine when he walked through her door. Lorraine would know immediately how she felt about Kevin, even though they were on the phone.

"Oh. Well, you have a good night, Ella. We'll talk again soon."

Despite herself, Ella blushed. It was silly, she knew, but that single word, "Oh," made her feel like a teenager again. "A teenager with a crush," she mumbled as she ended the call. Before answering the door, she started to smooth her hair, then gave up. "Whatever I look like is going to have to be fine," she whispered to Daisy. "Besides, why raise expectations so soon?"

It was obvious Kevin had just come from taking a shower. He had that slightly damp look about him with a clean, soapy scent emanating from his skin. She breathed him in, wondering what he looked like with his shirt off. She really had to get a grip—and soon—before she made an idiot of herself.

Ella smiled, pulling the door open wider. "That was quick! Come on in," she invited, stepping aside.

As he walked into her living room, Kevin frowned at her. "How did you know it was me?" he asked.

"It's eight o'clock," she answered. "Who else would it be?"

"Did you look out the window to check?"

She shook her head. "No. But even if you were *not* you and you were one of the bad guys, it wouldn't be so bad. By the time you forced your way in here, you—the good guy you, that is—would have come to my rescue to save me from you, the bad guy. So it all would have worked out fine, right?"

Kevin's face reflected his confusion. "I think I followed what you said, but do me a favor and check to see who's at the door from now on, okay?"

Ella laughed. "It's a deal. Before you begin laboring for my benefit, can I get you anything to eat or drink? Are you hungry?" The voice in Ella's head suggested she stop acting like Martha Stewart and just be herself. That voice sounded suspiciously like her mother, who always had a piece of advice for her daughters.

"I'd love a soda of some kind, but whatever you have is fine. And I'll never turn down an offer of food, but don't go to any trouble for me. I'm going to get started changing these locks right away. This shouldn't take too long."

"Do whatever you need to do. I'll be right back," Ella called over her shoulder as she headed toward the stairs. Once upstairs, she quickly checked herself in her bathroom mirror. She made a face at her hair, despairing at the disarray that was inevitable with high levels of humidity. Hurriedly, she fixed her hair as best as possible and applied a layer of lip gloss. "So much for the natural look," she thought. "I guess vanity eventually wins out." She was glad she'd changed her outfit earlier. "I don't want to look too obvious." With a final spritz of scent, she went back downstairs, wondering what kind of food he might like.

"How's it going down here?" she asked as she descended the steps. She stopped short when she saw Kevin opening the package with the new door handle and lock. "Wow, Kevin, there's a big hole in my door."

He laughed. "Don't worry. I'm replacing the entire thing. You'll have both a new lock and deadbolt installed."

"Thank you. This really is nice of you. I'll be right back with your drink."

In the kitchen, Ella prepared a tray. Uncertain as to what kind of food he liked, she simply loaded the plate with different types of cheese, crackers, and dip, along with a spray of grapes. Finger food seemed like the best choice since he was currently occupied. "Let's see if it's true what they say about the quickest way to a man's heart."

Hoisting the tray, Ella hesitated. Her hormones definitely took over when she was near Kevin, and she tried to take a moment to pull herself together. She wasn't sure why her thoughts turned indecent around him since he hadn't even propositioned her. Fluttery stomach feeling aside, she wondered what a straight-laced man of the law would say if he learned she was dealing with ghosts in the house. "That might be the stumbling block to a relationship."

It had been a long time since Ella was interested in dating anyone. In the recent past, she'd kept a careful distance between her and members of the opposite sex. Now that she'd met someone she liked, she wondered what his reaction to her life would be.

When she got back to the living room, Ella told him, "I put some light things on the plate for you. I wasn't sure how hungry you were."

Kevin slowly looked from the food to Ella. "Maybe we can share a real meal together on a real date sometime... if you're interested."

Ella couldn't stop the blush that spread across her face. Darn her bodily reactions. Raising her own glass in a mock toast, she answered, "That sounds great." Putting the tray on the coffee table, she told him, "If you need anything else, let me know. I'll be in the upstairs office doing some work."

Kevin took a long sip of his soda and asked, "What kind of work? I haven't even asked you what you do for a living."

"I teach college. Actually, this is my first teaching job here at the local college."

"Really? That's pretty cool. What do you teach?"

"Mostly anthropology courses. Some of the classes have an overlap into religion, and one of them is actually kind of whacky. I've been asked to teach a class about rationalist thought as it compares to bizarre spiritual practices in this country."

"What do you mean by 'bizarre?'"

"There are people who actually claim to be vampires, others claim that the end times are rapidly approaching, and some are so fundamentalist in their belief system that they're unable to understand or sometimes even discuss intellectual viewpoints with others. This class is supposed to examine all points of view, rationalist and spiritual, and lead everyone to an understanding of how it all functions in our society today."

Kevin frowned. "That's intense subject material."

Ella shrugged. "Don't look so upset. It may be intense, but it's extremely interesting and important for everyone to start to examine...why are you shaking your head?"

"I can't believe I didn't ask you this before. Have you wondered if these events in your house are in any way related to your job? How many people know about the classes you'll be teaching?"

Ella hesitated. Although the idea was farfetched, it bore consideration, especially in relation to the house being defaced.

"I'm not sure," she said slowly. "Let me think about this for a minute. Lorraine Endleby is the department head who hired me. She knows my schedule, but I have no idea if anyone else is aware of what I'm going to teach. I mean, obviously there are others, but I don't know who they are. We're supposed to have a faculty meeting next week, I guess that's when I might know more. I've managed to make a couple friends from the college, but I can't see them harassing me. In fact, they've been nothing but helpful."

Kevin put his soda down and paced for a moment. His face reflected concern. "It may even be someone you haven't met yet. The fact is, it sounds like the stuff you're teaching is fairly controversial. Talking to students, telling them that their belief system is nothing more than a system? If you're getting into things like creationism and evolution, believe me, that can and will produce some very destructive behavior in people."

Running a hand through his hair, he continued. "Last month, we got a call to go down to the Shack—you know, that bar out by the water?" he continued. "Some lady had the bartender all freaked out. Seems he had some kind of degree in biology or something and was talking about the stuff they teach in schools. Said he didn't want his kids learning, and I quote, 'that creationist crap.' This woman got so mad, she jumped over the bar and started hitting him on the head with her purse."

"All because of a conversation?"

"A little conversation and a lot of beer."

Ella was torn. Kevin seemed truly worried, which was flattering. But she didn't know how to explain the situation to him without sounding like a freak. Telling him she thought there was a ghost in the house would probably ruin any chance she might have to get to know him better; then again, maybe this did have something to do with the obnoxious message spray painted on the house. It was a small possibility, but one she needed to consider.

"I'll have to think about this. If it's all related, the college should be notified, but I don't want to say anything until we're sure this is about my work. I haven't even started yet. It's important to me that I do a good job, and I don't want to mess this up. Can we keep this to ourselves for now?"

"I don't know Ella—"

"I don't want to have to start looking for a job all over again," she pleaded with him.

"All right. For now, we can keep this between us," he relented, hastily adding, "but not for long. I don't want to see you get hurt because some hot-headed lunatic feels justified in terrorizing you."

It was a temporary reprieve, but one that she could live with. Ella tried not to think about what would happen when Kevin found out that she was trying to do research on a possible ghost. He'd probably write her off as insane, and that would be the end of that. Her hands twisted around the damp, cool glass as she traced lines through the condensation on the outside.

"I promise I'll be careful. Hopefully, we can have this figured out soon." For a moment, Ella debated asking if he knew anything about the disappearance of Hattie but decided he hadn't been in the area long enough. Besides, she didn't want him to start asking other kinds of questions. She had no doubt, though, that sooner or later the subject would come up. Maybe once he got to know her a little better, the whole ghost thing wouldn't be an issue.

Watching her face, he shook his head. "I don't know if this is the right thing to do, but I can't force you to do anything, especially when you look at me like that. Fine, we'll see what happens." As he reached for the food on the plate, he said, "Thanks, this is great. I can eat this while I finish putting in the new lock and chain."

As he continued working, Ella heard her cell phone ring from her purse in the kitchen. She knew who it was without even looking at the ID.

"Hi, Lisa."

"You're not gonna believe this."

Ella looked out the back door window. "Let me guess. You've done a little snooping and figured out what Dan was up to."

"That's right." Lisa sounded smug. "And let me tell you, you are *not* gonna believe it."

"He's taking you on a surprise trip? He's out buying you new jewelry?"

"Not quite. It's actually not a good thing—but it might turn out to be perfect."

Chapter Twenty-Four

THE THOUGHT THAT HER SISTER had been drinking flitted briefly through Ella's mind. "Lisa, you're not making any sense."

"Dan lost his job."

There was silence as Ella absorbed what her sister said. If Dan lost his job, why wasn't Lisa more upset? And how did that explain his whereabouts the other night? "So, where was he the other night?"

"He's been working part time at night for an accountant in town. He didn't want to tell me right away because he was so embarrassed."

Ella looked at the glass of soda in her hand, which was no longer fizzing with bubbles. "When did he plan on telling you? What was he thinking, anyway?" Her first reaction was anger. What right did Dan have keeping something that big from his wife? What were they going to do now? How were they going to survive on a part-time income? Lisa certainly couldn't make the kind of money her husband made, and Ella felt a twinge of apprehension.

"Are you guys okay? I mean, will you be able to pay the bills, keep the house and everything? Do you need help?"

Ella half-expected her sister to tell her that she felt deserted and alone since Ella had moved to Virginia, but instead her sister sounded excited.

"Nope, I think everything will be fine."

"Why? It sounds like there's something else."

"Dan's been looking for a job since before he got laid off. Apparently, he saw the writing on the wall and knew it wouldn't be long. He thought he had a little more time than they gave him, that's all."

Ella felt a tug of suspicion. "Did he ever talk to you about his job and what was going on?"

The hesitation on the other end of the phone said it all. "I don't know. He may have mentioned something at some point or other," Lisa said in a casual manner. "But it's all fine now, it really is. It looks like he found another job. And you won't believe this."

The sinking feeling in the pit of Ella's stomach told her that yes, indeed, she just might believe it.

"Believe what?"

"He found a job in Virginia!"

"Really? That fast? Don't these things take time?"

"He's been looking for months now, and he told me he actively pursued this company once he found out you were moving there. I think they'll make him an offer. Wouldn't that be great?"

Ella cleared her throat, trying to decide how great it would be if her sister moved south. "Lisa, you know that Virginia is a big state. Where is this job?"

"The company is in the city of Hampton. Is that near you?"

"I think so. Hold on." Covering the phone with her hand, Ella walked out to the living room. Waving her arm to get Kevin's attention, she whispered, "Are we anywhere near Hampton?"

"Yes, it's about a ten-minute ride from here. Paterson actually borders Hampton."

Ella wasn't sure how she felt about this. A lot of things were happening all at once, and very quickly. Uncovering the phone, she told her sister, "Hampton borders the town I live in. You'd be right next to me."

"Who were you talking to? Where are you?"

"That was a friend of mine. I'm at home."

"What kind of friend? Have you met a guy? Who is he? Oh God, be careful... you know how irresponsible you can be when it comes to making good choices. I hope you're not alone with him."

"Nope, not at all," Ella lied. "He's a police officer, and he's helping me with something. Anyway, I really have to go. Let me know how that job works out for Dan."

"Ella, I think you should ask that man to leave your house. You don't know anything—"

"Okay, bye, Lisa. I'll talk to you later." Ella disconnected the call, feeling a familiar mix of frustration and love for her sister.

She'd have to deal with whatever happened when it happened. She couldn't worry about the possibility of Lisa's moving yet. It might not happen. But Ella knew that if Lisa wanted something badly enough, she made sure she got it. The question was, how badly would her sister want to move to another state?

True to his word, it didn't take Kevin long to install the new hardware. Sooner than Ella would have liked, he was clearing his tools and saying good night to her.

"Thanks again for the food and all."

"All I gave you was some stuff I threw on a plate and a glass of soda. I can actually cook, too." Ella realized as soon as she spoke that her statement could be misinterpreted as a blatant lure to get him to come back to the house. *Isn't that what I want?*

"I'm sure you're multi-talented, Ella Giancetti," he spoke softly.

Ella drew in a sharp breath as her heart rate accelerated. Kevin Drake was one handsome man, and he was definitely flirting with her. Now if she could only get this part right and not come across as desperate for a boyfriend or geeky or anything like that.

"How about we go out to dinner first?" Ella asked. "It'll give us a chance to get to know each other." *Plus, it'll keep me from doing something stupid, like showing you where I sleep at night.*

"That sounds like a plan. I'll call you tomorrow, and we can figure out the details."

"Great," she said in what she hoped was an airy tone. "Again, thank you. Watch out for the mosquitoes out there on your way back to your car. Be careful driving home, and we'll talk soon." Mentally, Ella slapped herself. She needed to stop talking, stop sounding like an idiot.

Kevin looked at her intently. "Listen, Ella. I know I've already said this, but I think I should say it again. Lock the doors whenever you're in the house. Check to see who's outside before you let them in. And above all, don't be afraid to call the police again if there's anything suspicious."

Ella nodded. "Thanks," she said, wondering why he found it so important to speak to her as if she were being stalked. Then again, maybe it was because she threw the door open earlier without knowing who was standing outside her home. Or maybe it was that whole police incident earlier today when Kevin had to search the house. Oh, and don't forget those lovely messages on the house. Kevin definitely had a reason for expressing caution and telling her to be careful.

Kevin reached a hand out and lightly touched her cheek. "Cheer up. You look upset. Try not to worry, my overprotective nature makes me say stuff like that. Anyway, I'll call you tomorrow to make a date for next weekend. I actually have some time off on Saturday."

Smiling, Ella ordered her hormones to calm down. Kevin's sweet nature and good looks were a definite plus, but she did want to be careful. For her, casual dating may have been fine, but casual sex was not. And with the way she was feeling about Kevin at that moment, she wasn't sure she could stop herself from doing things that weren't in her best interest—like getting naked with him.

"That sounds great. You'll have to pick the restaurant since I'm new around here. How much do I owe you for the locks?"

He waved a hand at her as if brushing her aside. "Don't worry about it, it wasn't very much. Maybe someday you can cook for me, and we'll call it even, okay?"

She had more on her mind than cooking, but he didn't need to know that.

"I guess I should get going, but I look forward to talking to you tomorrow. Be careful, and remember what I said."

Waving goodbye, Ella closed the door and breathed a sigh of relief. She was confused. This was the first guy she felt any connection to in a long time, yet all she could think about was sex. It didn't seem like a particularly auspicious start for any type of long-term commitment. Sighing, she turned to Daisy.

"Come on, girl. Let's take a quick trip outside before we head in for the night."

The dog was taken care of, the lights were off, and the soft, humid air of the south wrapped around the night. Not bothering with a book, Ella closed her eyes. It had been a long, event-filled day, and she knew she'd have no trouble falling asleep.

***

Dreams always have a texture, Ella thought. Here I am again.

It was her house, but not quite. The afternoon sun brightened the kitchen, highlighting a room that looked entirely different from what Ella knew. The cream-colored wallpaper had a leafy green background, and the floor was brown linoleum. The countertops, obviously new, were white with a light brown speckled pattern. The ash cabinets gleamed as though they'd just been polished. The appliances were old, but only to Ella. In this place of dreams, they were barely out of their first decade. Sam Cooke played softly in the background, and a figure Ella recognized as Hattie stood at the stove, stirring something liquid in a pot. After a moment, Hattie tensed and turned. Ella gasped, though she doubted anyone could hear her dream self. A ray of light shone upon Hattie's face, illuminating bruising around both eyes and a split lip.

A single tear tracked down her cheek. She was looking at someone, but Ella could barely make out a shadowy figure in the kitchen doorway. He seemed tall, but it was hard to tell. Hattie didn't seem the least bit afraid.

"Hattie..." the voice cracked, the figure in the doorway obviously overcome with emotion.

Slowly, Hattie spoke. "I don't know if I can do this anymore... I don't know."

***

Across town, Jeff spoke swiftly into a cell phone. "I told you I was taking care of things and not to worry." With an exasperated sigh, he forced himself to calm down. "I know this isn't what you wanted. It's not what we ever want, but it's what we have to deal with. She's all right, like I said. She seems nice enough. The Yankee probably got a little scared, that's all, probably got spooked by a possum or something... who knows with women?"

A voice like sandpaper came through the cell phone, causing Jeff to stand a little straighter. "Make sure everything is taken care of. I don't want to have to do it myself."

Chapter Twenty-Five

ELLA OPENED HER EYES AS the morning sun streamed into her bedroom. Despite Kevin's warning, she'd left her window open to allow whatever breeze there might be to cool the room as she slept. She could have left the central air conditioning running through the night, but she preferred the night insects sing her to sleep. Without much traffic on her street, the crickets and an occasional owl hoot soothed her more than any electronic hum.

She yawned, stretched, and sat up. It was going to be hot again. The morning temperature was already uncomfortable, and humidity hung thick in the air—again. Ella was content with the fact that she'd slept undisturbed through the night, although she frowned when remembering her dream.

Coffee... I can't even think about it until I have coffee.

The scent of freshly brewed coffee wafted up the stairs and toward her, a morning ambrosia beckoning with its promise of wakefulness. *I love automatic timers*, Ella thought as she poured her first cup. Soon, the sugar and caffeine began to work their magic, and the fog that hovered in her head slowly lifted.

Opening the back door, Ella and Daisy stepped outside onto the deck. There were no mosquitoes, so Ella was able to sit on her porch quietly while she waited for Daisy to finish her business. She felt lazy as she sat in the warmth of the morning sun. Summer was almost over, and her new job started soon. Ella wondered how much time she'd have to enjoy mornings outside once she got busy with classes. She really needed to start on those course outlines.

Ella took a deep breath, enjoying the serenity of the moment. Watching her dog sniff through the grass, her thoughts returned to the drama of the previous day.

She needed to be honest with herself if she planned on staying in the house. *I think there are two different things going on here.* First, someone was trying to scare her, that was obvious. As Jeff had suggested, GO HOME YANKEE WHORE was definitely a hate crime. But being awakened out of sleep by the events in the kitchen was entirely different. *All those kitchen happenings have got to be a ghost.* Daisy trotted over and sat on the deck, looking at Ella expectantly.

"Yep, I think we live in a haunted house," she told her dog. The dog lay down and sighed, as if in agreement. Leaning back in her chair, Ella wondered about the ramifications of this. Would her kitchen continually be a mess, or would it slowly become worse, with flies on the windows and voices whispering at night?

When Ella saw the backyard shed, her breath caught in her throat. She'd almost forgotten her landlord's abrupt, surly attitude of the previous night. Despite the heat, she shivered, wondering if the shed held the key to her questions. Although she didn't believe any criminal activity could be taking place there, she hesitated. It wouldn't be very smart to do what she was thinking alone. She needed help.

Deciding on a plan, Ella went inside and got the phone. It was answered after only one ring.

"Hi, Katie. I hope I didn't wake you. I just realized how early it is."

Katie laughed. "Actually, I've been waiting to call you because I didn't want to call too early. How are you?"

Ella wasn't sure how to answer that, so she decided that a deliberate nonspecific answer was best. "I'm fine. I know you and Roland were coming over later, but I was wondering if you wanted to come a little early today, maybe have some breakfast with me. I can make an omelet, and the coffee's ready."

There was a brief hesitation before Katie answered. "Are you sure you're okay? I heard about what happened last night."

"I'm fine, really. It was nothing, but it did teach me not to take for granted the speed at which everyone finds things out. Lorraine called last night to check on me."

"I know, she called me, too," Katie said. "Anyway, yes, I'd love to come over for breakfast, but I don't eat eggs. I'll have some toast and coffee, though."

"Of course," Ella agreed. "Thanks, I'll see you in a little while."

After disconnecting the call, Ella thought about her new friend for a moment. She may have been risking the future of the friendship, but Ella needed someone to help her figure out what was happening. "Oh well, Daisy. If she thinks I'm crazy because of all this, then we probably weren't meant to be friends anyway."

Ella went back upstairs and changed into a pair of tan shorts and a camouflage t-shirt that read, *Ha Ha, Now You Can't See Me.*

She was cutting a watermelon into bite-sized pieces when Katie knocked on the door. "Come in," Ella called out, wiping her hands on a towel before going into the living room.

Belatedly, Ella realized she hadn't used the new chain and lock that Kevin had installed. She would definitely lock up later that night.

Katie walked in with a large shopping bag and hugged her. "I decided to bring breakfast. I brought you a loaf of honey pecan bread that I got at the farmers market this week."

Ella squealed in delight. "Thanks! I love different types of breads. Come on in, we can eat the bread with the watermelon I cut."

The two women carried the food and drink out to the back deck. After sitting, Katie turned to Ella and asked, "Okay, seriously, what's up? You know I'd come over anytime you need me, but I know there's some other reason you wanted me here early. Are you sure you're not upset after what happened yesterday?"

Ella sighed. "I don't know. I feel like I should be upset, but right now I just want answers to my questions. First, let me tell you about what happened once the police left."

Ella related how Jeff, her landlord, showed up at her door right after the police left. "It was fine at first. He was worried about me and checking to make sure everything was okay here. Then he got weird... really weird."

Katie's brow wrinkled. "What do you mean?"

Ella told her new friend what Jeff had said about the shed in the backyard and how his attitude quickly changed from nice to rude.

"He was seriously mean. I didn't let him see that it bothered me or scared me, but it did—all because he didn't want me going in that shed."

There was a moment's silence as the two women looked at the shed. The sun was higher in the sky, and the day's heat was continuing to build. Birdsong floated through the air. Katie's voice was quiet and even as she said, "You know what we have to do, right?"

Ella nodded. "Yes, and I was hoping you'd help me. I didn't want to do this alone."

Finished with breakfast, they got out of their chairs and brought their plates inside. "Do you have any tools?" Katie asked. "You know, in case we have to break the lock to get in."

Ella shook her head. "I have a hammer, nails, stuff like that. I wouldn't even know how to break in. Couldn't we see if the door is open or maybe climb through the window?"

Katie's brow wrinkled again, which Ella knew was a sign that she was thinking. "Okay," she finally said. "Let's see if we can walk in without breaking a window or anything. You probably don't want to leave any evidence you were in there, since Jeff acted so threatening about it. We'll check the lock first."

Ella acted brave for Katie's sake. She didn't want her friend to know that she was shaking inside. The old, gray barn-like structure was in obvious need of repair. With a slight lean, it was small, approximately the size of Ella's bedroom. Signs of flooding were obvious from the water marks on the bottom portion of the wood. The paint was starting to peel in some areas, and at least one of the darkened windows had a crack in the pane.

Ella tilted her head to one side and asked, "Is it me, or does it look crooked?"

Katie tilted her head to one side as well and answered, "Yep, it is definitely leaning. I hope it stands for at least another hour or so. Let's try not to knock it down."

Ella sighed. What were the odds of that actually happening? With her luck, about as high as the odds that her house was haunted.

"You okay?" Katie asked.

"Engaging in negative self-talk, that's all. The usual."

Katie's face was determined. "Well, stop that. I'm sure there's nothing wrong in here. Jeff can be a little peculiar, but he was probably doing what his dad asked him to do."

Ella looked at Katie. "You know Jeff and his dad?"

Katie nodded. "Of course. I might live in Yorktown, but it really is a small community here. Did you know that Yorktown and Paterson share a police department and courthouse? The population may have grown recently, but the families that have been here for a while all know each other."

This small-town personality was the exact reason Ella had moved to the area. She loved knowing that everyone knew everyone and history connected them all. An image of Kevin flickered through Ella's mind as she told Katie, "Remind me to talk to you about the police later. There's something I want to tell you after we get through this 'breaking and entering' thing."

Katie laughed. "Sounds good. I'll bet it has something to do with a man."

Noticing the look on Ella's face, she said, "Don't look so surprised. Why else would we talk about the police?"

Ella nodded. "True." Standing still for a moment, she thought about what would happen if Jeff or Kevin showed up for a surprise visit. "I have an idea. If we get caught, we need to have a reason for going into this thing. We can say that we thought we heard an animal crying."

"Oh, that's perfect," Katie exclaimed. "If something happens, we can tell everyone that we thought we heard a kitten or something crying in there and that Daisy was going crazy barking at the shed and all, and we had to save the poor little thing."

Ella and Katie looked over at Daisy, lying peacefully in the grass a few feet from where they stood. "She'll cover for us," Ella said. "Okay, let's get started. How do we get in there?"

"I don't know," Katie whispered.

"Why are you whispering?"

"Because it got so quiet. I don't even hear any birds singing, do you?"

It was true: silence had descended, making her back yard formidable despite the bright sun shining overhead. "Maybe it's getting too hot for the birds," she offered, knowing her explanation was weak.

"All we need now is creepy background music," Katie offered.

"I've got a t-shirt about that."

"Of course you do."

The two women stared for another moment as the sun beat down on the old structure. Ella shook herself. "No time like the present, right? Let's not let ourselves get spooked. We'll take a tiny peek, then go back inside and have another cup of coffee."

They tried the door first, which had a rusted padlock holding it shut. The lock wouldn't budge. Katie looked at Ella and asked, "Do you want to climb in the window, or should I?"

Ella sighed. "I will. This was my brilliant idea, so I should be the one who risks a broken bone." Dragging a lawn chair to the shed, they balanced precariously on it and managed to reach up and push a cracked, dirty window open. "I think I can fit. If we could both fit on this wobbly chair, I should be able to cram myself through this nasty old thing."

"Ready?" Katie asked.

Ella nodded. "Ready."

Katie waited in silence while Ella climbed up and through the window. For a full minute, she heard nothing.

"Ella!" Katie whispered loudly. "Are you okay?"

"This is really weird," Ella answered. "You have *got* to come in here."

Chapter Twenty-Six

KATIE CLIMBED THROUGH THE WINDOW with an elegance Ella didn't know was possible, given their circumstances. The two women stood on the dirt-packed floor, gazing open-mouthed at what they saw.

"There's nothing here!" Katie exclaimed, looking around the room.

It was true. There was a packed dirt floor and cobwebs in the corners; other than that, there was nothing. No tools, no shelves, no lawnmower or illegal substances anywhere.

"Why do I have to stay out of something that has nothing in it?" Ella demanded, growing angry at the thought of Jeff's rude words the night before.

Katie sneezed. "I don't even want to think about the bugs that might be hiding in this place. Let's get out of here."

Climbing out of the shed was harder than climbing in. They had to pull themselves up onto the rotting windowsill, without worrying about splinters or bugs. Ella tried to mimic Katie's gracefulness but still managed to fall out the window and land on her ass.

"I may have to take another shower," Katie said, standing outside and dusting herself off. "That place may be empty, but it gave me the willies standing in there."

"It's the cobwebs. They always make me feel spooked, then I start to worry about what might have gotten trapped in my hair."

Katie looked at Ella. "Your hair looks fine. I'm the one with dirt on my face."

Ella laughed, noticing the smudge on Katie's cheek. "How did you manage to do that?"

"I'm shorter than you, so getting out of that fire trap was harder. Come on, let's go back inside and get some more coffee. That's got to be the strangest thing I've done all summer."

While Ella poured more coffee Katie washed her hands and face in the bathroom. By the time Katie came out of the bathroom, Ella was pouring a cup of coffee for Roland, who was sitting at the kitchen table.

"Hey! When did you get here?" Katie asked.

Roland leaned back in his chair and smiled at Katie. "Have no fear, my lady, the cavalry is here to protect and assist." Ella knew Roland was joking, but she wondered again if perhaps he had a crush on Katie. The look in his eyes was a blend of humor and seriousness.

Ella made another mental note to talk to Katie privately. There were times that Roland looked at Katie with more than friendship in his eyes. That conversation, though, was going to have to wait until she could get Katie alone again.

Katie snorted. "I'm sorry to tell you, Sir Galahad, that you and your services are no longer needed. Ella and I have taken care of everything, thank you very much."

Roland sat up straight in his chair. "What are you talking about? I was kidding. Did something happen?"

Ella groaned, belatedly realizing that she should have called him. There was no use lamenting the fact now, though, since they'd already done the deed. "No, we're fine," Ella told him. She went on to relate the story she'd told Katie about Jeff and his comments concerning the shed. "If he'd asked nicely, I never would have thought that there was anything strange about it," she said petulantly. "But no, he had to go and be a jerk, which made me think he was hiding something."

"And that made you two decide to investigate the shed?" Roland finished, looking from Ella to Katie. "What if there was something in there? Or what if you got caught by Jeff, or trapped or hurt? Did you two ever think of that?"

"Actually, we had an excuse ready if we got caught. We never thought about being trapped or hurt. I guess we should have taken our cell phones with us," Katie mused.

Roland heaved a sigh, crossed his arms over his chest, and leaned back. "I don't know why I talk sometimes. You're missing the point entirely. The man said—no, the man *strongly warned* you to stay away from something, and what did you do? You walked right into what you were told to stay away from."

Ella nodded. "That's right."

There was a short silence as the three of them stared at each other, lost in thought. Ella was surprised to realize that she was feeling relief at not having found red spray paint in the shed.

Finally, Roland exploded. "Well?"

"Well, what?" both women asked simultaneously.

Roland shook his head. "What did you find?"

"Nothing. There was absolutely nothing in that nasty, old, falling-down building except dirt, cobwebs, and who knows how many spiders," Ella answered. "What do you think, Katie? Why do you suppose Jeff told me I couldn't go in there?"

"I'll tell you why," Roland interrupted. "Because it's an old, falling-down structure that you could get hurt in if you poke around. You have no reason to use it. Didn't you tell me the yard services were all taken care of?"

Ella nodded. "There you go," Roland said, satisfied. "You don't have to store a lawnmower, and you can keep your bicycle in the spare bedroom. It's as simple as that. Don't go in the shed."

Ella had only seen Roland act this protective once before, when he first toured her house. She wondered if he knew more than he was letting on, but she decided he would have at least told Katie if he were aware of anything sinister. She highly doubted Roland was the kind of person to allow her or any other innocent person to be put at risk.

"He didn't have to be so rude about it," Katie pouted. "Where were his manners? And telling her right after she had that episode with the police here and everything... why, he ought to be ashamed of himself. That's no way to speak to a lady, and he should know better."

Roland laughed. "Sorry to offend your sense of decorum, Katie, but sometimes even the most sophisticated Southern gentleman can be driven to a lapse in manners when dealing with a Yankee girl." He winked at Ella to let her know that he was joking. She almost believed him.

"Let's forget about it," Ella said. She didn't want to dwell on the fact that she was fairly certain there was something else behind her landlord's mannerisms. She and Jeff had been having a perfectly pleasant conversation until the subject of the shed came up, but there was no point in describing it in detail to her friends.

"Anybody hungry or thirsty?" Ella offered, going to the refrigerator. "I've got juice, coffee cake, fruit..."

"Lord, you keep feeding me, and I'll never be able to fit into another shed window again."

"Did you say cake? That sounds like a good breakfast." Roland took a sip of coffee from the cup Ella had set in front of him. "After we eat, we can plan our strategy. Ella, tell us what needs to be done, and we can prioritize. Did you want to move some furniture?"

Ella nodded. "I was thinking of rearranging the living room. The day the movers came was such a blur. I wasn't really thinking clearly when they asked me where I wanted everything. My usual method of furniture moving is to push and drag, but this time I'm afraid I might scratch the floors."

Katie nodded. "I think Mr. Bartok had these floors refinished after the last tenants moved."

"Why did the last tenants move?" Ella asked, hoping for some insight.

Roland shrugged. "Don't know. They probably couldn't pay or something because they weren't here for long. I think they lived here for about three, maybe four months."

Once again, Ella marveled at the amount of information her friends had regarding townspeople. It truly boggled the mind. "Do you guys know everything that goes on in everyone's house around here?" she asked.

Roland and Katie looked at each other guiltily. Katie paled and Roland shifted his gaze to the floor.

"What?" Ella demanded. "Tell me now, or I'll withhold all food until you speak. What aren't you telling me?"

Chapter Twenty-Seven

KATIE LOOKED SHEEPISH. "WE REALLY don't know all that much about everyone's business. But this house has such a history, I think everyone has heard something. There have been rumors for years about strange things happening here."

Roland snorted. "Strange things happen everywhere."

Ella agreed. "That's true, but some things are more strange than others."

"What are we really talking about?" Katie asked.

"Nothing," Ella hurried to say. "Do you two have department meetings this week, too?" Ella still wasn't sure she wanted to discuss her suspicions with her new friends. She couldn't imagine what they'd think once they found out she believed she was living with a ghost, much less what they'd tell any of her other co-workers. And since she'd never told anyone but Jeff about the most recent incident of nasty words on the house, there was no point in bringing up that little piece of information.

"Department meetings? Where have you been, woman?" Roland asked. "Have you had your head stuck in a book all week or something?"

Ella nodded. "Actually, yes I have. I don't really like television all that much, so I've been reading—"

"It doesn't matter what you were reading, you need to switch on the news every now and then!" Roland said. Turning to Katie, Ella shot her a questioning look.

"A hurricane might make landfall around here in a few days," Katie explained. "The weather folks still aren't sure if we're going to take a direct hit or not, but they're telling everyone to prepare. Because of that, all department meetings might be cancelled."

Ella felt silly. A hurricane was a major event, and she'd been so caught up in what was happening in her own little world that she hadn't paid attention to what was going on around her. "Oh. That's why Lorraine said we may have to change the meeting."

"Hurricane season can be nasty here," Roland said. "Paterson is especially prone to flooding. You might want to think about where you and Daisy will stay if we take a direct hit. Make sure you have all your important papers and computer so you don't have to deal with replacing anything. You'll probably lose power, too. Your neighbor, Alice, usually leaves."

"You and Daisy can stay with me," Katie offered. "I would love to have you over for a couple of days. I have a cat, but she won't mind the dog at all. And I don't live in a flood zone, so it's safe."

"Thanks, Katie. I might do that. I'll have to watch the weather tonight and see what's going to happen."

"Unless, of course, a tree or something falls on the house," Katie added. When Roland and Ella looked at her in surprise, she said, "There are a lot of trees around my house, you know."

"You should stay with Katie, trees or no trees," Roland said. "You don't want to be home alone during a violent hurricane, despite Katie's optimistic outlook for her own house."

Ella was not used to hurricanes. "How bad is this going to be?"

"They predict this one will reach land as a Category Two or Three," Katie answered. "Last year, most of this town flooded when we got hit with a tropical storm. This could be devastating. Y'all flood so easy out here."

Ella shook her head, resolving to stay more aware of what was going on around her. She'd been so caught up in her own worries about the events in the house, it never occurred to her to check the weather, especially when it had only been hot and humid since her arrival. Plus, there was the nagging concern that she had about getting ready to teach. Maybe the hurricane would force her to stop procrastinating and get those course outlines written.

"When did you say this is happening?"

"The weather lady said it will get here on Wednesday."

"That's in two days!" Ella exclaimed. "Wait, now I remember Jeff saying something about storm supplies. He must have assumed I knew a hurricane was coming. And even Kevin asked if I needed a flashlight or batteries... I feel like such an idiot."

Roland shook his head. "If you don't watch television or listen to the radio, I can see where that would happen. Who's Kevin?"

Ella blushed. Leave it to Roland to pick up on the other thing she wasn't sure she wanted to talk about. "He's one of the police officers who came to the house last night. I heard noises downstairs, so I called 911."

Roland smiled. "So, Kevin came rushing out here to protect you?" Seeing Ella's blush deepen, he hurriedly added, "Sorry, I'm just teasing. Are you okay? I heard that the police didn't find anything or anyone when they came out here."

Ella nodded. "Yes, I'm fine, and no, they didn't find anything. And why am I not surprised that you know all about it?" She couldn't stop the shiver that ran up her spine as she thought about the reason for her night noises.

Noticing the shiver, Katie said, "It is cold in here, isn't it? It feels like the temperature has dropped about twenty degrees in here."

"Yeah, I thought kitchens were supposed to be warm," Roland added.

"Sometimes it gets cooler at night, but I don't remember the kitchen feeling this cold when we came inside earlier," Katie commented.

Should I tell them? Would they think she was crazy, or would they believe her? In the midst of her mental debate, the phone rang. Relieved at not having to make a decision, Ella grabbed the receiver.

"Ella, hi. I'm glad you're home. It's Kevin."

Ella smiled and put her head down. "I know. I recognized your voice."

"There's something I need to talk to you about. I'm working right now, but I decided to take a quick break to let you know what I found out."

Dread took root in the pit of Ella's stomach. "What you found out?" she asked, feeling silly for echoing his words.

"Remember when you mentioned that none of the other officers seemed concerned about the possibility of an intruder? I thought it was kind of strange, so I've been asking around at the station. I thought maybe someone might know something about your house."

Ella swallowed, wondering if she wanted to hear his explanation. "What did you find out?"

"This isn't the first time we've been out on a call like this to your place."

Of course it wasn't, but she had to ask anyway. "What do you mean?"

"A couple of the guys here, they've been on the force for about ten years or so. They said that in the past seven years they've gotten the exact same phone call from other tenants there."

Ella felt like she was underwater, where everything was blurry and she couldn't quite hear properly. "I don't understand. Other people have called with the same complaint?"

"Not just the same complaint—the exact same situation. People hear noises in the house, we come out to investigate, the kitchen is a mess, and nobody knows why it's happening."

"What happened to all these people? Was anybody hurt?" she asked.

"No one was hurt; they just moved out. I can't say that I blame them."

"What do your co-workers think of all this?" Ella held her breath.

"Some guys think that the local kids have started doing this as a prank, and others think the place is haunted."

"What do you think?" Ella's voice sounded small to her own ears. It was one thing to debate telling her thoughts to her new friends, but she was fairly certain that telling a police officer that she believed in ghosts would hamper any relationship beginnings, if not outright kill them.

"I'm willing to bet that it's the local kids. I seriously doubt your house is haunted. But don't worry: extra patrols will drive by from now on. We'll figure this out. In the meantime, keep your doors and windows locked."

"Right." Ella bristled at his casual attitude toward ghosts. "Thanks for the information. I'll talk to you later, okay?"

"No problem. Are you sure you have all your supplies? This might turn out to be a rough week with that storm."

Not wanting Kevin to know that she'd just found out about the storm, she answered, "Yes, I'm fine. I think I'll stay with my friend Katie."

"That's a great idea. I'll feel better knowing you're not being washed away by flood waters." Ella stifled a giggle at the mental image of her and Daisy floating down the street. The stress of everything was starting to wear on her.

"So what did your new boyfriend have to say?" Roland teased.

"He's not my boyfriend," Ella defended herself.

"Mmmm-hmmm." Katie examined her manicured nails.

Her decision made, Ella took a deep breath. "He wanted to give me information about the house. My phone call to the police last night wasn't the first. Previous tenants had problems here, too. Lorraine said something about rumors and strange stories. Do you two know anything about this?"

Another look of guilt passed between Katie and Roland. "We don't know specifics," Roland hedged.

"But you've heard the rumors?" Ella persisted.

Katie nodded. "We've heard… things," she finished. "Is it getting colder in here, or is it my imagination?"

"It is getting colder in here," Ella said. "And let me tell you what I think: I think there's a ghost in this house. I think I've moved into a haunted house."

Chapter Twenty-Eight

SO MUCH FOR DISCRETION. AS soon as the words were out of her mouth there was no turning back. A silence hovered over the table. She couldn't tell what they were thinking; their faces were carefully neutral.

Finally, Ella couldn't stand it anymore. "Do you think I'm crazy? Are you ready to send me to the asylum?"

Roland shook his head. "No. Actually, I'd like to hear more about why you think this place is haunted. You might wear funny t-shirts, but I think you're a smart, capable woman who never struck me as prone to hysterics. What's going on here?"

For the first time all morning, Ella relaxed. As she took a deep breath, some tension moved out of her neck and shoulders. "Thanks. I appreciate that you believe me."

"Of course we believe you. Now start talking, because you haven't told us everything," Katie added. Ella looked at Katie, grateful to have met people who had her back, so to speak. Now she had to tell them the story—all of it.

"It started the day I got here, I think."

"You think?" Roland asked, eyebrows raised.

"I didn't know what was going on, but the idea of a ghost didn't occur to me. Daisy had started acting really weird. She didn't want to explore the yard, and she got really anxious in the kitchen."

"What do you mean by 'anxious?'" Roland asked. His questions were sincere, as if there were nothing odd about Ella's story.

"She started whining, and her hackles came up. At first I thought maybe a raccoon or something was running around back here, but I didn't see anything."

"Did you smell anything?" Katie asked.

Ella scrunched her nose and looked at Katie. "No, why? Do ghosts have a smell?"

Katie looked sheepish. "I was thinking it was possible a dead mouse was in the cabinets."

"No, I would have noticed that smell. Besides, I did a thorough cleaning in here before I unpacked all my stuff. I hate the thought of putting dishes into a dusty cabinet."

"What happened next?" Roland asked gently.

Ella proceeded to tell them about everything: her experience with the screaming, pans floating in the air, a vision of a mysterious woman, freezing temperatures in the kitchen, and Daisy's reactions to these occurrences.

Even though she felt that the vandalism was a separate event, Ella talked about that, too. They knew about the first graffiti incident, and in the interest of full disclosure, Ella told them about the second time, as well.

"That's not all," she said in a quiet voice.

"There's more?" Katie sounded horrified. "Good heavens, you haven't even been here that long. I can't imagine how you've been able to sleep at all. What else is happening?"

"It's not something that's happening outwardly, but I have a very strong feeling that this is somehow related to what's going on in this house," Ella answered.

"*What* is related to these happenings?" Roland asked.

This part of the story got really strange, even for Ella. She knew how it was going to sound, but if she were going to come clean to her friends about what was going on in the house, she had to tell them everything.

"I've been having dreams, but they're not really like dreams. Obviously I'm asleep and everything, but there's something different about this. In these dreams, I think I'm seeing Hattie and Lorraine."

Roland frowned. "Do you think your dreams have been influenced by what we told you?"

"We've been talking about that situation a lot lately," Katie added. "Maybe your subconscious is running with it."

"That's what I thought at first, too. But the dreams started before I knew the story, and they have a different quality to them. Somehow, I feel as if I'm actually there, watching them—and I think they almost saw me once. These dreams seem to be telling me the story of Hattie. I can't help but wonder if..."

Ella stopped. There had been times in her life when she'd experienced strange things, times when she knew what was going to happen before it happened. She'd even had visions of the past in other dreams. But never before had her dreams been so clear, and never before had she had a series of them. Her family knew about this, and they accepted it. Ella never told anyone outside her family about her experiences, and now her stomach clenched from nerves. Katie and Roland had seemed okay with everything so far, but really, how much more could they hear before they thought she was some kind of freak—or worse, delusional?

"If what?" Katie prompted.

"If they're true," Ella finished, speaking softly. "I know it sounds crazy, but I think I'm going back in time and witnessing what happened."

"Tell us about the dreams. What do you see?"

Ella recounted seeing Hattie and Lorraine together reading in the woods, going to the general store, Hattie's insistence that she was in love, and Hattie standing in the kitchen. At that point, Roland raised his hand.

"Stop," he said. "I have an idea. Do you have a notebook or piece of paper?"

Ella walked to a kitchen drawer, opened it, and took out a yellow pad. "Why?"

"Before you tell us anything else, write this stuff down. Write all the details so we can verify if these really are dreams. We should be able to find information about certain things easily enough."

Ella let out her breath. This was good news—he was at least willing to listen to her—and, if there were enough evidence, maybe even believe what she said.

"That's true," Katie exclaimed. "What did the store look like? How were the girls dressed? Those are details we can confirm to see if you're on the right track." After a moment's silence, Katie added, "I knew something was going on in this house."

Pushing her hair off her face, Ella twisted a curl in her hand and looked at Katie. "How did you know?"

"It wasn't difficult to figure out," Roland said.

"True," Katie agreed. "Most of the tenants don't stay for long. And we knew about Lorraine and her friend. When I found out you were living here, I was so excited!"

"Excited about me or my house?" Ella asked.

"Goodness, I'm sorry, that sounded horrible!" Katie said.

"You seem to have forgotten your proper Southern manners." Roland smiled.

"I am so sorry, Ella. I didn't mean to imply I was only interested in your house." Katie looked at Ella with rounded eyes. "When we first met, I really liked you and hoped we could be friends. I was trying to say that I thought it would be exciting to be able to see this house after hearing about it for all those years."

Ella laughed, more relieved than she wanted to put into words. Her friends not only believed her, they'd already been thinking about the possibilities here. "I have no doubt that you're my friend, and I probably would have had the same reaction."

Roland pointed at her. "Start writing. The sooner you get this on paper, the sooner we can help you."

Ella nodded. "You're right." She sat at the kitchen table, pad in front of her, and began scribbling. For the next thirty minutes, while Roland flipped through the newspaper and Katie straightened up the kitchen, Ella wrote everything she could remember about the dreams. Because of the vivid nature of what she'd seen, they weren't difficult to recall.

Finally, she looked up. "I stuck to the facts. It's difficult to find words to describe the feeling of those dreams."

Roland nodded. "The facts are all we need. We believe there's a ghost in the house, and that fact seems to be backed up by the steady turnover of renters. But visionary dreams need to be researched. Don't worry about feelings. I want to know what color the walls in the kitchen were in your dream." He reached over and took the pad.

Ella closed her eyes. "I almost forgot. In one of the dreams, the girls mentioned something odd. They said, 'Remember the Lovings,' and then something about the Lovings being put in jail. I've been thinking about that because I remember reading about them."

Katie and Roland exchanged a look of confusion.

"They were the married couple, right?" Katie asked.

"Yes, they were an interracial couple who married in 1958," Ella answered.

"When it was illegal," Roland added.

Ella thought about the history of the couple. Mildred and Richard Loving had been married in Washington, D.C., in 1958. While their marriage was legal in Washington, D.C., interracial marriage was illegal in Virginia. Upon their return to Caroline County, Virginia, they were placed under arrest and jailed. To stay out of jail, the couple agreed to leave the state, a move they later regretted after leaving family and friends behind.

"I think Hattie might have been having a relationship with a white man. I mean, it makes sense since I remember Hattie saying she was in love."

"I guess that would be a possibility, as long as what you're dreaming was real."

Katie shook her head. "I don't think so. Wouldn't we have heard rumors? That would have been an amazing piece of gossip."

"And not something anyone in polite company would want to discuss," Roland reminded them. There was a brief silence, then Roland sighed. "As much as I hate to suggest this, maybe we should ask Lorraine."

Ella felt a moment's anger toward Lorraine. Where would Hattie be now if Lorraine had spoken up? This whole situation might have had a very different ending, and Ella might not have to deal with a ghost in her house. "Maybe Lorraine should have already told people about things."

"You can't be mad at her," Katie gently admonished her. "She really did care about Hattie, but if she'd been seen as being friendly with the 'colored folk,' it would have been very dangerous for both of them. People were killed for less back then."

Ella inhaled sharply, recognizing the truth of what Katie said. It was easy to forget that not so long ago, social attitudes might have prohibited people from being friends—or getting married. And attitudes sometimes led to murder.

"That's true," Roland said slowly. "We'd better get to work. Hattie may have something to tell us." Notepad in hand, Roland stood and paced as he read Ella's words. The two women watched him, a look of intensity crossing his face. They were so focused on the moment, all three jumped at the knock at the door—sharp as a gunshot.

Chapter Twenty-Nine

"IT'S ME." ALICE OPENED THE back door and entered the kitchen. "So, you've been having some dreams, have you?" she asked as she carried a bag into the kitchen. "Just as Albert said you would. I've brought your lasagna plate back. Where should I put it?"

"I'll take it." Ella hurried to take the glass dish from the older woman. *Do I really want to hear what Albert thinks of all this? Maybe he knows something I don't...*

"What does Albert think?" Ella said.

Alice sighed and shook her head. "Albert thinks you've got trouble coming. In fact, he said we've all got trouble coming. Me, I think he's worried about the storm. I told him not to worry; I'm going to stay with the grandkids in Richmond. I'll be leaving tonight, which is why I wanted to get your dish back to you."

"And what do you think about all this?" Ella asked carefully.

"I think you've got a ghost in here—and Lord knows you're going to have to take care of that situation before you get a good night's sleep."

Roland stood and offered Alice a chair at the kitchen table. "I wonder if I could ask you a few questions," he said. Alice hesitated, obviously torn about wanting to leave, yet not wanting to refuse helping them. Roland reassured her. "It won't take long. I wanted to ask you if a few things Ella wrote down were true or not."

Alice sighed. "I reckon you could ask me those questions. But I don't have long, young man; I have pies I need to make that I'm going to bring to Richmond with me."

Roland smiled his most charming smile. "Well, I'm sorry to hear that you can't stay long, Miss Alice. I do enjoy your company."

Alice swatted a hand at him, pretending to be annoyed. "Oh, go on and ask your questions."

Roland sat next to her. "I think I only have two questions. First, do you remember a general store around here that —"

"I don't think we can use that one, Roland," Ella interrupted. "I just remembered, I visited that store before I dreamt about it. That wouldn't count, would it?"

Roland shook his head. "Good catch. No, we can't use that. Okay, how about this..." Flipping the pages of the pad, he pointed to a spot on the paper. "At the very end, you wrote about the kitchen. Alice, do you know what the kitchen used to look like in this house in 1960?"

Alice scrunched up her face in concentration. "Sure enough, I ought to remember that. I came over here many times and brought clothes and whatnot to that ornery old man. I brought them for the boy, though. He was a cute little one, but his father always acted ungrateful—like I was some busybody who couldn't mind her own business. Why, I was trying to look after that poor, motherless boy in a neighborly way." She slowly shook her head. "I guess some people don't take kindly to what they think is charity."

"So you were in this kitchen?" Katie prompted, trying to get Alice back to the subject.

Alice's eyes took on a faraway, dreamy look. "Yes, let me see...oh, that's right. There was wallpaper of some sort that had some kind of flowers...no, it was a leafy sort of ivy on it. The floor was different, too. It was brown, and the countertops were white-speckled Formica. The cabinets were the original ones. These are the same cabinets, except they've been painted over and have fancy new handles on the doors. They used to have the original wood finish on them, and Hattie would polish them so much, they shone."

Everyone stared in silence at the white-painted cabinets. After a moment, Roland cleared his throat. "Well, yes. Thank you Alice."

"Well?" Alice demanded.

"Well what?" Roland asked.

"Did she get it right? Did Ella describe the kitchen like it used to be?"

Roland looked down at the paper. "Yes. She wrote it exactly as you said."

Ella had known that as she heard Alice speak, but having the confirmation voiced aloud made her feel better. Now nobody could point a finger at her and accuse her of being crazy—or, as her sister Lisa liked to say, "having a little too much imagination."

Alice nodded. "Just as I thought." She stood abruptly, almost knocking her chair over. "I've got to go. Albert told me not to stay too long. He said things were about to happen, and I should mind my own business this time."

Katie hurried to move the chair out of Alice's way. "It was so nice to see you, Miss Alice."

Smiling at Katie, Alice told her, "You be sure and say a big 'hello' to your family." Turning to Ella, she asked, "Are you planning on staying here during the storm?"

"No," Ella answered. "Katie very nicely offered to let me stay with her, and I'm going to take her up on that offer." Ella shot Katie another grateful look, thankful to have a safe place to weather the upcoming storm. It might be good for her to get out of this house, and it might also spur her to start her lesson plans. Then again, if there were a hurricane coming, nobody really expected classes to start, right?

"Good. I'm glad you'll be safe." Alice hesitated for a moment at the door before telling Ella, "You might want to think about mentioning those dreams to Lorraine. I would think she'd be the one who could tell you what did or did not happen. She was there for most of it."

Alice turned and quickly walked out the back door. There was a moment of silence before Ella asked, "Do you think she's mad at me?"

"Why would she be mad at you?" Katie was puzzled.

"She was so abrupt. She came and left so quickly, and she didn't stay to chat or anything. I thought she might be mad about me dredging up this old issue." *And she's probably not going to be the only one.* Ella didn't dare say that out loud. After what her friend Ed had mentioned when she first moved in coupled with what she knew of the town's history, she wondered again if there were some sort of conspiracy in town to keep the past buried. Why else wouldn't this situation have been dealt with before?

Katie shook her head. "No, that's the way she is. When Albert tells her something, it's imperative she listens. If he told her not to spend too much time here, she's darn well not going to spend too much time here. And it's sort of eerie, too."

"What is?" Ella asked.

"Sometimes it seems as if Albert really *does* know what he's talking about," Katie said, shrugging. "Like everyone else, at first I thought she was going batty or something. Then Albert would have these little messages for people, and it turned out he was often right about things. I think most people around here have accepted that Albert's ghost is hanging around

Alice these days. At least he doesn't cause as much of a disturbance as… well, as some of the other area ghosts," she finished, looking sheepishly at Ella.

"Southern disturbances," Ella muttered.

"What?" Roland asked.

"I said, 'Southern disturbances.' It's my polite southern way of saying there's a haunting, a ghost, a spirit causing trouble in this part of the world."

Katie laughed. "I think you're finally catching on. Down here, there's always a more polite way to say things." After a moment, Katie sobered. "Ella, are you sure you want to live here? Never mind us and our ghost hunting enthusiasm; you can always do what the previous tenants have done and find another place to live. We can help if you want."

Ella would not be bullied by some long-dead person or even some local trying to scare her off. It was bad enough her sister Lisa tried to push Ella around; she wasn't going to let spirits take up where Lisa left off. Plus, a part of Ella was wistful. Maybe if the door were open for her to see one ghost, she might see others—and not just any other ghost. Maybe the door would be open for her mother to appear…

"I appreciate the offer, but I moved 500 miles only four days ago. Not even a ghost can make me do it all over again so quickly."

Roland agreed. "That's true. You can't let some little old ghost chase you away. So, now that you know you're staying, do you have any plans?"

Ella looked at her friends blankly. "Plans?" she echoed.

Katie sighed. "Aren't you supposed to be the expert on this type of thing?"

"No," Ella cried. "I'm an expert on indigenous rituals, customs of different tribes. I know nothing about actually dealing with ghosts except what I read on the internet and that show I've watched on television."

"The ghost hunter show," Roland said, and Katie nodded.

Ella's eyes narrowed as she regarded the two of them. "Both of you seem suspiciously calm about all this; in fact, neither one of you had a moment's hesitation when I told you what was going on around here. What's up with that? Do you know something I don't know?"

There was a moment's silence in the kitchen while Ella regarded Katie and Roland. Both of her friends seemed to be looking everywhere except at her. Ella crossed her arms and waited, knowing they had to tell her eventually.

Roland began. "It's not that we know anything, but remember, we grew up with ghost stories and talk about this house. There have been so many rumors flying around over the past decade that it's a wonder anyone ever dared to move in here at all."

Chapter Thirty

"**EVERYONE EXCEPT THE YANKEE,**" **ELLA** mumbled.

"We don't mind that you're a Yankee," Katie said. When Ella looked at her sharply, Katie smiled. "I'm kidding. Anyway, the concept of ghosts is really not so foreign to us. Remember, both the Revolutionary and Civil wars were fought here. We expect some leftover spirits to be wandering around. This is especially true in Yorktown, where I live. In my neighborhood, too."

From what Ella could discern, the past was a living entity in the South, with different eras sometimes overlapping as if time were superimposed upon itself. Even in books and movies, the ghosts of the South were very much a part of everyone's lives, and she wondered if others in the area could see people long gone walking down the streets as if it were nothing.

"I'm seriously hoping both of you know what I should do next, because short of calling in a priest to splash some holy water around, I have no idea what to do about all of... this." Ella waved her arm to indicate the entire house.

Roland stood and went to the refrigerator, opening it and staring into its depths for a moment. "My understanding is that if a place is truly haunted, then usually the spirit left behind wants something."

Katie walked to the refrigerator, took out a pitcher of lemonade, and closed the door. Getting a glass from the cabinet, she poured the lemonade and handed it to Roland as he continued to speak. "The trick is knowing whether it's a true haunting or simply an imprint. Do you know what that is?"

Ella shook her head, amazed at Katie's abilities to know both what

Roland wanted and effectively direct him at the same time. "I have no idea. I assume it has something to do with ghosts?"

"Yes. In fact, an imprint is not a true haunting," Roland told her. "Like I said, a haunting is usually a spirit that hasn't crossed over to the other side. Most times, that spirit has unfinished business, but sometimes there are other reasons."

Unfinished business...like the kind of unfinished business that a racially divided town might encounter. "What are the other reasons?" Ella asked.

"It depends on the personality of the person while they were alive. Sometimes the ego, or personality, clings to the spirit and makes them forget what they're supposed to do or who they really are. Then the bits and pieces that make up a person's character, the parts that dictate if they're nice or ornery or flighty or whatever, those pieces remain with the spirit and get it confused and cause it to wander around. It doesn't happen often, but when it does that can be difficult to handle. Those spirits need intense cleansing, a sort of 'ghost therapy,' but they don't often want it."

Ella thought about what Roland said. It made sense, but that did nothing to alleviate her sense of unbalance. And, if she were honest, she was a little afraid. It briefly flashed through her mind that Roland knew a lot about ghosts, but maybe that was part of being a Southerner.

Ella continued. "Let me see if I get this straight. If I'm a ghost, it could be for a couple of reasons. Maybe I was murdered, and I want to see that the murderer is caught, so I hang around and try to drop clues and tell people it was no accident that I'm dead."

Katie and Roland nodded. Ella took a breath and went on. "And this other part, I think I understand. If I died and retained my personality, then my ghost would forever wander around, wearing T-shirts with sayings on them, right?"

Katie burst out laughing. "That's perfect. I can see you now, drifting through town with a shirt that says, 'I told you I was sick.'" Both Ella and Katie started giggling uncontrollably at the image; however, Roland stood, watching them with a serious look on his face.

"Speaking of the spirits is serious," he said. "You need to understand that this isn't something to be taken lightly."

Ella caught her breath and stopped laughing for a moment. "That's true. This is serious, Katie. I'm certain that if I were to wander around after I died, my T-shirt would say, *'I knew this would happen.'*" Once again, the women erupted into a fit of giggles. Roland walked into the living room, sat on the couch, and waited. Eventually, both Katie and Ella joined him.

"Sorry," Katie told him, wiping her eyes as she sat next to him.

"It's okay," Roland answered. "I figured I'd come out here to wait for you to stop." He looked at Ella. "Are you nervous?"

She nodded. "Yes, but I don't know why. You'd think I'd be less nervous now that I have friends who believe me, and I know I'm not going crazy."

"We've probably made it worse for you," Roland said. "By telling us your story, and by our acknowledgment of it, everything became more real. Now you can't hide behind the idea that this is all in your imagination."

Ella nodded slowly. "So what happens next? How do we know if this is a true haunting or an imprint, and what do I do? And what exactly is an imprint?"

Roland leaned forward with his hands clasped. "We'll know it's an imprint if the exact same thing happens at the exact same time. Do you think your experiences have been identical?"

Ella scrunched her face as she thought. "It's hard to tell, really. The problem is that both times I was woken out of sleep. I don't really function at my best when I first wake up, especially if it's abrupt."

"We'll have to try to pay close attention the next time something appears," Roland announced.

"We need to do research," Katie added. "Find out more concrete details about this house and everyone who lived here, not just the Bartoks. Maybe even information related to what might have happened on this land before the house was built."

"I tried to do some research," Ella admitted, "but I didn't get very far. I couldn't find any mention of Hattie in any newspaper or historic paper, not even an obituary. The only thing I found was information related to Hurricane Donna." She hesitated as a thought occurred to her. "How do you both know so much about this? You know more than most of those ridiculous ghost websites I visited. Have you dealt with this in the past?"

Katie and Roland looked at each other for a moment, then finally Roland answered. "Katie may have learned much of what she knows from her own history or listening to me talk about my experiences. Most of the knowledge I have comes from family experience."

Ella waited a couple beats before asking, "You were raised by ghosts?"

Roland laughed. "No, my family dealt with matters of the spirit. But that's not important; that's a story for another day. Right now, we need to work on a plan of action."

True. I can learn their story once this is done and life gets back to normal.

"Right now, we need to figure out what exactly is going on in our little world," Katie said as she turned on the television. As Katie used the remote to change the channel, the phone rang. Ella answered, spoke for a few minutes, then went into the kitchen. After about ten minutes, she returned to the living room, her face ashen and her gaze unfocused.

"What's wrong?" Katie asked.

How could it be that less than a week ago Ella was arguing with her sister in Connecticut, and now she lived in a haunted house in Virginia?

"That was Lorraine. The staff meeting is cancelled because of the storm. Since I had her on the phone, I went ahead and asked her some questions." Ella hated it when her dreams were more than just dreams.

Roland frowned. "She was okay with you asking questions about Hattie? I thought she'd be more sensitive about the subject. What did she say?"

"She opened up to me for some reason... I'm not sure why."

"Maybe she wants you to finally solve this mystery," Katie offered.

Ella scoffed. "It's not like I'm some great detective. I hardly know what's going on myself."

"But she trusts you," Katie added softly. "That changes everything. It doesn't matter what or who you know; if there's anything to discover, you'll do your best to get to the bottom of it all."

Ella shrugged, feeling unaccountably embarrassed. She hadn't known Lorraine for very long, and she sure wasn't doing so well in dealing with the ghosts of her own past. It puzzled her why Lorraine would trust her to find answers that had remained hidden for almost half a century. "I hope I didn't get her hopes up. We had a little talk about some of my dreams."

Katie and Roland leaned forward as Ella continued. "Most of the stuff I saw actually happened. Amazingly, Lorraine remembers some of the conversations she had with Hattie, and they were the same as what I'd heard in my dreams."

Ella hesitated, uncertain about saying what she had to say next. It was one thing to talk to friends from her own past about racism in the South; it was another thing entirely to discuss the situation with people who lived there.

"There was one other thing Lorraine wanted to talk about. Hattie had a boyfriend."

"White?" Katie asked.

Ella nodded. "Not just white, but older. According to Lorraine, Hattie was seeing Mr. Bartok."

There was a stunned silence in the room. "That nasty old man must have done something bad to her," Katie said with surprising vehemence.

"We still don't know what happened," Ella interrupted. "In fact, we don't even know what this information means."

"It means we need to get to work," Roland announced.

Chapter Thirty-One

ELLA FELT LIGHTHEADED. FOR DAYS now, she'd been struggling with the thought that she had a ghost in her house—which was scary—but for some reason, knowing she was having revealing dreams about the past ratcheted her anxiety level several notches. Was this always going to happen to her? It was one thing to have dreams of what her old neighborhood looked like before she was born or where her father's watch was hidden, but now her dreams were about people she didn't know. *I don't like seeing the past or the future. Not at all.*

"Are you okay? You don't look well," Katie asked.

"I'll be fine," Ella told her in a shaky voice.

Katie rubbed Ella's back lightly. "It's a lot to take in, I'm sure. And on top of all that, you just moved, and you're starting a new job..."

That I haven't been preparing for, Ella thought but kept silent on the issue.

"And a storm is coming, so we've got to get to work," Roland said. "Let's divide up the work so tomorrow we can get some serious research done."

"Wait a minute," Ella protested. "Listen, I'm grateful for your help, but we need to talk about the big picture."

"What do you mean?" Katie asked.

"What happens when we have the story of why this place is haunted? What do we do with the information once we find it? Should we ask the ghost to leave, or do I live with this forever?"

Roland smiled. "That's an excellent question. I can't believe I forgot to mention that part."

"I can't believe he's excited about this," Katie muttered.

"Once we find information, who it is and why the spirit is here, then we make plans to help it go home," Roland began. "We're assuming the spirit is Hattie, right? We can guess Hattie was probably a practicing Christian and went to church every week, read the bible, stuff like that. That's important, because now we know that something non-Christian, like Hebrew prayers, will have no effect on her. We need to work within the belief system of the spirit in order to send it home."

"So... if we have a Wiccan ghost, we need to draw a pentagram?" Ella asked.

"Or if we have a Hindu ghost, we'd say prayers in Indian. This is especially important if the spirit is particularly nasty; religious ceremonies have an interesting effect on nasty spirits."

"That's quite a theory," Ella said.

"It's not a theory—it works. I've seen it work. Where I come from, we send spirits back all the time. If we don't know who they are, we try several different approaches to see what works best. You'd be amazed at what—or who—is wandering around out there, causing trouble."

Ella remained silent, but she wondered exactly where Roland was from. It never occurred to her to ask the philosophy professor about his beliefs in ghostly matters; she had incorrectly assumed that he was like everyone else. She didn't know what to think about his expert opinions on the matter.

Katie leaned over to Ella and whispered in her ear, "Don't think about it too much; it'll drive you crazy."

"We'd better hurry and get our work done," Katie announced as she stared at the television. "It looks like that storm is turning our way and might even hit sooner than expected."

"Sooner than expected?" Ella wasn't sure she was ready for her first hurricane in her new home. Blizzards she could manage, but hurricanes were much scarier.

Katie's eyes were glued to the television screen. "I don't know when it was expected, but the weather person just said that it's gained a significant amount of speed and will reach land sometime tomorrow night."

Ella shuddered, realizing that 'significant amount of speed' meant it could be plenty bad.

Roland took charge. "This is it, then. Let's divide our assignments and get through this. Ella, you talk to Lorraine and see how much more information you can get from her. Try to find out specifics about Hattie, if she went to church, where she went to church, anything at all. Also see if you can get her to tell you what she really thinks happened. She may know something she doesn't realize she knows. Katie, you go talk to the old man."

"What?" Katie exclaimed. "Why do I get the difficult job?"

"Because, darling," Roland drawled, "you are a charming, beautiful Southern lady. I believe the senior Mr. Bartok would perhaps open up to you better than any of us in this room."

Katie relented. "Fine. Maybe I'll bring some flowers or something for that place, try to brighten it up a little."

"What place? Where is he?" Ella asked.

"He's in the Baymoore Convalescent Home. I suppose it's okay, as far as those places go, but I hate walking in there without something for the residents. I imagine it's depressing living there."

The women turned to Roland. "What are you going to do?" Katie demanded.

"I'm going to look at property records at town hall. They should have information regarding this piece of land, such as who owned it and when. I might even get some insight into the owners if I can match the names with local census records. Those records can tell me things like how many people lived here, who might have died, and what the heads of the household did for a living."

"I had no idea there was that much information at town hall," Ella said.

Everyone stopped talking for a moment. Despite the incoming warmth from the day outside, the temperature in the living room carried a chill. Dust motes danced in the beams of light that lazily spilled through the windows, and the momentary silence held the occupants hostage in time. Music drifted through the room, dancing with the light.

"What's that?" Roland whispered.

"I don't know," Ella whispered back. "I hear it all the time and assumed it was one of the neighbors. It must be something popular because even the movers were humming the tune by the time they left. I can't quite place it."

"Ella Giancetti, don't you ever go to church?" Katie demanded.

"Yes, but I still don't recognize the music. Is it church music?"

Katie sighed. "I guess you have to go to certain churches to hear it, but you've probably heard that song on television and in movies. It's called 'I'll Fly Away.'"

"Isn't that a song about dying?" Roland said.

The three of them looked at each other. "That's a little... spooky," Ella whispered.

"It's not supposed to be," Katie insisted. "Really, it's supposed to be an uplifting song about entering God's kingdom after death. The song should be imbued with hope. We sing it all the time in our church."

The music had stopped, but the echo lingered in the air around them.

Finally, Roland cleared his throat. "I wonder..." he began.

"What?" Katie prompted.

"I wonder if this is another message."

There was silence as they thought about that. "It makes sense," Ella said. "Especially if this ghost needs some sort of wrong to be righted. As soon as that's done, she—or he or it—can go home."

Roland stood and headed toward the kitchen. "I need another drink. Does anybody want anything?" Both women shook their heads no before he went into the other room.

"What do you think?" Katie asked quietly.

"I think I'm glad you guys are my friends," Ella answered. "And I think it's no coincidence that this spirit and the music and the dreams are all happening more often. I also think that the coming storm may be contributing to whatever is happening here." Ella reflected on the similarity between then and now. First, there was a hurricane coming, like when Hattie disappeared in 1960. Second...actually, there was no second; the similarity ended with the hurricane.

Katie looked at Ella with concern. "Did the police ever figure out who vandalized your house?"

Ella shook her head. "I'm sure they'll find him soon. I have a feeling whoever did this is finished, and hopefully that's the end of it." She was fairly certain she'd been targeted by her coffee shop friend, but the question remained: was her instinct right and he was finished, or would he be back to try to scare her again? Either way, she was ready.

Roland came back with a can of soda in his hand. "Roland, why can't you be civilized and use a glass?" Katie teased.

"Because I need this one for the road," he answered. "Come on, Katie, we've got to get going. Things need to get done so we can be back here before it gets dark. Actually, I'd like to be back before dusk."

"We didn't drive together. You can go anytime you want," Katie answered.

"You've got to pack," Roland told her.

"Why should she pack? What does that have to do with our research for tomorrow?" Ella asked.

Roland sighed. "I thought it was fairly obvious: Katie and I are going to spend the night here tonight."

Chapter Thirty-Two

"YOU DON'T HAVE TO DO that." *But it would be nice.* She was on edge and nervous, even with a plan for the ghost. But that wasn't fair to her friends. "You can always come back in the morning," she added.

"No, Roland is right," Katie told her. "We should stay here tonight. It sounds like things are escalating, and we can help you through this. Besides, this might give us some insight into what's going on."

"Remember, Ella, there's also a very small possibility that this isn't a spiritual issue, but a human one instead," Roland added in a serious tone. The possibility gave all three of them pause.

"That might be scarier than a ghost," Ella whispered. She could handle nasty words spray painted on her house, but if someone were going to the trouble to make the house look haunted by breaking and entering, then that became a whole new level of creepy.

Katie nodded. "I agree. But look on the bright side: you can always have a hunky policeman save the day." Katie winked. *How much does she know about my future date with Kevin?* For that matter, Ella wondered if there was anybody who *didn't* know about her future date with Kevin, considering the speed at which gossip spread through town.

Ella cleared her throat. "Before you go, let's sit outside for a moment so you can answer a few more questions for me."

Roland looked at her. "Sure, but why do we have to go outside?"

"Because Daisy said so." Everyone looked at Daisy, who stood expectantly, wagging her tail.

"Have you thought about installing a doggie door for her?" Katie asked as they walked into the back yard. "What happens when you're not here?"

"If I'm not here, she's usually good at waiting. She hasn't had any accidents yet. But this isn't my house, and I'm not sure I can convince my charming landlord a doggie door would be a good idea. Besides, it also provides another access point for other critters—animal and human."

They went outside and sat on deck chairs, and Ella took a moment to gather her thoughts. Everything was happening quickly, and she felt like she was losing control of the situation—if she ever had control, that is. At least she had the illusion of control. "I want to make sure I get this straight. We'll do some research and try to put together the story about who might be haunting this place so we have a better idea of what we're dealing with?"

Roland nodded, so Ella continued. "Then what? What do we do to send this thing down the tunnel, or back to the light, or into the television, or wherever it needs to go?"

Roland smiled. "We never send spirits into the television; it always messes up the programming. Spirit entities would start creating bizarre reality shows and strange talent contests."

"Too late," Katie commented dryly.

Roland snorted. "True. Anyway, what we'll try to do, like I mentioned, is send the spirit home. In order to do that, we have to communicate with it by using prayers it will recognize. For instance, if our resident ghost was a Christian, then we recite one of the Psalms or a passage from the bible—an appropriate passage, that is. We should also have relevant artifacts available, like crosses or torahs or whatever will work."

Ella thought about what he was saying. "That sounds simple." Was it too simple? Did Roland really know what he was doing?

Roland nodded. "It *is* simple. Of course, we'll prepare the house before darkness falls. I'll smudge the place, and we can surround the outside with sea salt."

"Do you have a smudge stick?" Ella asked.

Roland looked at her and said, "What do you think?"

"Pardon me, but can someone please tell me what a smudge stick is?" Katie asked.

"A smudge stick is a bundle of herbs, usually cedar and sage. When the stick is lit, the smoke is alleged to purify or clear an area of negative energy. It was used mostly by Native Americans, but the New Agers kind of laid claim to smudging in recent times." Ella looked at Roland. "I never would have thought of you as a New Agey kind of guy."

He shook his head. "I'm not."

Before Ella could ask any more questions, Katie interrupted. "So we clear the area of unwanted negative energy with a smudge stick. What's the sea salt for?"

"Protection." Ella answered. "If you surround an area with sea salt, it's supposed to provide some level of protection against unwanted darker energies from entering."

"See, you *do* know something about all this ghost stuff!" Katie teased.

"No, this is a side benefit of reading all those weird books when I was a kid."

Roland interrupted. "What we really hope to do is communicate directly with the spirit. If we're lucky, she'll show herself to us."

"That would be lucky, all right," Ella muttered. She wondered about that kind of luck. What kind of luck allowed Ella to see the ghosts of people she never knew but didn't allow her to see her own mother? Maybe it had nothing to do with luck at all. Maybe Ella's mother was already long gone to wherever people go when they die. Her feelings weren't necessarily reasonable, but then again, feelings never were.

Katie nudged her. "Are you scared?"

"Yes," Ella admitted.

"They can't hurt us, you know. Besides, if this really is Hattie, I don't think she wants to do any harm. I think she's probably trying to tell us what happened." Katie was trying to be reassuring, Ella knew, but she still felt uneasy. Roland was making this sound relatively simple, but she wondered if he forgot to mention anything.

"I don't know... something doesn't feel right to me." Ella decided to come out and tell them. There was no point in hiding her thoughts now, not when they were all in this situation together.

"That's probably because of your dreams," Roland said. "You are very close to this situation, and for some reason the spirit is communicating with you in the dream time. As we get closer to answers, you may be feeling some of the pain or discomfort that the spirit has felt. It's only natural."

Ella wondered how Roland's idea of "natural" could be so very different from hers. "Flowers and sunshine are natural," she told him. "Getting rid of ghosts in your house is *not*."

Roland laughed. "Maybe not for you, but this is something that people have been dealing with for centuries. Don't worry; all we have to do is stay focused and not lose sight of the ultimate goal. Try not to get scared or freaked out. We'll invoke the protection of the ancestors, as well as any other spirit you may be close to."

"Any other spirits I might be close to? I have no idea what you're talking about." An image of her mother flashed through her mind.

"Guardian angels, totem animals, any source of protection that may have roots in the religion or spiritual practice that you follow."

"I haven't been to church in years," Ella said. She didn't feel like mentioning that the last time she'd been in church was for her mother's funeral.

Roland shook his head. "That doesn't matter. Ask your relatives to be with you, and if you have a belief in guardian angels, ask them to be here as well. But try not to worry; those details will work themselves out."

Ella thought that those details were the kind that should be worked out beforehand, but Roland seemed to know what he was talking about, or at least she hoped he did. *This time I'll let go of the details and trust that it will be fine.*

As the phone began to ring, Ella realized she should call her family. *If they heard about the incoming hurricane, they'll be worried.* Glancing at the Caller ID, Ella was surprised to see the word 'Unavailable.' *Maybe Dad's calling from a different phone.*

The raspy voice whispered, "Go home, Yankee bitch," then the line went dead. Ella stood, shaking. Somehow the sound of that voice scared her more than any message scrawled on the house. She reached for the business card she'd affixed to the refrigerator and dialed the number on the back.

"Kevin? I have to tell you something."
***

Walking back outside, Ella tried to compose her face behind a mask of calm, not wanting her friends to see how shaken she was. "So, we have a plan, right?" she asked them as she sat on a deck chair.

"How's lover boy?" Roland teased, stopping when he saw her face.

I can't keep this from them. If they were going to stay in the house with her, they needed to know other kinds of danger might be present. "He wasn't the first phone call. I called Kevin after." She went on to tell them what the caller had said and sounded like, so they could make their own decisions about whether or not to stay with her.

As he listened to Ella's story, Roland frowned. "Sounds like some of the town's good ol' boys have been bothering you."

She nodded. "I think I know who it is. I had a sort of confrontation with one of them at the coffee shop the day the movers got here." As she told them the story, she cringed. She really should have kept her mouth shut that day, but her temper had flared at the man's disrespect.

"That's what I was trying to tell you that first day we came over." Roland stood and started pacing the deck. "You can't piss off these people; some of them are downright nasty."

Katie agreed. "Not everyone here is like that, Ella, but some of those idiots can be dangerous. I'm glad we're going to be with you tonight, and you'll be with me after that. You absolutely cannot stay alone until the police stop him."

Ella wasn't sure if she felt gratitude or wariness. "Are you sure? This puts a whole new slant on things, and you might be putting yourselves in danger by staying with me."

"Do you think we'd leave you alone to deal with those dopes?" Roland asked in amazement.

Grateful, Ella didn't mention her heightened her sense of unease. With a mix of real people and ghosts harassing her, who knew what was going to happen? Maybe it was time to give up and move to a more urban area, get away from the small-town attitude and haunted house. Unfortunately, it was highly likely that if ghosts truly existed, they would not be confined to small, suburban towns; in fact, there might even be *more* of them in the cities.

Ella was struck by a sudden idea: this could be her proof of life after death. She forced her tears back. She hadn't realized she was looking for proof, but the thought had taken hold in her mind. She'd need to process everything later, maybe after her ghost-banishing adventure.

"What did your police guy say about the phone call?" Katie asked.

"He told me to be careful and that they were going to step up patrols on this street. He also said they might have a lead on who it might be, but that was all he could tell me right now."

Roland leaned back in his chair. "When all this is done, you might not want to stay here anymore," he said, echoing Ella's thoughts. "We should get going so we can pick up our stuff and come right back. I don't want to leave Ella alone for too long. Tonight is for observation; tomorrow morning we'll do some research, and then we'll send your ghost packing before the storm hits."

Katie started, "Shouldn't we—"

"We need to see what we're dealing with first," Roland said firmly.

Chapter Thirty-Three

AFTER FRANTICALLY DIGGING THROUGH THE house, Ella found her purse and keys under a pile of clothes in her bedroom, then left to go shopping. A couple of hours later she was home, armed with supplies. Dragging as many bags as she could carry, Ella trudged up to the front steps, managed to get her door unlocked, and went in. Closing the front door with her foot, she dragged her bags into the kitchen.

"Geez, Daisy, you wouldn't believe how crowded all the stores were. It's kind of like it gets back home right before a blizzard. Lots of shelves were empty, and I was lucky to get any batteries. It took me forever to find a parking spot, and the lines at the cash register were incredibly long. But, I did buy a brand new flashlight in case we lose power at Katie's house." Daisy cocked her head. "I know, I'm sure she has her own flashlights, but I don't want to show up without supplies. I even bought a few gallons of water."

The idea of enduring a hurricane was both exciting and a little frightening. She thought about calling Kevin just to check in with him, but she assumed he was busy dealing with all the people that were out and about. She could call him later; instead, she picked up the phone and dialed her sister's number.

"Lisa, I wanted to let you know that I'm going to be staying at my friend Katie's house for a day or two."

"Why are you going to do that? Is something wrong with your house? I told you to be more careful about picking a place to live. Why you thought it would be okay to choose some random place off the internet is beyond me. What happened? Did something fall down?"

Ella suppressed a sigh. "No, a hurricane is coming up the coast, and I think it would be better if I stayed somewhere else. I'm fairly close to the water, and some flooding is expected here."

"Ohmygod—a hurricane? Do you get them much down there? I'm going to have to talk to Dan about this. I don't know if this is going to be such a good idea after all."

Ella was confused. "Well geez, Lisa, it's not like you have any control over whether or not there's a hurricane. You can't call Dan and tell him to cancel the storm."

"That's not what I'm talking about, and you know it!" Actually, Ella had no idea what her sister was talking about, so she kept quiet as Lisa ranted. "I told you we were seriously considering moving down there, but if it's going to be nothing but one hurricane after another, I don't know."

Understanding dawned: her sister was thinking of moving. Right. To Virginia. Near Ella. She'd conveniently forgotten that piece of information. "Oh." Ella was silent, trying to find something positive to say... *Nope, I've got nothing.* "Yeah, I think hurricanes might actually be a problem here. It's definitely something you want to look into."

"I will. When are you going to your friend's house? Call me after the storm hits so I know you've survived."

"I'm going to stay with Katie tomorrow because it's more likely I'll lose power before she does. I'll call you in a couple of days."

"Fine, I've got to go. You wouldn't believe how stressful my life has been lately, and now I need to rethink this whole moving thing."

"That's probably a good idea," Ella said, then added quickly, "not that I wouldn't love it if you moved to Virginia, but you can't be too careful, you know?"

"Obviously," Lisa retorted. "Although, I don't know if we'll have much choice. Dan might have already accepted the offer."

"Hmm...well, I guess it will be what it will be, right?" Ella realized she was speaking more to herself than her sister. "I've got to go. I'm going to call Dad, too, and I've got a ton of work to do."

After disconnecting from her conversation with her sister, Ella called her father and let him know where she'd be staying. He took the news in stride, not really worried about a hurricane. "You've been through blizzards that have probably been worse," he said.

After her phone calls, she took a quick shower. She still felt dusty from her adventure in the shed outside. Changing into denim shorts with a T-shirt that read '*Eve was Framed,*' Ella thought about her morning's adventure.

It didn't make sense to her that Jeff was so uptight about the backyard shed. Maybe he was worried about someone getting hurt, but nothing was in there. She wondered if he was worried about getting sued, or if his father was worried about getting sued. *Doesn't matter, does it? One way or another I'm going to get to the bottom of this.*

This was it. Tonight she would have some answers and get rid of a ghost, with a little help from her friends.

Deciding to see if she could get some research done before anyone arrived, she sat at her computer. The first thing she accessed was the Paterson town website. Sometimes assessment information could be found on a municipal web page. Scrolling through the menu, she found a resource entitled 'Property Information Look Up.' Maybe she could find something interesting in there. After clicking on the title and filling in her address when prompted, an information sheet filled the screen. The details of her house were in front of her, including square footage, materials used, number of rooms, and yard size. There was even a small picture of the outside of the house. The owner of record was listed as Jeff Bartok. According to the records, Jeff Bartok purchased the home seven years earlier from William Bartok, who had purchased the home in 1952 from Daniel Whitmore.

Ella realized that seven years ago was around the time Mr. Bartok went into the nursing home. If the police have been receiving weird calls about the house for the past seven years, that would be around the time it started being rented.

She looked to see if there was any more information, but nothing else looked relevant. After printing the pages, Ella tucked them into a folder to show her friends later. She may have a good start, or she may have found nothing worthwhile.

After stopping for a quick sandwich break, she went back to work, determined to use her time to find out as much as possible. A couple of websites claimed to have online census records, but a subscription was needed to view the information. *Forget it*, she thought. *I'll wait until Roland goes to Town Hall and see what he can unearth.*

A knock sounded at the front door. She ran downstairs and threw the door open before remembering to check first. *Good thing it's only Katie and Roland.* They stood on her front steps armed with suitcases and shopping bags.

Katie dragged her suitcase in and threw herself on the couch. "Lordy, I think people have gone plumb crazy. I declare, I haven't seen so much pushing and shoving since the last 'buy one get one free' Duke's mayonnaise sale last year."

Ella looked at Roland and asked, "What is she talking about?"

Roland laughed. "Katie becomes more Southern under stress. Apparently, her trip to the store was taxing."

Katie stared back at him indignantly. "And what did you do with your time, Mr. Smarty Pants?"

"Filled the gas tanks on my bike and truck, turned up the refrigerator, and put new batteries in my flashlights."

"Oh." Katie deflated. "You're always so prepared. I had to go get the batteries first, never mind trying to figure out where my flashlights are."

"Don't worry, I bought a new one. At least we'll have one to use if we lose power," Ella reassured her. "I got batteries, too, as well as water and nonperishable food. But you're right, people were crazy. I think it happens no matter what kind of storm is coming."

The energy from the incoming hurricane was building, that much was certain. People were frantic, and even Daisy was unsettled, pacing the house as if searching for something. Not wanting to be caught unawares again, Ella left the television turned to the local weather station for updates.

"Okay, kids, let's see what we've got for tonight." Roland unpacked his cloth grocery sack. "Microwave popcorn, cheez doodles, and chocolate bars. That's my contribution for the evening."

Ella and Katie looked at each other, and Ella shrugged. Katie folded her arms over her chest. "Honestly, Roland, you'd think you spent your childhood at nothing more than girl's slumber parties. What made you buy that junk?"

"What do you mean 'buy' this? This is the kind of stuff I eat every night," he teased. "I wasn't sure what we were going to do for dinner, so I decided to take care of dessert and snacks."

"Thanks, Roland," Ella said. "I was going to make chicken cutlets and salad, if that's okay."

Katie and Roland nodded enthusiastically. Ella smiled and shook her head. "I don't know why I bother asking. I think you two would eat almost anything I put in front of you."

The trio made their way into the kitchen, where they continued unpacking bags and talking. Ella filled them in on what she'd found on the internet earlier. "I printed the pages, and I was hoping it would save us time tomorrow. From what I can tell, this house was built in 1936 and has had only two owners—well three, I guess, if you want to count Jeff, the son. But the father, William Bartok, bought the house in 1952, and it has stayed in the family ever since."

"Do you know how much they paid?" Katie asked.

"No, that was listed as 'no data.'"

"Can I see the sheets you printed?" Roland asked.

"Sure. I left them upstairs. I'll be right back."

"While you're doing that, I have to go out to my truck and get some more stuff. I'll be right in."

"You have more?" Ella was incredulous. "What else could you have possibly brought?"

"Sleeping bags," he answered. "I wasn't sure if you had three separate beds, and if you only had one and Katie slept on the couch, I wanted to make sure I was prepared."

Katie sighed. "A regular Boy Scout."

"It's part of my heritage." Roland grinned at her and went out to his truck. Ella turned to Katie. "What exactly is his heritage, anyway?"

"You mean you couldn't guess? He's part Native American, part Irish. His dad was from the Mattaponi tribe, not too far from here. His mom was Irish."

Ella nodded, wondering what his heritage had to do with being prepared. Walking upstairs, she called over her shoulder. "I guess that explains everything."

Chapter Thirty-Four

AS ELLA WALKED BACK DOWNSTAIRS, Roland dumped his sleeping bags in the living room. "Here's the papers," she said, handing them to Katie and Roland. "I made copies for both of you."

"Thanks, this will be useful. Now that we know Mr. Whitmore was the first owner of the house, we can research their family background, see if there were any kind of murders, disappearances, that type of thing."

Katie shook her head. "We could do research, yes, but I'm willing to bet my money on the fact that it's Hattie haunting this house. It's too obvious, with her having gone missing and nobody ever knowing what happened to her."

"I'm willing to agree with you. That's one of the reasons I wanted a night to observe, though; I wanted to see if we could get some clues to the identity of this thing so we could focus our research tomorrow."

"Sometimes you can be pretty smart, you know that?" Katie gazed up at Roland. Ella could have sworn she saw her friend bat her eyelashes at him, something she didn't think actually happened outside of books.

"All right, you two, let's be practical for now. Where do you want to sleep? I have my bedroom, which Katie is welcome to stay in with me. I also have the office upstairs, which has a daybed in it. The third bedroom is downstairs, behind the kitchen. I have to tell you, though, that room has always made me uncomfortable. I wanted to use it as the office, but I always felt sort of creeped out in there. Does anyone want to try to sleep in it?" she offered brightly.

"Thanks," Katie said drily. "I really don't want to sleep downstairs, if that's okay with ya'll."

"I think that's a good idea," Roland said. "Let's stay in different bedrooms. Katie can sleep on the daybed, Ella can stay in her room, and I'll take my sleeping bag into the downstairs bedroom; this way, we'll have different perspectives on what may or may not happen tonight. Also, if anyone tries to break into the house, I'll be downstairs to take care of things."

Katie sighed. "My hero," she said, placing a hand over her heart. Ella pretended to swoon and added, "Thank goodness there's a big strong man in the house now."

"Okay, you two, cut the crap. All I'm saying is that if someone is trying to mess with you, they're going to have to go through me first, at least for tonight. I'm no hero, and I don't want to be a hero. But I can handle myself well enough if it comes to that."

Ella immediately sobered. "I don't want you fighting," she said. "I don't care if someone is breaking in, call the police and get out of the way. Fighting would be foolish. What if they have a gun? It won't matter how well you fight, if they have a gun, it's over. And we already know some wacko is trying to scare me. Promise you will not provoke anyone tonight."

"You're right," he admitted. "I'll sleep with my cell phone next to me in case I need to call the police. Is that better?"

Both women nodded, clearly relieved. Ella, though, again started feeling stirrings of unease. What if something went very wrong tonight and somebody got hurt? It would be her fault. *I hope the worst thing that happens is a ghost showing up.*

"Don't worry; it'll be fine," Katie reassured her. "I seriously doubt that somebody has been breaking into this house for seven years trying to scare people. That doesn't make any sense. I'm sure the worst thing that will happen tonight is that we'll all be scared."

Ella nodded. "You're probably right. I feel guilty about getting both of you involved—this might turn out to be dangerous. I wasn't thinking too clearly before, and I don't want anything to happen—"

"Like Katie said, we'll be fine," Roland interrupted. "Why don't we stop thinking negative thoughts and try to relax and do something fun? How about we watch a movie, maybe some sort of comedy?"

"Or a romance," Katie suggested.

"Oh, there's this great new movie out about this woman who falls in love with this guy, but he's so busy taking care of his mother he never notices her, so she—"

"No." Roland was firm. "I'm not sitting around watching some chick flick." After a few minutes of debate, they finally decided to watch a classic from Ella's movie collection, *Harold and Maude*. Working together in the kitchen, the three made a dinner of the chicken cutlets and salad that Ella had planned. Once everything was ready, they carried their plates of food out to the living room to watch the movie. By mutual consent, no alcohol was served. It seemed important to remain clearheaded for their upcoming evening.

After the movie, everyone cleaned up, then Ella took Daisy outside. The night air was warm and felt soft against her skin.

"I know I should be worried, Daisy, but I really do feel better having them here." Ella looked at the clear sky with millions of stars outlined before her. "What would you do, Mom? Are you watching over me, or are you so far away right now that you don't know what's going on in your daughter's world? Are you out there, or are you here with me and this so-called ghost?" As if in answer, a gentle breeze caressed her face. Ella took a deep breath, determined not to cry. *I don't know why I'm constantly thinking about my mother now*, she thought, *but I really, really miss her. It's weird; sometimes I feel like she's right here with me, helping me through this.* Ella wrapped her arms around herself, warding off the cold. The night air was warm, but she found herself shaking from a chill that seemed to come from inside her.

Maybe her imagination was getting the best of her. She turned to go inside, then stopped. There was a whisper around her, soft words being spoken...but if Ella was the only person out there, who was talking?

Chapter Thirty-Five

DAISY WHIMPERED AND LOOKED UP at Ella. Soft as a baby's caress, the night air moved, no sound evident. Ella wondered if she'd simply imagined the voice.

Sighing in frustration at what had become her very strange life, Ella fully opened the back door. Maybe all those ghost stories were getting to her. Maybe what she was hearing was nothing more than her imagination. Or maybe she'd officially gone around the bend.

Roland turned to Ella when she entered the kitchen. "Are you talking to yourself again?" he asked.

"Absolutely. Sometimes I even answer myself."

"Ha. You're going to fit in just fine in the South," Katie declared. Looking at the clock, she added, "I don't know about you two, but I'm exhausted. I had to get up early and help my friend here break into the backyard shed. I think I'll get ready for bed."

"I'm trying very hard to forget about your shed shenanigans. Maybe we should all go to bed," Roland added. "We don't know if we'll have a good night's sleep or not, so we should at least try to get as much rest as we can."

"That's true," Ella said. "We should all retire for the evening." She looked nervously at her friends. "I sound like I'm in a bad Tennessee Williams play."

"Don't worry; we're going to be okay," Roland reassured her.

"Never met a ghost I couldn't handle," Katie told Ella.

Ella smiled. "According to Roland, you've never met a ghost."

Katie waved her well-manicured hand in the air. "Pshaw. The only difference is that the ones I've met weren't scary at all. They were regular old people."

"Except they were dead," Roland added dryly.

"Well, yes, except for that," Katie acknowledged. "Ella, let's get upstairs. Roland, are you all set down here?"

He nodded and held up his cell phone. "I'll be in my sleeping bag. I've got my phone, so Ella can keep the house phone by her bed."

"What about me?" Katie demanded.

"Don't you have a cell phone?" Roland asked.

Katie blew out a breath. "Yes, but you could have at least mentioned that my safety was a priority, too. Just so you know, I have a cell phone and a baseball bat."

Ella looked at Katie, eyes wide. "I have a baseball bat by my bed, too. Great minds and all that, right?"

The two women laughed, dispelling some of the fear that had been building for both of them. "Are you ready?" Roland asked. "Remember, I'm downstairs if anything happens. I'll lock all the doors and put the chain on. Anyway," he added, shooting a look at Ella, "I'm sure that the police department will be here right away once we call from this address."

Ella tried not to let any reaction show at the mention of Kevin. Instead, she took the mature approach to Roland's comment: she stuck her tongue out at him. Laughing, Katie took her arm, and the two of them went upstairs.

Naturally, Daisy kept tabs on everybody; she traveled upstairs and downstairs, checking on the guests and Ella, making certain everything was as it should be. Finally, after climbing into each bed and jumping onto Roland's sleeping bag, Daisy decided to adorn her usual sleeping spot at the foot of Ella's bed.

The house settled into an evening quiet, the kind that has only the hum of the refrigerator and occasional creak of the house settling. It was a little after ten in the evening, and Ella was wondering how she'd get to sleep when she was feeling so wired about the potential for the night's events. As she lay there, unable to stop her mind from traveling in circles, the music began. She sighed, threw back her covers, and opened the door to the hallway. Katie stood there, looking like Ella felt.

"What does he think he's doing?" Katie asked.

Ella shrugged. "I don't know. Let's yell at him, then we can go back to bed." She called down the stairs. "Hey, Roland, turn the music off. We can't get to sleep with all that racket!" Turning back to Katie, she asked, "What is that, anyway?"

Katie was standing stock still, her head cocked to one side as she listened to the music floating up the stairs. "This is really weird," she told Ella. "It sounds like the punk rock version of *I'll Fly Away.*"

"That does it," Ella muttered as she marched down the stairs. Roland was in the living room, looking up the stairs.

"What did you say?" he asked. "I couldn't hear you."

"Don't play innocent with me, asking 'what' and trying to look like a little angel. What are you doing?"

"I was playing some music to try to get to sleep," he answered, eyes wide.

"That was not just some music." Katie stomped down the final two steps. "That was the song we discussed earlier, the one that's been heard around here. Why on earth are you playing that version of the song?"

Roland shrugged. "I'm not really into gospel music, but when I found this punk band cover of it, I hoped it might be a kind of invitation for our spirit to come out and visit tonight, that's all. Sorry I woke you."

"We weren't actually asleep," Ella corrected. "And while I agree that it might be a good idea to play that particular song, perhaps you could play it a little more quietly."

"A lot more," Katie added.

"No problem. I understand I'm keeping the old girls up, so I'll turn it down."

"Ignore him," Katie said as they turned to walk upstairs. "I swear, he is just trying to annoy us." Ella grinned at her friend's back, thinking about all the times she'd seen the exact opposite happen. "It's a two-way street, my friend," she said to Katie. *What next? This has to work.* Closing her bedroom door softly, Ella got back in bed and stared at the ceiling. Much later she managed to drift into sleep.

***

August in Virginia has existed in the same way for decades: slow, hot, and humid. Ella watched, as if from a distance, wondering how people survived before central air conditioning. Hattie stood in the kitchen, carefully putting dishes into the overhead cabinets, then turned toward Ella. Ella knew Hattie was seeing someone else, but no matter how hard she strained her eyes, she couldn't tell who was in the room with them.

The fan against the back wall made a clacking sound, providing the only movement of air in the house. Hattie opened her mouth to speak, then closed it again. She then turned away and started to wipe down the counters, shoulders slumped. Ella knew it was a dream; still, she wished she could at least reach out a hand and touch her, perhaps find a way to provide comfort. Somehow Ella knew that Hattie was in emotional pain, and she felt a surge of sympathy for the young woman, and more than a little trepidation at what might lie ahead.

"I'm sorry," Hattie spoke without turning around. "This is the way it has to be, I guess. If I don't do what he asks, there's going to be trouble—big trouble. I don't want anybody to get into any trouble... I just want..." Her voice broke as tears ran down her face. Ella could feel her heart shatter, and she wasn't certain if it was her own heart or Hattie's despondency that she felt.

"I should have known better," Hattie said again, still turned toward the counter. "I wish it weren't so, but wishing doesn't change anything, does it?"

***

Cold air permeated everything when Ella woke, her body shivering. Wondering if she was dreaming, she looked out the window. A fog hovered outside the glass. *I can't open the window; the fog will wrap around me and hold me.*

From downstairs, there came a series of thumping noises, followed by silence. Grabbing her bathrobe off the rocking chair next to the night stand, Ella opened her door and crept into the hallway. Daisy slunk off the bed, reluctantly following. As Ella's eyes adjusted to the lack of light, she could see another figure standing there. "Katie?" she whispered.

"I'm right here," Katie whispered back. "What was that noise?"

"I don't know, but I think we should go downstairs and find out. Roland might need us." Another thump sounded. "C'mon, there might be trouble." The two women ran, stopping abruptly at the foot of the stairs.

The outside moonlight illuminated a portion of the room, causing Katie to gasp and Ella to stand in stunned silence. The scene before them was bizarre because it was so silent; outside of the occasional thump, there was no noise. There, in the center of the living room, they could dimly make out Roland's form as he struggled against a shadowy attacker.

Finally, a scream let loose.

Chapter Thirty-Six

DESPITE THE URGENCY OF THE scream, the darkness of the night held them in place. Ella and Katie were frozen, unable to speak, watching in soundless horror as Roland wrestled with the dark figure. It was unclear who had screamed, but whoever it was stopped.

Daisy let out a short bark, cowering behind Ella. A grunt from the struggle in front of them stirred Ella into action. Moving quickly, she felt along the wall, her hand searching for the light switch. Once she found it, she flipped it on, and as light filled the room and chased the shadows away, Ella's first thought was, *My God, it's human.* Her second thought, however, banished any horror she may have initially felt.

"Meg?" Ella was incredulous. What was her friend doing in her house, over five hundred miles away from her own home, in the middle of the night? "Let go of my friend; she's not going to hurt anyone." she told Roland. "Oh, God, are you okay? What are you doing here?"

The two figures stopped struggling and looked at Ella. "You know this person?" Roland sounded dubious. Looking Meg up and down, he said, "I thought it was a girl." Long hair in disarray, Meg looked fierce in her bright orange tank top and faded Levis. Her big brown eyes glared at Roland, daring him to lay another finger on her.

Straightening to his full height, Roland brushed himself off, folded his arms over his chest, and demanded, "Would you like to explain yourself?"

Meg responded in a fury. "Me? You attacked me... who the hell are you, anyway?" Daisy whined and walked over to Meg, licking her hand.

"Poor Daisy," Meg murmured, leaning down to pat her on the head and rub her belly. Fuming, she looked up at Roland. "You've even upset the dog."

Roland shook his head. "I wasn't trying to hurt you. I was trying to stop you from hurting anyone else."

"Hold on a minute," Ella interrupted. "Meg, I had no idea you were going to be here. I'm sorry, I hope you're all right." She put an arm around her friend, who was sniffling. "This is Roland, and he's in charge of guarding the house tonight. It's nobody's fault this happened." As much as Ella wanted to glare at Roland—maybe even kick him—she couldn't. He was only doing what he'd said he was going to do. At least he hadn't called the police.

"I think we'd all better get ourselves something to drink and sit down. This is going to be a long night," Katie mused from her spot on the stairs.

"Nobody asked if I got hurt," Roland muttered.

Everyone found a seat, except Ella, and for a moment there was an awkward silence. "Does anyone want anything to drink?" Ella asked. "I have a feeling we might need some... fortification."

"I brought a six pack," Meg piped up. "It's at the door. In fact, I was carrying all my stuff in before I was *attacked*." She said the last part with venom, looking at Roland.

Katie walked over to the door, grabbed a beer, and twisted the cap off a bottle. "I think I'm going to need this."

"What are you doing breaking into people's houses in the middle of the night? Why didn't you ring the doorbell, like any normal, sane person would have done?" Roland demanded.

Meg found a spot on her pants to pick the lint off, then started fussing with an overnight bag. "I wanted to surprise Ella. When I pulled into the driveway, I saw a car I didn't recognize, so I thought she might be... you know, busy."

"How did you get in?" Katie asked. "Roland said he was locking all the doors."

All eyes were on Meg as she defiantly answered. "He did; I had to climb in the window. If I knew that nobody was getting busy in here, I would have knocked on the darn door."

There was a short silence while everyone stared in disbelief at Meg. Ella then burst out laughing. "When was the last time you came to visit me and I was 'getting busy,' as you so delicately put it?"

"Never. I was hoping the new house or new job brought some luck for you in that department." While Katie and Roland stared at Meg, she winked at Ella. "You haven't mentioned meeting anyone in particular, but I thought since we hadn't spoken in a couple of days, maybe you met some Southern cutie pie and hit it off. I thought I'd crash on your couch for now. Then I got in and this big gorilla came at me, and... well, you know the rest. So anyway—surprise!"

"Why didn't you scream?" Roland asked.

Meg smiled ruefully. "When you tackled me, it honestly didn't occur to me to scream. I didn't think I was in any real danger. Then it felt like there were all these other people in the room, and that's when I screamed. Just once, though."

"It was your inherent femininity kicking in," Katie added, taking a swig of beer straight from the bottle. "We've been trained since we were children not to be loud, not to yell, and above all, not to cause any trouble. Screaming is probably the single most difficult thing a woman can do when she's being attacked, yet it's one of those things that will help her the most."

"I don't know... my mother never had any trouble screaming at all of us kids," Roland said. Katie poked him in the ribs, letting him know it was time to behave.

Ella shook her head. "I'm so amazed that you're actually here. Thank you for coming and surprising me. Things have been a little strange around here... anyway, let me get a beer and sit down, and I'll tell you all about it. Oh, and these are my friends, Katie and Roland," Ella pointed to each one in turn, then turned back to Meg. "And this is my best friend from Connecticut, Meg." Once she finished the introductions, Ella went to the front door to retrieve Meg's bag. Looking inside, she gave a cry of delight. "Oh, I love this stuff! It's cranberry beer!" She held a bottle aloft for the others to see.

Roland gave a snort of disgust. "Girlie beer."

"Hey, if you don't like girlie beer and girlie movies, maybe you shouldn't hang out with the girls. Go find yourself some manly men." Katie poked him again in the ribs, this time a little harder.

He answered quickly. "I could do that, but there aren't any cute ones around here."

Ella sighed. "Roland, do you want a bottle?" She wasn't surprised when he held his hand out for the beer; at that point, they all needed a drink.

"What's going on, anyway?" Meg asked. "I had some time off, and I wanted to surprise you with a visit. Remember the night before you left? I hinted that you should expect me?"

Ella nodded. "Yeah, I thought you were being silly. I honestly had no idea you'd show up. That is a seriously long car ride."

Meg waved an arm in the air. "There's no way I was going to drive all by myself. I flew into the Williamsburg airport and rented a car. Now, tell me everything."

Ella leaned back and started talking. It was strange; a few days ago, she would have hesitated to tell people about having a ghost in her house for fear of being laughed at or thought of as strange. But everything poured out in the retelling. Except for the part about the words on the house. She knew Meg wasn't going to like it, but she knew someone else who'd like it even less. "Don't tell Lisa," she pleaded.

Meg shook her head. "There's no way I'm telling your sister about this. I have no desire to get in the middle of that conversation." Relieved, Ella continued, telling Meg about the day the movers arrived and the events at the coffee shop.

"So let me see if I have this right," Meg started. "You've been awakened by strange noises, you've periodically heard gospel music, you've had nasty words spray painted on your house, you have dreams you think might have been about real people, and you saw what you think was a ghost... did I forget anything?"

"Actually, there is one more thing I wanted to share." Ella hesitated. She couldn't be certain that the dreams she was having actually meant anything; they could have simply been the product of an overactive imagination. But instinct told her otherwise, and since she'd come this far, she might as well share what she'd dreamt earlier that evening.

"I had another dream tonight. This time Hattie—or the girl I've come to think of as Hattie—was telling someone that there was going to be trouble. She said she had to leave, and it wasn't what she wanted, but if she didn't go there was going to be some kind of big trouble."

"Who was she talking to?" Katie asked.

Ella shrugged. "I tried to see, but I couldn't make out a face or anything. Whoever it was never answered, or at least I never heard an answer. All I heard was what she said to this person, and she was so...dejected. I mean, it was all I could do not to hug the poor girl."

"You can't hug a dream," Meg told her.

Ella pushed away her annoyance. "I know that. But lately I'm starting to think that the only impossible things are the ones we decide on." Ella put her beer down on a coaster on the side table. "Anyway, it's obvious that Hattie was in some kind of trouble, and she needed to get away. I'm starting to wonder if she left town on her own."

Chapter Thirty-Seven

ROLAND SHOOK HIS HEAD. "IF she did, at some point she would have contacted Lorraine. There's no way she would have let her suffer all those years of not knowing what happened. At the very least, Hattie would have sent some kind of coded message. They were best friends, and best friends don't do that to each other."

Meg looked at Ella. "As much as I hate to admit it, he's right. You and I wouldn't disappear on each other. Anyway, I know that I'm hearing this story for the first time," at this point, Meg shot a look at Ella that said they'd discuss the situation at a later date, "but it seems to me you're all making lots of assumptions."

"Really?" Roland asked, leaning back and looking down at Meg.

"Yes, really. First, you're assuming that this Hattie person was indeed a nice person. What if she wasn't? What if she was stealing something from someone and had been caught doing it and didn't want to pay the price? Or what if she decided that living around here wasn't worth it, for whatever reason, and she left? People do that all the time; you see it on the back of milk cartons."

Katie nodded. "I hear what you're saying, Meg, and you have a good point. However, we know a couple of people who told us the kind of person Hattie was, and I don't see her doing that. She was smart and kind, and she had at least one good friend who cared about her. That makes a world of difference, you know? Although I suppose it is possible she left on her own, we're still left with the question of why she never contacted her best friend."

"There's something else you guys really need to think about," Meg added. "My friend here is a very nice person, but what happens once everyone in town finds out about this? Will people know that she's nice, or will they think she's stirring up trouble? Because I have to tell you, I've heard stories about things that happen down here, and it's not pretty."

"It's not like that anymore," Katie said.

Meg raised her eyebrows. "Really? Are you sure about that?"

Ella was silent, remembering her experience on moving day. How could Katie have forgotten so quickly? But this was a conversation for another day. For now, things needed to happen.

"I wonder what Jeff thought of Hattie?" Ella asked. The room fell quiet as everyone considered that. "We know he was young when Hattie left, but even if he doesn't remember anything, if his father was dating her he probably had some attachment to her. Children often pick up on their parents' feelings."

"Is that the landlord guy you told me about?" Meg asked.

Ella nodded. "Yes, and he lived in the house while Hattie was working here and dating his dad. He was only a little kid, but still..."

"That's a good question. Who wants to ask him?" Roland asked. For a moment, nobody answered. "I think Ella should."

"What? Why me?"

"Because you have a sort of relationship with him," Roland answered. "Besides, you're from out of town, so of course you've heard all these stories. The next time you see him, ask. He should be stopping by any day now, right?"

Ella sighed. She would ask Jeff about Hattie, but she had a bad feeling about what his reaction would be. After all, he'd been fine right up until she mentioned the shed, then the conversation completely fell apart. Hopefully, the question about Hattie would go better than the question about the shed, but she knew better than to assume anything about her landlord, especially when it came to prying information out of him.

"I'll ask, but I'm not expecting much. He's not exactly forthcoming with small talk, you know? In fact, he creeps me out. Not all the time, just sometimes."

Roland defended the man. "I know you've said that, but remember what I told you about him? He's had a hard life, and without a mother I don't think he learned some of the more, uh, important social skills."

"You mean he doesn't know how to talk to women?" Meg asked.

Roland nodded. "He's fine when he's hanging out with the guys, but if you put him in a room with a woman he gets all flustered."

"Has he ever had a girlfriend?" Meg asked.

"Why? What difference does that make?" Roland asked.

"Oh, I don't know… a guy who gives my friend the creeps, who's socially inept, probably lived at home all his life… let's see, should I be worried that he's going to chop her up in little pieces and put her down the garbage disposal?"

"Meg, really; he's not that bad. He may be a little awkward, but I don't think he's a serial killer."

"Maybe he killed this woman that you think is haunting the place, whats-her-name, Annie."

"Hattie."

"He was way too young to be chopping up bodies," Roland said dryly. "I think you'd have to be at least a teenager to have the strength for that."

"Whatever. Anyway, my point is that you never really know what people are capable of. Honestly, Ella, I can't believe that you've been here less than a week, and you're already in the middle of this great big drama."

"I know. But all this stuff started happening; I didn't go looking for it."

"And you're sure there's no one else trying to scare you? Maybe whoever spray painted the house?" Meg eyed Roland with distrust.

"I think I'm dealing with two different things. I've managed to annoy some of the locals, like dirty T-shirt guy and the cable guy, but I can say with certainty that they had nothing to do with the woman in my kitchen. She was just not… alive."

Ella wondered how to phrase what she wanted to tell them. Sometimes the only way to say something was to come right out and say it. After all, they'd come this far.

"You know, there are times like earlier tonight…I swear that it's more than Hattie. I think I have my own ghosts here, too."

Chapter Thirty-Eight

"WHAT DO YOU MEAN?" ROLAND asked.

Ella felt tired, deep-down tired, drained by her grief. "There are times when it feels like my mom is here, looking in on me to make sure I'm okay. It's weird, because I know she isn't really here. Maybe I wanted her to come back so much that I've been imagining it."

She wasn't sure anymore that it was such a good idea to tell her friends how she felt. Everyone was looking at her with sympathy, the kind that gets suffocating after a while.

"Ella, not all ghosts appear to people like Hattie has appeared to you," Roland told her. "Sometimes it's nothing more than a feeling, a sort of knowing that someone is there with you, watching out for you or dropping in to say, 'Don't worry, everything's fine over here.'"

Meg looked at Roland in disbelief. "Are you for real? I think my friend would know if her own mother was dropping in to say hello. Like she said, she's wanted her to come back so badly that she's imagining it."

Ella shook her head. "Maybe not, Meg. I don't know, but have you ever wanted something so much that your perception of things gets distorted? I think that happened with my mom. I wanted to see her again because I miss her so much but part of me didn't want to see her again because it's not really her, she's not really here anymore. She's dead, and she's not coming back."

Katie began to speak. "Ella, honey, I know that losing your mom—"

She was interrupted by a low, mournful howl coming from the kitchen. Roland paused, beer midway to his mouth, while the other three looked at each other. Once again, a howl echoed through the house.

"That's Daisy. It sounds like she's in the kitchen," Ella whispered.

"Why are you whispering?" Meg whispered back.

"Because we don't know what the hell is causing her to make that sound," Katie said.

"Let's check it out," Roland told them.

Meg glanced at him, adding "Yeah, maybe you can tackle someone else tonight."

"Ssssshhhhhh," Ella and Katie said in unison. As another low, agitated howl filled the air, Ella felt goose bumps on her arms. Passing through the kitchen doorway, her hand found the wall switch and turned on the overhead light. Everyone stopped short, staring in fascinated horror.

Daisy was backed up against the cabinets in front of them, hackles raised, ears flattened. In the middle of the kitchen stood a young, African American woman, arms outstretched. She was dressed in a plain khaki skirt with a white shirt that had a peter pan collar. Although clearly visible, she still appeared translucent—as if she were made of thickened smoke. Pans spun around her, circling in mid-air as she reached out beseechingly.

Frozen, all four friends watched as the woman began yelling, clearly upset. Her face contorted, and her eyes flashed as she raised a palm to the onlookers. The anger abruptly switched to fear, and her yelling stopped. Arms over her head and sobbing, the young woman stumbled back, cringing against the kitchen sink. A stunned look then crossed her face as she collapsed, arms raised in an awkward defense while pans rained upon her, crashing on her head as if she were being beaten.

For one endless moment, the scene was frozen and everything was still as the vision faded, leaving nothing but debris on the floor. The tightness in Ella's chest made it hard for her to catch her breath, and her words sounded raspy as she whispered, "Please tell me I'm not the only person who saw that."

"You're not the only person who saw that," Meg said quietly. "If I ever for a single moment doubted you, I apologize. What the hell was that?"

"That was Hattie," Katie answered.

"Are you sure?" Ella asked.

"Yes." This time both Katie and Roland answered.

"Lorraine has a picture of Hattie," Katie said. "That was her."

"I agree," Roland said before lapsing into silence.

The four of them stood, shivering in the kitchen, trying to process the vision that had appeared before them. The temperature was freezing, but Ella wondered if that was the only thing making her tremble.

"It feels like I'm cold on the inside, too," Ella complained.

"Now what do we do? I don't know about the rest of you, but I don't think I'm going to get much sleep tonight." Meg spoke softly, a slight tremor in her voice. She turned to Ella. "What on earth has been going on here, anyway? Have you been playing with Ouija boards or something? Why is this ghost haunting you?"

Ella sighed. "Haven't you been listening? I think she's been haunting everyone who's lived here for almost a decade. Like I said before, she disappeared in 1960, and I suspect she has something to tell us about what happened to her."

But what the hell is she trying to say? The chirping of crickets outside combined with the ticking of the kitchen clock; the juxtaposition of normalcy blending with the supernatural made Ella dizzy.

Roland ran his fingers through his hair and took a deep breath. "First things first. Let's clean the kitchen, then we can figure out what's next."

Working together in silence, they cleared the kitchen, making sure to wash and dry all the pans before putting them away. Trooping back into the living room, everyone sprawled in various states on the furniture to debate their next move.

"Here's the first question," Roland began. "Was the experience tonight like the other experiences?"

Ella thought for a moment before answering. "Sort of, but not really," she finally said. "The image of the woman was more clear, and tonight she seemed to be talking, or yelling at someone. I've never seen her do that before. The fear on her face was new, too."

Katie nodded. "Yes, it looked to me like she was having an argument with someone before she tried to defend herself."

"Right," Ella said. "That's all new to me. The other times I've seen her, she was standing there looking really upset. The pans in the air was the same—except there weren't as many as there have been in the past. And nothing got broken tonight."

"This is some pretty freaky stuff, here, people. I mean, we saw what we think is a ghost, and we're all sitting around discussing it like it's some sort of classroom experience." Meg shook her head. "I don't know about the rest of you, but I'm pretty creeped out."

Katie agreed. "Me, too, but I'm not going to let this chase me away. We're in this together, right? And I don't think that the ghost—or whatever you want to call her—is going to hurt us. It's just rather... odd," Katie finished haltingly, looking at the others to see if they agreed.

Roland nodded. "It is odd, that's exactly the word for it. I think we'll have to step back from this thing if we're ever going to figure it out. Let's make a huge assumption here. Let's assume, for a moment, that what we're seeing is what we refer to as a real haunting."

"As opposed to an imprint, a repeating image stuck in time," Meg added. When everyone looked at her in surprise, she answered indignantly, "Hey, I know my ghost stuff. I've read the books."

"What books?" Ella asked in exasperation. "I've been trying to find ghost information for days, and all I can find are either weirdos who go to houses with recording devices or New Age quacks who claim to channel the words of the dead. What books do you have?"

"I have a bunch of books on the subject at home. I'll send you some when I get back."

"Fat lot of good that's gonna do me," Ella grumbled. She was starting to feel unaccountably annoyed. She was trying to deal with the ghost of a woman who had disappeared for some unknown reason, and she'd bet anything that her disappearance was related to her race. What kind of a world was this where people were judged by the color of their skin instead of who they really were? Sometimes there was no getting around it: people were mean.

"Let's get back to the subject," Roland interrupted her thoughts. "Since we're in agreement that this particular ghost has something to tell us, we should proceed as planned tomorrow." He turned to Meg. "We agreed that we needed to do research and get as much of the story of this spirit as we could. Maybe you could help Ella."

"That's a great idea," Meg said. "Point me in the right direction, and I'll be happy to help clean this house up."

"I'm glad you don't think we're all crazy." Katie leaned forward, speaking directly to Meg.

Meg looked at her in amazement. "How could I possibly think you're crazy? I saw the same thing, remember? If you're crazy, then it must be something in the air because I am, too." Meg hesitated for a moment, looking at Ella. "I'm sorry I doubted your story and asked so many questions. I should have listened to you."

"No, I think it's good that you asked questions," Roland interjected.

"You do? Ten minutes ago, we were in the living room arguing about this whole thing."

"Yeah, but ten minutes ago we didn't know what we do now. It's important to ask questions; otherwise, you become passive. When you start to accept what everyone tells you as reality, that means you're open to lies and deceit."

"Glad to know you're such an optimist about human nature," Ella said wryly. "Must be the philosopher in you." She didn't mention that he'd echoed her earlier thoughts about the dismal state of humanity.

He nodded. "Where would we be if philosophers through the ages didn't question what came before them? As wonderful as the historical philosophies are, we have to look at truth in a substantive—"

"I know I'm interrupting, but there's one thing I'd really like to say." Meg was adamant.

"What is it?" Ella valued her friend's advice and was eager to hear her thoughts. After her initial shock at seeing Roland grappling with a stranger in her living room, she found herself full of gratitude for having her close friend so near during such a bizarre time.

"I think that whatever research or planning we need to do has to get finished tomorrow. In fact, I forgot to mention earlier how lucky I am to be here right now."

"Lucky? Well, we certainly are lucky to have you, that's for sure," Ella said.

"El, honey, I barely made it here. I think I got the last plane out. Everyone else is going the other way. We need to hurry the heck up since we don't have much time."

There was a brief silence as everyone looked at each other, realizing what Meg was trying to say.

"We need to get our act together," Meg continued. "That hurricane barreling up the coast is moving fast, and it's scheduled to hit Paterson anytime now."

Chapter Thirty-Nine

"**ACTUALLY, IT'S NOT SCHEDULED TO** make landfall until tomorrow night sometime," Roland corrected her.

"Meg's right," Ella said. "It's not like this is some little thunderstorm headed our way. Besides, I have a feeling that the storm is actually going to help us."

"Has the heat down here melted your brain? How can a storm help us?" Meg said.

"Hattie disappeared in 1960 during Hurricane Donna," Katie explained. "I think Ella is seeing a similarity here. First, we need to get some sleep. I don't know about ya'll, but that beer made me drowsy." Katie started up the stairs, then turned back to Meg. "Meg, it was nice meeting you. I look forward to seeing more of you after we're well rested. Perhaps we can find a way to give you a more proper Southern welcome." Smiling, she turned and went up the stairs.

Roland agreed. "Katie's right. I'm sorry I jumped on you. I didn't mean to hurt you, but I thought you were trying to hurt Ella."

Meg laughed. "I totally understand. I would have done the same thing to me if it was me." She shook her head. "That didn't make much sense, but you know what I meant, right?" Roland smiled at her and nodded.

"Katie's right, though," Meg continued. "It's been a really long day, and if I'm going to help my friend catch a ghost, I need sleep."

"You can stay upstairs with me," Ella told her. "We'll leave Roland as the downstairs guard. He seems to be doing a fairly good job." After making their final 'goodnights,' Ella and Meg went upstairs, followed by Daisy, while Roland returned to his sleeping bag in the back room.

Once in Ella's bedroom, Meg asked, "Seriously, are you okay? This seems so... weird," she finished awkwardly.

"I know. It is weird. But you saw what we saw in the kitchen. This has been going on pretty much since I moved in. What do you think?"

Meg took a deep breath. "I don't know. Now that I'm thinking about it, I can't help but wonder if we were having some sort of collective hallucination. Is it possible that the suggestion of ghosts caused us all to see one?"

Ella snorted. "No. Come on, Meg, you saw this with your own eyes. How much more proof do you need?"

Meg sighed. "Maybe I'm tired. Maybe this is some elaborate hoax someone is playing on you. Maybe it's the dirty T-shirt spray painter."

Ella shook her head. "I know that's what Kevin thinks, too." She was almost disappointed in her friend's reaction, but it was late and nobody was thinking clearly. "Whatever it is, we're not going to figure it out by standing here talking about it. Let's get some sleep."

Despite the evening's warmth drifting in from the open window, Ella settled herself under the sheet. Looking around her bedroom, she had that slightly off-balance feeling again. Everything looked normal, but she knew unseen forces were at work. Meg startled her out of her reverie.

"Who's Kevin?"

"A police officer who came to the house when I called 911 on the ghost."

"And?"

Ella laughed at Meg's tone. "Yes, he's cute. *Seriously* cute. He came over later that night and changed the locks on the doors. He's supposed to call me so we can make plans for a real date."

"Well, hallelujah! I'm so glad you finally met someone you're interested in. When do I get to meet him?"

"Not until after our first date." There was no way Ella was going to subject Kevin to Meg's scrutiny, no matter how much she loved her friend. It would be almost as bad as introducing him to her sister Lisa before their first date. A girl had to make sure her relationship was stable with a man before exposing him to certain elements in her life.

"Are you going to have sex with him?"

Ella pretended to be shocked. "Meg, how can you think of such a thing? Of course not!"

"Really?"

To her own dismay, Ella blushed. *Damn hormones; always ready when you don't want them around.* "Really."

"But you want to, I know you want to."

"Just because I want to do something doesn't mean I'll do it. Yes, I'm attracted to him. Yes, he seems like a nice guy. I'd like to take it slow. Besides, what do you think he's going to say when he finds out about all this? He's a police officer, for God's sake—not a wizard or ghost hunter. He might dismiss me as a lunatic and decide he wants nothing to do with me."

"Then you're better off without him." Meg's loyalty was endearing. "Oh, God, have you told Lisa anything?"

Ella was incredulous. "Are you kidding? She's hard enough to deal with on a normal basis; there's no way I'm going to talk to her about my house being haunted. Can you imagine what she'd say?"

Laughing, Meg imitated Ella's sister in a nasal tone. "I knew it, Ella! I knew you'd end up in a haunted house. Oh, how could you? You've ruined our reputation!"

Ella joined in the laughter, then sobered and said, "Ask me about her again tomorrow. I'm seriously tired, but there are some updates I've got to tell you."

After Meg changed into a pair of red pajamas, she climbed into the other side of Ella's bed. Daisy jumped up and managed to wiggle her way into the middle of the bed between the two women. Ella and Meg giggled at the expression on the dog's face, which seemed to say "Don't leave me alone."

"I guess if Daisy believes in ghosts, I do, too," Meg mumbled before drifting off to sleep.

"Don't worry. Stick around for another day or so, and you won't have any doubts at all."

***

The dream came quickly because it was time for the story to be told. Ella recognized the kitchen from 1960 and felt a ripple of unease as Hattie stood stiffly in the middle of the room. Something was very wrong. "No, sir, I did not engage in those types of activities." Her voice was small and soft and laced with fear.

"Don't believe her—she's got a gun!" The cry came from a middle aged black man standing behind the others, sneering at a young, uncertain Hattie.

Hattie looked at him in despair. "Uncle Samuel, why you tellin' them that? I don't have a gun... where would I get such a thing?"

The others in the room formed a semi-circle around Hattie. The man's voice, raised in anger, accused, "You did! Admit it—you'se doin' exactly what I done tol' you not to go an do! I got nothin' to say 'bout this, 'cept you'se gonna get what you deserve."

The others drew their Smith & Wessons on Hattie. "Ma'am, we don't want anyone to get hurt here. Just admit what happened, hand us your weapon, and you can be on your way. Come on, now, we can't have this sort of thing going on in our town. You've broken the law, and we don't take too kindly to that."

"Leave her alone! I've lived in this town my whole life, and this is my house, and I'm telling you she did nothing wrong... just leave her be." The voice coming from the side of the kitchen cracked with futility at the end of the sentence.

"Why don't you go on in the other room, Mr. Bartok? We'll take care of business in here."

"She's gettin' what she deserves, bringin' this into my house when I done given her a place to stay an' all." Hattie's uncle glared. "I'm lettin' you live in my home, girl, and this is how you repay me?"

"But I'm not hurting anyone," Hattie cried.

"No, I won't leave. She's not going to hurt anyone..."Mr. Bartok yelled before breaking into sobs.

"I'm tellin' you, she's got a gun—and she ain't afraid to use it."

Even in dreams we cry, Ella thought, numb by helplessness to stop history. Mr. Bartok reached in desperation to wrest the gun away from one of the intruders, struggling with the man as he aimed at Hattie. As shots rang out, Hattie's lover ran to her side, powerless to stop the life from bleeding out of her. One of the men in blue laid a hand on Mr. Bartok's shoulder while the others watched, shaking their heads as if they were witnessing a man who simply did not understand the realities of life.

"C'mon, Bartok, we'll help you get this all cleaned up."

Chapter Forty

THE FOLLOWING DAY DAWNED HOT and clear. At seven a.m. it was already seventy-five degrees as Ella stood in her kitchen, yawning and measuring coffee to brew the first pot. Amidst all the drama from the night before, she'd forgotten to set the automatic timer. She stood at the counter, impatient for her first cup, staring out the window. Residual emotion of last night's dream lingered, a sadness she knew would stay with her for a very long time.

The house was silent. Lost in thoughts about spirits, she dumped flavored creamer into her mug and poured the first cup of coffee, unable to wait for the pot to finish brewing.

"C'mon, Daisy," she called softly, opening the back door to let them both outside. Standing on the deck, she cradled the coffee mug and gazed out at her back yard. The mosquitoes weren't out yet, which was a relief. The morning sun was not yet blazing, but it was only a matter of time before the outside temperature climbed into at least the nineties for the day.

Ella couldn't stop the thoughts of her mother. When she had been alive, Ella talked to her almost every day and visited her parents at least once a week. That routine had been a part of Ella's life for years, and although she'd visited and talked with her father just as much—if not more—since her mother's death, it wasn't always the same. "Why hasn't my mother's ghost visited me? Why do I get some stranger, someone who died before I was even born?"

The image of her yard swam before her as Ella's eyes filled with tears. She shook her head, vowing not to cry; it was fine to let go and let her grief flow unchecked when she was alone, but she didn't want her friends to find her crying. They would ask for explanations, and somehow she didn't feel like telling them. *People must be tired of hearing about my grief.*

She was frustrated by her sadness. After all, this was a parent, this was supposed to happen. People lost spouses or children all the time, which was a much bigger kind of heartache.

A gentle breeze stirred, caressing Ella's face and bringing with it a new scent. Ella lifted her head, sniffing the air. This was a scent she knew well: the smell of hairspray and cigarettes.

"Mom?" she asked softly. Ella wondered for a moment if she was going crazy, but a soft wind wrapped around her again, and with it came that same smell; her mother's scent.

Remembering Roland's words from the night before, Ella was comforted. "Thanks, Mom," she whispered. This wasn't something she'd share with her friends; this was a private moment meant only for her. *She's here, and she's helping.*

"It's nice to know you're here," she whispered again.

The sound of the back door opening broke her attention. It was Roland, carrying his own cup of coffee.

"Nice morning," he said, watching her from the doorway. "Am I interrupting?"

Ella shook her head, wondering if Roland knew that she'd been talking to her mother. There was no way he could have known, but she couldn't shake the feeling that he did.

"Come out and join me before the mosquitoes get here," she told Roland. "I'm having my first cup of coffee to try to wake up a little."

Roland joined her at the deck railing, looking at the back yard and the marsh beyond. "Did you sleep okay for the rest of the night?" he asked. When she nodded, he added, "I really am sorry I grabbed your friend last night. I—"

Ella laughed softly. "Don't worry about it. We weren't expecting her, so of course you thought someone was breaking in. It's not a big deal for her or me, and we're grateful you were downstairs guarding us." Ella hesitated for a moment. "How did you sleep last night? Was everything all right back there?"

Roland waited a few beats before answering. "It was fine. I see what you mean, though. There's something uncomfortable about that room; maybe it's the proximity to the kitchen. With so much paranormal activity going on in the kitchen, it might permeate that part of the house." He grinned at her. "Or maybe I had trouble sleeping because I was wondering if anyone else was going to show up."

Ella smiled, then Katie and Meg came outside with coffee of their own. "I started a new pot of coffee brewing," Katie told them. "I have a feeling we'll all need more caffeine today."

"She's right," Meg said, turning to Ella. "You mentioned something about research to be done today. What's our assignment?"

Katie interrupted. "Before we talk about all that, I want to say that I've asked Ella and Daisy to come to my house for the storm, Meg, and I hope that you join us. This isn't exactly the easiest town to be in during a hurricane. We tend to get a lot of flooding around here."

Meg nodded. "Sounds like a good idea to me. I'd planned to stay about a week anyway, so at least I'll be here to help with any clean-up efforts."

"Last night, I was thinking about what we had for emergency supplies," Katie continued. "And, Meg, I'm not saying this because of you, but I don't think we have enough. We should probably try to get more food, and definitely more drinking water. When I go home this morning, I'll fill the bathtub and some containers with water for flushing the toilet. We don't know how hard this storm will hit us, but I'd say it's safe to assume we'll lose power."

"She's right," Roland said. "Ella, why don't you and Meg get more supplies while Katie visits the nursing home like she planned? In the meantime, I'll check out other stuff."

Great, another trip to grocery-store-hell.

Meg stared at Roland, eyebrows raised. "What other stuff?"

Roland stared back. "It occurred to me that there might be one thing we missed, and I'm going to check it out."

"Could you be a little more mysterious?" Meg asked.

"Sorry." Roland said. "You're right, I'm not trying to… it's about Hattie's family. I don't think she had much family around here, but I wanted to check on them. Does that sound good to everyone?"

"Sounds good to me," Ella said. "In fact, I have a feeling we need to take care of this quickly. The fact that our otherworldly resident has appeared to all of us at the same time doesn't make me comfortable. In fact," she continued, "she probably wants something. She's become very persistent."

"I think Ella's right," Roland told them. "Meg, what do you think?"

"Whatever you need, I'm here to help. You'll probably have lots of storm damage." Clearly, Meg still wasn't convinced they were dealing with a ghost, despite what she'd seen the previous night.

It would be interesting to see what happened if Meg was alone in the house and Hattie appeared. Would her 'mass hallucination' theory fly right out the window? Ella was willing to bet it would.

Thoughts of the previous night's dream tugged at Ella, but she wasn't ready to discuss this last dream with anyone.

Even if she had an idea of what happened to Hattie, it wasn't the right time to broach the subject with the others. What she witnessed was too personal, too raw. *I'll tell them when it's time.*

Finishing their coffee, everyone grabbed a breakfast pastry before getting dressed for the day. Katie dressed in white Capri pants with a short sleeved navy blue top, while Roland wore jeans. Meg threw on a pair of shorts and a tank top, and Ella came back downstairs dressed in shorts and a T-shirt that read, '*Due to budget cuts, the light at the end of the tunnel has been shut off.*'

"Appropriate," Meg commented. "I would expect nothing less."

Holding the door open, Ella smiled at her. "Are you ready to brave the stores with me, my friend?"

Meg snorted. "I'll bet it's just as bad as when a snow storm hits."

"Worse," Ella told her. "But it must be done. Roland, can you and Katie lock up behind you?"

"No problem," came the muffled answer from the kitchen. Ella smiled and called out, "Pack up some food to take with you. Meg and I are getting more anyway." She loved that Roland had a healthy appetite since feeding people was one of her favorite things to do.

Daisy will guard the house. The last thing Ella heard was a short whine, followed by the thump of paws on the stairs as Daisy ran to the second floor. She didn't want to think about why the dog may have run upstairs to hide.

Chapter Forty-One

IT TOOK MUCH LONGER THAN anyone expected to complete the day's errands. When Meg and Ella finally returned to the house, it was almost five o'clock. The skies had grown progressively darker during the day, and strong winds blew the rain sideways as they rushed inside with their packages.

"It started off as such a nice, sunny day," Meg commented while shaking the water off her clothes as she stood on the front porch. As Ella fumbled with the lock, she said over her shoulder, "We should have realized how quickly this storm was coming when we were having lunch. The skies opened up like someone was dumping buckets of water on us."

"I cannot believe how crowded the stores were. C'mon, let's get inside so I can go upstairs and dry my hair before it's totally ruined and we have no power. Do you think the others got anything done?"

Opening the front door, Ella nodded. "I'm sure they did. Those two strike me as extremely efficient."

"Tell me again why they aren't dating each other?"

"Refusal to see what's right in front of them," Ella said as they stepped into the living room. "Let's put this stuff away, then we can pack the cooler and throw a few clothes in a suitcase to take with us."

Meg smiled. "I didn't unpack my suitcase last night, so I can just grab it and go." Following Ella into the kitchen, she asked, "So, what did you want to tell me about your evil sister? Is she offering you any poison apples?"

"Worse," Ella answered. "She's moving here."

"You have *got* to be kidding me."

"Nope. Dan got laid off from his job, but he happened to find a new job here—of all places."

Meg let out a short laugh that sounded more like a bark. "That's a load of you-know-what. There is no way he 'happened' to find a job in this part of Virginia; she can't stand that you're getting on with your life without her. Jeez, I can't believe the nerve of that woman. I hope she's not planning on staying with you while they house hunt?"

Ella stopped and looked at her friend. "Actually, that might not be such a bad idea. If we're not successful in getting rid of our resident ghost, I'm sure Lisa's presence will scare her off."

Their laughter was interrupted by a knock at the front door, followed by Roland's voice from the living room. "It's me, don't attack!"

Meg scowled. "Maybe I should, just to pay him back for last night."

"Be nice," Ella said quietly. "He's helping us, remember?"

Roland entered the kitchen, carrying a backpack. "This storm is moving quickly. Did you get everything you need?" When Ella nodded, he said, "Good. I brought some materials, too. I've got my smudge stick, crystals, and salt, and I grabbed a bible in case we need it." He looked out the window, worried. "It's getting worse out there. I thought we'd have more time, but if we stay too much longer we won't be going anywhere."

Ella's anxiety rose. She had no control over when Hattie appeared or didn't appear, and if they had to leave because of the storm they might not be able to carry out their plan. She'd been assuming this situation would be taken care of before the storm hit.

"Do you think there's a real hurry?" Meg asked.

"Didn't you look around on the way home, or did you drive with your eyes closed? The wind is picking up speed, branches are falling all over the place, and you can hardly see a thing the way the rain is coming down. Besides that, there's a tornado watch out now, too. You definitely don't want to be in a car for that."

"Hey, ya'll!" Katie's voice carried to the kitchen, and Ella noted the look of relief that crossed Roland's face when he heard her.

"We're in here," Ella called out. Katie walked into the kitchen, looking as if she'd just climbed out of a pool. "What happened to you?" Ella asked.

Katie sighed. "This has got to be one of the worst days I've had in a long time."

"Oh, God, sit down," Ella told her, pulling out a chair. "Are you all right? I'll make you a cup of tea."

"I'll get you a towel," Roland said. He walked into the bathroom and returned with a large, fluffy towel, then handed it to Katie. Meanwhile,

Daisy danced around Katie, sniffing at her to make sure she was okay.

"Thank you," Katie sighed. After drying her arms and legs, she wrapped the towel around herself and sat. "Everything kind of went from bad to really bad." Turning to Ella she added, "A cup of tea would be perfect."

"Of course," Ella hurried to boil the water.

"Did you go to the nursing home?" Roland asked.

Katie closed her eyes, taking a moment to compose herself. "Yes. Everything started off fine. I've been there as a volunteer, so some of the people were happy to see me. They weren't busy like I expected; I guess places like that are always prepared for storms and emergencies." She drew in a deep breath. "Anyway, I went into the social area and sat around chatting with folks, saying hello. Then I asked for Mr. Bartok, and they told me he generally stays in his room, so I went upstairs. I found his room, and he was in bed, staring at the television, almost as if he wasn't really watching it. So I went in, introduced myself, and asked him how he was doing." She gratefully accepted the cup of tea that Ella put in front of her. "That was quick," she told Ella.

"So what happened next? Did he talk about this house?" Ella wasn't sure if she wanted to hear the answer or not. She already knew what happened, but there was no way around it; Mr. Bartok's story would be painful.

Katie shook her head. "I tried to steer the conversation that way, but he got strange and kept talking about other things. He seemed nervous, but I wasn't sure if that was because he didn't recognize me. Then I finally decided I didn't have that much time left, so I jumped right in and asked him about Hattie."

"What did you say?" Ella asked.

"I said, 'Mr. Bartok, do you remember a woman who used to work in your home a long time ago? She was your housekeeper, and her name was Hattie. I was wondering what you could tell me about her.' That's when things got really bad." Katie's hands were shaking as she put the mug of tea back on the table.

"What do you mean?" Roland asked.

"As soon as I asked the question, he started yelling at me." Katie shivered. "It was truly awful. His face got red, and he screamed that some things were none of my business and who did I think I was and leave him alone... as you can imagine, the nurses came running because he was causing such a commotion. He tried to throw something at me, but it sort of fell on the floor when he tossed it. The nurses asked me to leave."

"Why do you think he yelled at you like that?" Meg said.

"I have no idea, but it was a very unpleasant experience. That man had no manners at all."

Ella stifled a laugh; she found it funny that Katie equated bad manners with yelling at people. It was a good thing Katie never had to sit through one of Ella's family dinners, where all her aunts, uncles and cousins screamed at each other from one end of the table to the other.

"Hey, Ella, good thing you never invited Katie to your house for a major family dinner," Meg said, smiling. Ella and Meg looked at each other and started laughing.

"Why?" Katie wanted to know.

"I'm sorry. I'm not laughing at you," Ella explained. "It's just that I grew up with everyone yelling in my house. They weren't angry; it's the way they talked to each other. Usually, you had to yell back just to be heard." She took a breath to stop herself from laughing anymore; this was not the time for humor. "Anyway, what happened after you left the nursing home? Why are you soaking wet?"

"I stopped to check in with my parents and make sure they didn't need anything," Katie continued. "After that, I went and had a late lunch. When I came out of the restaurant, someone drove by too fast through a puddle that ended up all over me. Then, with all that rain coming down..." She shook her head in disgust, exasperated.

Taking another sip of the tea in front of her, Katie added, "But I'm better now. I think we should go soon, though."

Again, Ella wondered what the point of all their preparation was if they left because of the storm. She tried to focus her attention back on Roland, who was talking.

"I agree. We don't want to wait too much longer. Let me quickly tell you about my visit to the historical society, then we can get out of here."

"They were there today?" Ella was incredulous.

"Today is a day that their genealogy library is supposed to be open, so yes, someone was there. Also, I think they wanted to make sure everything was up high or protected in case of flooding. I helped them stack boxes, so when I asked a bunch of questions the ladies didn't mind talking to me. They gave me some very interesting answers."

"Did they answer all your questions, or did they try to avoid them?" Ella asked.

"No, they answered everything. In fact, do you remember hearing that Hattie had an uncle that she lived with?" When Ella nodded, he continued. "Well, it seems that this uncle was not a very nice person. In fact, both of the ladies at the historical society remembered him well."

"Is he dead?" Meg asked.

Roland wrinkled his forehead. "We're not sure about that. The last anyone knew, he was serving time at the state penitentiary for murder."

Katie gasped. "I never heard about this."

"It gets worse," he continued. "It seems that this guy—his name was Samuel—was married. About ten years after Hattie's disappearance, he and his wife had a baby, a little boy."

"This can't be good," Ella muttered. She hated stories about cruelty to children or animals; the thought of those types of things happening made her nauseous.

"It's not a good story," Roland confirmed. "Samuel murdered his son by drowning him in the river. According to the ladies I spoke with today, Samuel admitted to doing this at his trial. He told the jury he didn't believe the child was his, and he couldn't abide the bastard boy in his house anymore."

"He actually used those words?" Katie whispered.

"Hard to believe, isn't it?" Roland said softly. "Especially since it was only a baby."

"What happened to the baby's mother?" Ella asked.

"Nobody knows. Samuel went off to prison, and she disappeared. I can't blame her, really; she probably wanted to get as far away from this place as possible. Can you imagine what it would have been like for her? First, Hattie disappears, then her husband murders their child. It must have been awful for that woman."

Some things were too horrible to conceive. Ella struggled again with the idea that people allowed such violence to shape their world.

"Did they say anything about Hattie or have any ideas about what happened to her?" Ella asked.

Roland shook his head. "No, but I have a feeling they knew something. They wanted to talk, but there was one point in the conversation when one woman sort of hesitated, as if she was going to tell me something, but then thought better of it."

"Do you think this means anything? Do you think maybe the uncle could have—"

A pounding at the door caused them all to jump. "Who on earth is at your door right before a hurricane?" Katie asked. "Do you have any more friends coming to visit?" Ella shrugged, then started toward the door.

"Wait, don't answer that." Roland put a hand on her shoulder. "Make sure you look to see who it is first. Judging from that pounding, I'm pretty sure it's not Alice."

As the four of them walked into the living room, the door burst open. Jeff

Bartok strode inside, anger evident in his every step. His face was furious as he stepped forward and pointed a finger at Ella. "You've gone too far this time. What the hell do you mean by barging into my father's home and getting him all riled up?" he demanded.

Ella took a step back. Daisy stood by her, a low growl starting in her throat. "She didn't do anything; I did," Katie said, folding her arms over her chest. "And I'm terribly sorry he got so upset. That wasn't my intention at all."

Turning to face Katie, Jeff snarled at her. "Oh, really? And what was your intention? Trying to get information from my father? He's an old man. Why can't people leave him alone? That's all he ever really wanted was to be left alone—but no, you had to play little Miss Nosey and get him all worked up, didn't you?"

"Listen, nobody meant to upset anyone. Why don't we sit down and talk about this?" Roland interjected in a calm voice. As she watched the scene before her, Ella's hands were shaking. She didn't think Jeff would harm them—but does anyone really know who has it in them to hurt others?

Silence built as Jeff stood before them, face reddening. "Well, it looks like you're gonna get what you want," he snapped, taking a step toward Ella.

Chapter Forty-Two

"**WHAT DO YOU MEAN BY** that?" Ella asked. At that moment, a low, moaning sound emanated from the kitchen. Ella closed her eyes. *Not now... not with Jeff here and a storm coming. I don't think he's supposed to be here.*

Everyone froze at the sound, uncertain of what to do. The moaning continued, gaining in intensity as Daisy started barking frantically in the direction of the kitchen. Ella glanced over at Jeff, whose face had gone completely white. "Are you okay?" she asked her landlord softly. For all she knew, this ghost was nothing new to him, but the look on his face suggested otherwise.

"What's that noise?" Jeff asked in a ragged whisper.

"We don't know," Meg answered. "But I think it's time we find out." Turning, she walked toward the kitchen, expecting the others to follow. They did, and when they all stepped into the kitchen, there was the ghostly figure, arms outstretched. For a moment, the silence in the room was deafening as the figure lost its transparency and solidified.

"Impossible." Jeff spoke to no one in particular.

Roland was the first to move to action. "Meg, hand me my backpack, quick!" As Meg grabbed it from the kitchen chair and handed it to him, Ella heard a thump behind her. Turning, she saw Jeff on the floor.

Roland swore under his breath, shoving his backpack at Ella. "Here, take this and get the stuff out of there. We have to work quickly."

"Is he okay?" Ella asked, worried.

"He'll be fine." Roland was terse. "He fainted, that's all. I'll drag him out to the couch in the living room so he doesn't wake up in here."

"Shouldn't someone stay with him?" Katie asked. She had to speak loudly, as the moaning rose in intensity.

"Don't worry. We'll deal with him later," Roland shouted.

Roland half-carried, half-dragged Jeff out to the living room, then hurried back into the kitchen. Ella cringed at the sound surrounding her; it was as if the noise came from all directions. With a cold breeze flowing through the kitchen, Roland's efforts to light the smudge stick were hindered. Frustrated, he called out to Katie. "Come stand over here, will you? I can't get this thing lit."

"She's trying to tell us something," Katie said, barely loud enough to be heard. Instead of helping Roland, she stepped forward and spoke directly to the figure before them. "What is it you want to tell us? Is there something we need to know?" She hesitated for a fraction of a moment before asking, "How did you die?"

The apparition looked up, seeming to hear Katie's question. Her lips formed a word that she repeated over and over, but no sound came out.

"I've got it! The smudge is lit!" Roland cried.

"Wait, we need to know what happened to her first," Katie said, looking at him. "Ella, help me out. Don't let him send her away yet."

Ella looked at the woman she knew as Hattie. She remembered her dreams, and her feeling that she'd missed knowing someone truly interesting. "I'm sorry we never got to meet," she said, trying to catch her breath as she spoke. "I'm sure we would have liked each other. I really like your friend, Lorraine." Hattie's face appeared to crumble at the mention of her old friend, tears welling in her eyes. Ella continued. "Hattie, I think you're here for a reason. I've been dreaming about you, you know." The smell of cedar and sage drifted through the kitchen, a pungent aroma that seeped into all the crevices of the room. As she grew in essence while Ella spoke, the image of Hattie began to change slightly, and a glow began to emanate from the figure.

Ella ignored the shaking that had started in her body. "Hattie, speak to us... tell us what happened... did someone kill you?"

Sinking to the ground, the figure of Hattie looked up and nodded.

Yes, she had been murdered.

"Did Mr. Bartok kill you?" Ella asked gently. Hattie's eyes grew wide as she shook her head wildly. "He wouldn't do that to you, would he?" Ella commented, almost to herself.

Katie spoke to the ghostly figure. "I think that leaves only one person, then. But where did he hide your body?"

Another long, low moan came from the ghost before them as Hattie shook her head from side to side. "I don't think she agrees with you, Katie," Ella commented. "Hattie, it was a group, wasn't it? They came in here to get you, right?" The figure before them nodded, resigned to the fact of her own death.

"It's time, Ella. She's got to begin her next existence now," Roland said, stepping in front of Ella. He gently placed three crystals on the ground before them and proceeded to wave his smudge stick.

"Wait," Ella called. "Who pulled the trigger?" Katie put her hand on Ella's arm in encouragement as Ella continued to ask questions. "Was it one bullet that killed you, or more? Do we need to know the names?"

Pans flew from the cabinet and rained down upon the ghost of Hattie. The apparition cowered, trying to cover her head from the onslaught of objects assailing her.

From behind her, Ella heard Meg begin to recite from the bible. "Ella, let her go...the Lord is my shepherd..." Inside the kitchen, a fierce wind blew, causing the lights to extinguish.

"Stop! I need to know if it happened like I saw in my dream!" Ella cried. "Hattie, I saw them come to arrest you for breaking the law, which I'm guessing was because you were involved with Mr. Bartok. He tried to stop them. It wasn't his fault; it was the police officer's gun that went off. Mr. Bartok tried to stop it from happening."

Hattie's eyes filled with tears, and a wave of grief washed over Ella, grief for the life that was lost, grief for the love that never had a chance to grow, and grief for people who couldn't see past skin color to understand the depths of a person's soul.

"Ella, she has to go home now; it's time. You're seeing the history in your dreams, and we know how it happened. Let her go." Turning to Hattie, Roland told her, "We'll get to the bottom of this, I promise. We'll figure out who did it." At that, Hattie lowered her arms and nodded once in acknowledgement. As the wind in the kitchen increased, pans lay scattered on the floor.

Roland walked through the room, sprinkling water around the edges and muttering phrases that were too low for anyone to hear.

"...and yea, though I walk through the Valley of Death, I shall fear no evil..." As Meg's uneven voice intoned the psalm, the wind inside the house began to die. Hattie looked up at the people before her and smiled. Lifting her hands, she slowly faded away until they could no longer see an apparition before them. All that remained was frigid air, and even that was quickly dissipating.

For a moment, there was only the roar of silence; everyone was too shaken to speak or move. Finally, Roland looked at Ella and asked, "Are you sure?"

Nodding, Ella answered. "I saw it last night. I wasn't ready to talk about it, but I had another dream. There were four of them, police, and I think one of them was her awful uncle. The uncle knew what would happen, but he was so mean he may have even hoped for it to happen. He kept telling the police she had a gun, but she didn't. I guess they got nervous because they aimed their guns at her. Mr. Bartok tried to take the gun away from someone, but it went off. The thing is, since they were all armed, I'm not exactly sure who fired the shot. Maybe it was one, maybe more... I don't know. They were supposed to uphold the law, and look what they did."

Meg sounded angry. "They made their own laws around here."

The four of them stood silent for a moment, absorbing the information. After a full minute, Ella inhaled sharply. "Listen...do you hear that?"

In the distance, the strains of music, the ending to a song that had become so familiar.

"*I'll fly away, oh glory, I'll fly away...to a land where joy shall never end, I'll fly away...*"

"She's gone home," Katie said softly. "Thank God, she's finally gone home."

Chapter Forty-Three

"ELLA! ARE YOU OKAY IN there?" Kevin's voice called from the front of the house.

"We're in the kitchen," Ella called.

Out of breath, Kevin appeared in the doorway. "What happened here? Who's that guy on the couch? Is Jeff Bartok here?"

Everyone stood silent for a moment, wondering how to explain the situation. Finally, Ella asked, "What made you come out here?"

With a frown, Kevin explained that he'd heard on the radio that there had been a problem at The Shack. "When I heard the dispatcher say that Jeff Bartok was disturbing the peace, I remembered he was your landlord. I figured with all the trouble you've been having I'd better get over here."

"Well, you were right; he's here. He's the one on the couch," Meg told him. "I'm Meg, Ella's friend."

"Does he need medical attention?"

"Doesn't look like it," Meg said wryly. "Look who's come back to life."

Jeff was standing awkwardly in the living room as if he were afraid to join them in the kitchen. She realized he was probably terrified by what he'd seen in the kitchen, and she felt sorry for him—but mad at the same time. He didn't have to come busting into the house the way he had, screaming at Katie and acting all tough.

Still, he was only human. "Are you okay?" Ella asked.

"You had a rough time of it today, didn't you?" Kevin said as he walked toward him in the living room. "What brings you out here?"

Jeff shook his head as if trying to clear it. "I'm sorry for the way I burst in here. It's just… she was real, wasn't she? She was here when I came in… I saw her."

"Do you know what day it is?" Kevin asked.

Ella interrupted. "He's fine. We had a little bit of a scare here." She realized that the story was going to come out, but she felt strangely at peace talking about what had happened. She wouldn't be able to date someone who didn't believe her, regardless of how outrageous the story. If Kevin decided he wanted nothing to do with her because of some little old ghost, so be it.

Kevin looked at everyone standing awkwardly in the room. "Had a visit from the ghost, did you?"

This day keeps getting stranger and stranger.

"No matter what happened here, you all need to leave now. It's time to get to higher ground, so to speak. Ella, do you need a ride to your friend's house?"

Mute, Ella shook her head. Kevin was acting the big, strong and sexy cop, and he was definitely in charge. She liked that side of him very much—the big, strong, sexy part.

"Then let's get out of this house. Grab your bags and lock up; you are officially out of time. It's bad enough out there now, and it's only going to get worse."

***

"What happened down there that's got you in such a weird mood?"

"Nothing." Ella knew that she'd never be able to tell Lisa about Hattie, it was something she might not tell most people. Maybe this was why there were so many ineffectual examples of ghosts out there; maybe nobody was able to describe an encounter with the dead.

"Did you ever feel like Mom was with you after she died? Did you ever see her in dreams, or…" Ella faltered for a moment, then determined that this was something that had to be talked about. "Did you ever have a vision of her?"

Lisa's sadness carried through the phone. "No. Not ever. Not once. You?"

"No."

"Really?" Lisa's surprise was evident. "Are you sure?"

"Of course, I'm sure. This isn't something that you sort of remember; it either happened or it didn't."

"Wow." Lisa's voice was soft, almost a whisper. "I figured that you had dreams or visits or something from her."

"Why would you think that?" Ella sounded sharper than she intended.

"Remember when we were younger and Mom's nickname for you was 'sort-of-psychic'? You know, because of all the stuff that you sometimes seemed to know or see?"

"Guessing where Dad left his watch is way different than seeing Mom's ghost," Ella retorted. But Ella did remember being a child and knowing things or having dreams that eventually came true. It was part of who she was, then and apparently now. That piece of her that was 'sort-of-psychic' was a part of herself that she tried to keep buried away like an unwanted crazy cousin, but Ella eventually realized there were some things you couldn't change about yourself.

"It was more than that, and you know it. Remember when we were little and you used to have dreams about the neighborhood? You were able to tell Mom and Dad what the streets used to look like back in the fifties, right down to the color of the houses. That used to scare me. I always assumed that you knew and saw things that you'd stopped telling us about, mostly because I gave you such a hard time about it." The last comment was said almost sheepishly.

"I would have given me a hard time about it, too, if I were you," Ella admitted. "I haven't ever seen Mom, but maybe I never really wanted to. Sometimes it seems like I can catch a faint sense of her, like maybe in the wind when I smell hairspray—"

"Or cigarettes," Lisa interrupted, laughing through what sounded suspiciously like tears.

"I miss her, and I feel like I should be able to see her or talk to her or something." But her truth was that she couldn't always control what she knew or saw any more than she could control anything else in the world. Some things happened just because.

There was a hesitation on the phone. "I think I was jealous because I figured you were having these amazing conversations with her, and I was left out of the whole thing. You know, since you're slightly psychic or something. I was even kind of mad at you about that for a while."

"Hmmm. That explains a few things."

"What do you mean?"

"Lisa, we were both affected in different ways by what happened in our family. I guess it's only natural, and I'm just figuring out that it's okay to grieve for a parent, even though it feels like I have no right to do it." Sharing this with her sister was a big deal, and Ella knew that. She also knew it was time for them to move on in their relationship and get beyond the power differential and juvenile bickering that occurred on a regular basis.

"Of course, you have a right to your grief. What made you think you didn't?"

"It doesn't matter now. What matters is there's a whole heck of a lot of things I've figured out that I didn't know."

"And why is that at all relevant? There's things I don't know either, but if I need to know I'll figure it out, or someone like Dan will help me."

Ella struggled to put her feelings into words. "I don't mean that kind of not knowing. I mean the bigger kind of not knowing... what I don't know is the big picture, why things happen the way they do and what the point is. I don't know the purpose or the meaning to it all, and I don't know where we'll end up. I do know, though, that I don't need to know everything, but I do need to at least trust that things are what they're supposed to be, and if I do my best to be kind in all ways then at least I'm somehow making a difference."

"Wow, what a speech, Pollyanna. I didn't know you had it in you."

Ella grinned. Some things with her sister would never change, and maybe that was all right, too. It would make for an interesting world, especially since Lisa and her family were due to arrive in Virginia within the next month—permanently. Now all they had to do was work on getting their father to move south, which shouldn't be too difficult; after all, his two favorite girls were going to be there.

Ella checked the time on the wall clock. "I've got to go. I'll talk to you later."

"What's the hurry?"

Ella smiled. "I've got a date."

***

Kevin looked exceptionally handsome standing on her doorstep with a bouquet of flowers in hand. It was only when Ella looked carefully at his eyes that she could see the weariness. The storm, digging up Hattie's body, and the story of her murder had taken a toll, and Ella could see faint lines of stress around his eyes. Stepping inside, he hesitated only slightly before leaning in and placing a soft kiss on Ella's mouth. Heart hammering, she looked up at him, briefly wondering if they'd make it through dinner without her doing something stupid like climbing on top of him or dragging him back to her house.

He smiled at her with warmth in his eyes. "Hey. Are you ready to eat?"

"I'm ready when you are."

Ella had wondered what Kevin's feelings would be about this situation. He'd taken the news about a ghost rather well; then again, most of his co-workers had confirmed that there was, in fact, a ghost in the house and had been for years. But it was one thing to accept that a house was haunted; it was an entirely different thing to come to terms with the reality that it was the alleged good guys that had made it haunted, the guys who were supposed to uphold the law in the first place. Ella knew from her conversations with Kevin that he had a very clear sense of right, wrong, and justice, and this situation was bound to be bothering him.

Opening the door for her, she climbed into his spotless Tahoe. "Wow. You could practically live in here."

He laughed. "It's great for camping. Especially when I don't feel like staying in a tent during a thunderstorm."

"Are you okay with us going out tonight? We can do this some other night." Not really, but Ella wanted at least to appear somewhat supportive.

"I can't think of anything else I'd rather be doing." His answering smile made her insides quiver, and it also made her glad she'd worn her matching underwear that night. "I thought we might try the new Thai restaurant that opened in Williamsburg. What do you think?"

Since she loved Thai food, it sounded like a great idea to Ella. Conversation between them was playful during the car ride as they traded jokes and laughter. Once they were seated in the restaurant, Kevin looked over the top of the menu at her. "Thank you."

Ella wasn't sure she knew what to say. She understood why he was thanking her, but it made her a little uncomfortable. "I needed some relief from the past week, too. It seems like I've been spending a lot of time having serious life and death conversations."

"Is Jeff still having a hard time with all of this?"

Ella nodded. Instead of being relieved that his house was no longer haunted, Jeff Bartok was feeling a huge amount of guilt about the situation. "I told him yesterday that none of this was his fault; he was a kid when it happened. He insists he should have spoken up sooner, though."

"Hard to do when your old man is calling the shots," Kevin answered.

"I guess Mr. Bartok never really got over all this. I think he mentally crumbled from the strain of it all."

"I've seen that happen before. Some people can handle an amazing amount of crap that life throws at them, and others go a little crazy from it all. He probably felt a ton of guilt at the whole situation, and I'm sure it didn't help that his first wife abandoned him."

Ella studied the menu, uncertain where to go with the conversation. She didn't blame Mr. Bartok for his actions; she might have done the same thing.

"I hear they brought the forensics team to recover Hattie's body."

Ella nodded. She had been in the house while they worked, but she had witnessed the body bag being removed from the shed. "I don't think that shed ever got used after he buried her under there."

Kevin put his menu down. "I don't understand that. He didn't shoot her, so why would he go and bury her body like that? Why didn't anyone report it?"

Ella was incredulous. "Kevin, the police shot her. What was he going to do? They already knew what happened, and it was obvious they didn't care."

He shook his head. "I can't believe there wasn't someone he could go to and demand justice. It's not possible that everyone on the police force felt the same way."

Ella reached across the table and took his hand. "This isn't a reflection on the police, Kevin. This is a reflection on a small town and friends who let their prejudices get in the way of what they knew was right. Those guys who came to his house that day were people he'd known his whole life. How do you think he felt? How was he supposed to know who he could trust? I would have done the same thing."

Kevin looked at her in surprise. "Why would you do a thing like that?"

"Maybe because I wouldn't want to go to jail." It seemed to Ella that Mr. Bartok had done the only thing he could. Why risk going to the police when you don't know what they would do? For all he knew, they'd pin the murder on him and he'd have been thrown in jail. He had a young son to consider, and he couldn't risk ruining the boy's life, too.

Kevin ran his hands through his hair. "It's like anywhere else, I guess; there's good cops, bad cops, you name it. I just have to do my job and hope for the best."

Ella squeezed his hand. "I have an idea. Why don't we agree not to discuss the Bartoks or ghosts or police for the entire night? Let's just get to know each other a little bit." Her insides fluttered as she imagined a host of ways that they could get to know each other. When he smiled at her, she knew he was thinking the same thoughts.

"Sounds good to me."

Chapter Forty-Four

THE INSISTENCE OF THE ALARM clock had always bothered Ella. Why, when she was warm and safe and curled in bed with a hunky man, did she have to get up? Even Daisy was curled up asleep at the end of the bed.

"Time to go to school, Missy," Kevin laughed, brushing a curl of hair off Ella's forehead.

"I don't want to get up." She pulled the blanket over her head.

"But today's an extra special day."

Crap. Kevin was right. Today was moving day. Double crap. In less than eight hours, her sister would be showing up, family in tow. Ella had a feeling her life was going to change. Again.

*What we have here is a failure to communicate...*Ella smiled as she always did when she heard Kevin's cell phone. She was inordinately amused that a police officer would choose that as his ring tone.

The mattress moved as he climbed out of bed, leaving Ella alone with her thoughts. She supposed it was okay that Lisa was moving south—at least it would be for Ella. She wasn't so sure about the Southerners, though; just wait until the cable guy showed up at her house. Ella had spent the past couple of weeks preparing Kevin for the onslaught of her family. It was hard to describe Lisa, but she'd given it her best shot. It was even more difficult to describe Lisa's relationship with her husband.

"So, let me get this straight," Kevin had asked the night before. "Her husband went out and got a job in another state without her knowing about it?"

"Yep."

"Forgive me for saying this, but that seems like an awfully ballsy move for him to pull on what you've basically described as a pit bull of a woman."

Ella struggled to explain the workings of someone else's marriage. "He wanted to make her happy—that's all he ever wants—and he figured keeping her close to me was the way to do it. Obviously, it worked, because they're on their way."

Kevin's voice interrupted her thoughts. "Ella, we have to talk."

She turned to face him as he sat on the bed next to her. He put his hand on her face, hesitating for a moment. "It's over."

She couldn't believe she heard him correctly. "What's over?"

"That was the chief on the phone. He wanted to let me know personally what had happened."

Was it possible? Did they discover who had shot Hattie? "Did they find the shooter?"

Momentary confusion crossed Kevin's face. "The shooter? Oh, no, they didn't. They'll probably never figure out who did that. I'm sure there are people in town who know, like Mr. Bartok, but they're not talking. And with no evidence or DNA, we've got nothing to go on. No, I'm talking about the guy who was threatening you."

"Threatening me?"

Jeff blew out a breath in exasperation. "I know you never took the spray painter seriously, but those were some nasty messages he left for you on the side of the house. They caught him early this morning."

Ella couldn't believe what she was hearing. How did they know it was the right person?

"He wasn't here, though. There haven't been any messages in a while. How do they know it's him?"

Kevin's face was stern. "There's no doubt about this. He broke into the college before dawn this morning and sprayed the words 'Yankee Whore' before security stopped him."

"In my classroom?" Ella was incredulous.

"Yeah, in your classroom."

"On my new whiteboard?"

"It's not so white anymore."

Ella felt a surge of anger. "I hope they can get that cleaned off."

"Don't you want to know who it was?" Kevin sounded almost amused.

Ella waved a hand in the air. "Dirty T-shirt guy, right? So, are they cleaning my room, or do I have to use a different classroom?"

"His name was Bobby. We've had our eye on him for a while, and I think he's the person you told me about that you had trouble with at the coffee shop."

"Yes, I know. It's the dirty T-shirt guy, like I said. He's not very smart, is he?"

Kevin laughed. "No, he doesn't seem like the brightest bulb in the chandelier. I'd have to say that breaking into a college to do what he did sure falls into the 'Stupid Criminal' category."

"So what happens now? Will he go to jail?"

Kevin sobered. "Probably. He'll be charged with a hate crime and sentenced accordingly. But the important thing is that now you can take out a restraining order against him to make sure he stays away from you."

Ella's mind was racing as she got out of bed. She had to change and get down to the college. Maybe they hadn't cleaned the words off yet. She might be able to use the spiteful message as part of the day's lecture, incorporating ideas of tolerance into the lesson.

As she scrambled to find clean clothes, Kevin's gaze followed her around the room. "It's never going to get boring, is it?" he asked.

She paused, considering his question. "I hope not."

Reaching out, he grasped her hand before he spoke. "I really like you, Ella."

Puzzled, she looked at him. "I like you, too."

He shook his head. "I want you to know, I'm in this for the everything."

She watched him with a question in her eyes. "Everything?"

A slow smile started on his face. "Everything. I'm in this for the happy ever after, and I think we can have that together."

Ella tilted her head slightly. "Does happy ever after mean that I do your laundry, cooking, cleaning, and take care of the kids while we both work?"

Kevin pulled her onto his lap. "Happy ever after means that we share everything, good and bad, lawn mowing and dishes, diapers and Happy Meals, ghosts and dreams."

When he put it like that, how could she refuse? Except for the part about the ghosts; that was one thing she could definitely live without.

"Sounds like a deal to me."

**Turn the page for an exciting preview of the next book
in the series...**

Revenge of the Past

A tale of love, revenge, and recovery...

Why is it so hard to listen when Hannah, the family ghost, issues a warning? Probably because she says things Katie doesn't want to hear, and she only shows up when there's trouble.

In 1861, Irish immigrant Hannah Donovan is unjustly accused of murdering her employer, Titus Foote. Hoping to leave memories of that awful time behind her, she flees Connecticut and migrates south, to Yorktown, Virginia.

After a century and a half Titus catches up to Hannah, seeking revenge. He still believes she killed him, and he vows to annihilate her descendants.

Cleve Farrington is the handsome new stranger in town, and it seems he has his eye set on Katie Hollister. But Katie has a secret, and it has nothing to do with the fact that she lives with the ghost of her great-great-great grandmother. Katie's secret is starting to unravel, and she finds that even her old friends Roland and Ella may not be able to help her in time.

As revelations about Katie's obsession come to light, she is faced with enemies so powerful they could destroy her, body and soul.

Chapter One

Katie wondered if this was the night her life would end—from a heart attack. Her heart pounded in her chest, painful and ready to burst. It was a good thing she didn't have to run right now, or she'd be dead.

"I really don't want to do this."

"C'mon, it'll be good for us," her friend Ella encouraged.

"'Good' as in, 'Vegetables are good for you', or 'good' as in 'My boyfriend is a police officer, and he's making me do this so you should come with me' sort of good for us?" Katie scrunched down in the front seat of Ella's car, hoping a magical traffic jam would appear and make it impossible to get to class.

"Katie Hollister, how can learning self-defense be a bad thing?"

Katie shook her head. "It's not a bad thing, and philosophically I have no objection to this."

Ella continued as if Katie hadn't spoken. "Besides, it's for women only, and it's taught by law enforcement, so it's bound to help keep us safe, right?"

"Says the woman who still doesn't lock her doors," Katie muttered.

It amazed Katie that Ella was so blasé about home security. They lived in a relatively low crime area, but that didn't mean there was none. Crime still happened. This past summer, Ella had dealt with more than a few problems in her new house. First, there was the ghost of a woman murdered there decades before, while at the same time some of the less enlightened locals spray painted nasty messages on the side of the house. Katie closed her eyes, wondering how her friend was able to maintain a positive outlook on life, considering the prejudice and horror Ella had faced.

But the real reason Katie didn't want to go to this class had nothing to do with ghosts or local attitudes. Katie wasn't afraid of ghosts. If she had been, she wouldn't have been able to live in the house she'd grown up in.

And she wasn't afraid of learning self-defense techniques, either. It might actually be good for her.

If she could get away with only taking the first week of class, that would be perfect. But Ella had asked, cajoled her into it really. Ella's boyfriend, Kevin, suggested the class, saying it was important that they learned the techniques. In order to take this class, though, Katie had to commit to being there for all the nights of instruction.

Which would be fine, except...

...the final night was a test of sorts. It was a simulated attack, performed by the police officers that were teaching it. They would wear protective gear and attack the women, creating real life scenarios. The test would be if the women were able to use what they'd learned and escape.

Being attacked, even for a benign purpose, scared Katie spitless.

She knew she wouldn't be able to handle men coming at her, even if they weren't actually going to hurt her.

She didn't want to do this class, but Ella had talked her into going to the first one. Then, when it was too late and she'd already signed up, she found out how it would end.

Badly, she was sure. What was going to happen when they knocked her down or roughed her up or did whatever they were going to do and Katie couldn't escape? What was going to happen when she ended up lying on the floor in a heap of fear?

But she had promised Ella, and she always kept her promises to her friends.

Katie crossed her long legs at the ankles, jamming her ringless fingers into her fleece jacket pocket. She'd fortified herself for the night, knowing a drink or two would help calm her nerves. Nobody would smell the vodka on her breath, and it would help her get through the ordeal.

Good thing she'd done that because it looked like there wasn't going to be any traffic jam to help her out.

They had arrived.

*****

"Straight kick, go!"

"Straight punch, go!"

Reuben's voice, naturally loud, barked out commands that ripped through Katie. She was tired, sweaty, and starting to feel more than a little cranky. They'd been practicing kicks, punches, and blocks for a solid thirty minutes.

If she'd known it would be this grueling, Katie might have filled her entire water bottle with vodka.

The overhead fluorescent lights of the school gym made a buzzing noise, an annoying sound that added to Katie's emerging headache. Maybe it was that school gym smell that triggered it, but memories of physical education classes gone wrong were drifting through her mind. She tried in vain to suppress the particularly distasteful ones that involved rope climbing and gymnastics equipment, unsuccessful activities during her school experience. She didn't want to relive those moments for anything, and she tried not to think about it. Right now, she needed to endure Reuben and his barking commands.

Reuben might be tough, but he wasn't the boss of her. Maybe she'd just stop, on the pretext of needing a breath of fresh air; then she could wait out the rest of the class. Or maybe she could twist her ankle, sort of accidentally on purpose.

"Hollister!" Reuben yelled.

Katie sighed. *Now what?*

"How tough are you?"

"Not very," she admitted.

"Yeah, well, that's not going to do you much good when you're being abducted."

Katie shook her head. "Nope, it's not."

"You got a death wish or something? Let's see you put a little more effort into those punches. Nothin' to be afraid of here; this is the place you get to practice this stuff."

She knew he meant well, but Reuben was starting to be a real pain in the ass.

*****

"Katie-love…"

Every muscle hurt; yet another divine benefit from class the night before. And on top of that, she was dreaming about Hannah again, dreaming that the ghost was right there in the room with her. Not that there was anything wrong with dreaming about a ghost, but a part of Katie's mind wondered if Hannah was real. True, she'd believed in Hannah as a child, the same way she'd believed in fairies and unicorns. But that was a different time, and her childhood was long gone.

"Katie-love, you have to listen to me this time. There's a danger coming to you…"

Katie could barely hear the lilting Irish voice trying to speak to her. The words sounded like they were far away.

"Really, this is very, very important."

The voice was insistent, which made Katie not want to listen. What kind of dream did this, anyway? It was just her luck to get the nagging sort of hallucination.

Katie heard a ghostly sigh. "Fine then, have it your way. I'm starting to fade, anyhow. But I'm afraid you're going to have to get up, since your mother is waiting for you downstairs." After a moment's pause, the voice added, "There are pancakes, too. Blueberry."

Katie opened her eyes a little at a time, adjusting to the bright sunlight spilling through the windows. Boxes were stacked in every corner of the room, jewelry spilling all over the lace runner on the bureau, and a hodge-podge of clothing and shoes scattered about.

Although her stomach was queasy, she eased herself out of bed, driven by the thought of pancakes. A good, solid breakfast would probably go a long way toward making her feel better about life in general.

It was moving day for the Hollister family. Not for her, though; she'd already packed everything she owned and trucked it all the mile and a half to her parents' house. All of her things were lying in boxes, waiting to be unpacked. This was her new life—her new life, that is, in her old childhood home.

Times are tough for everybody these days, Katie reasoned as she struggled to pull a brush through her long blonde hair. Spraying a bit of conditioner in to help tame her usually manageable straight hair, Katie couldn't help feeling a bit of remorse over being forced into this move.

The truth was, she was broke. Her salary wasn't enough to cover all her expenses anymore, and the bills kept piling up. Katie was desperately afraid of losing her house. She was only twenty-eight years old, and she reasoned that ever since the economy tanked it was difficult for many people to pay their bills. Luck was on her side, however, and within a month of listing her house with a real estate agent, Katie received an offer that was too good to turn down—especially for someone who was facing bank foreclosure.

Things could be worse. I could be living at home with Mom and Dad. That would truly be a nightmare.

Her father, a retired minister, was looking forward to living in a different part of the country. Her mother, a retired bank manager, seemed equally enthusiastic. Not only were they leaving behind the working life, they were moving to Scottsdale, Arizona, a place they had often traveled to and felt most at home.

"Scottsdale, watch out," Katie muttered, throwing on an old sweatshirt. "Here comes Belinda and Paul."

About the Author

Narielle Living is a freelance writer based out of the tidewater area of Virginia. In addition, she is the editor of the Williamsburg magazine Next Door Neighbors and has written hundreds of do-it-yourself articles for online magazines. Her mysteries include *Signs of the South*, *Revenge of the Past*, and *Madness in Brewster Square*, and she co-authored *Chesapeake Bay Karma—The Amulet*. Her fiction also appears in the anthologies *Chesapeake Bay Christmas Volume I*, *Chesapeake Bay Christmas Volume II*, *Chesapeake Bay Christmas Volume III*, and *Harboring Secrets*. She edits both fiction and non-fiction, and loves helping other writers achieve their goals. Narielle is currently working on the next books in the Brewster Square series as well as other fun writing projects.

For information about her books or workshops, visit www.narielleliving.com or find her on Facebook and Twitter.

* 9 7 8 1 9 4 8 8 9 7 9 0 2 3 *